Beguiling Anne

A Mystery Dripping With Passion

C J Maust

Cover Art Designer: Kyle Clark

Category: Mystery/Romance

Description: *An online word game brings Anne and Troy together half a world apart. The games, the stakes, and the consequences could get intensely complicated and irreversible.*

Paperback ISBN:

Ebook ISBN:

First Edition

Contents

Acknowledgment

I am so blessed that I had the opportunity to write this book. My friends and family have been so supportive and I can't thank them enough. I need to mention some of them specifically out of love and respect for their encouragement.

Dan, my wonderful partner of 25 years listened to every word I wrote, sometimes with raised eyebrow, but mostly with words that kept me going. His suggestions throughout the process were invaluable.

My daughter Dawn named the book. She's so clever and she rescued me when I was struggling. My daughter Shellane is the epitome of *"Atta Girl"* go for it! Both of my girls supported me with unquestionable positivity.

Many conversations in this book were offered by an Aussie who gave me information and permission to use his words to be the "captain of this ship" for the intent of writing this work of fiction.

My writing coach Marie encouraged and nudged me gently with her voice of experience to keep at the project until I felt I had fulfilled my passion.

The graphic art designer, Kyle Clark, who is part of my extended family, is the professional who created the amazing cover for *Beguiling Anne*.

To my family and wonderful friends, thank you for the love you have bestowed on me these many years.

C J Maust

About the Author

CJ Maust is a prolific writer. She is the kind of disciplined author, who, once you hear the words on the page, read aloud with passion and often humor, makes one want to up their game. Those moments are revelatory and often convicting, challenging us, ever so gently, to bring our stories to life. Her writings are a wonderful meal of art and intrigue.

I first met C J when she attended my workshop for women writers. She was there the first day and is now a fixture. She has written three books in the short time since Would- Be-Writer's was formed. The workshop serves as a support group, as well as a teaching, and learning class, for those who have a story to tell.

We are all writing a major work in varied genres and voices and all are encouraged to share their knowledge and ideas with our like-minded women.

C J's contribution is not only allowing us to take the journey through her world, but her advice, expertise, kindness, and compassion are welcomed. She is an encouraging voice to the writers and we value her input. Writers have improved, taking her suggestions to heart and applying them. I refer to C J as our "Romance Counselor."

Beguiling Anne is a fun and riveting read, as you frolic with her through the pages, the games, and travel to Australia to meet up with a stranger. His stories about himself are questionable at best and could be a setup for Anne devised by this dangerous man.

Bon Áppetit!

Marie Plauche' Gustin

Creator and Coach of Would-Be-Writer's Workshops

Founder, Artistic Director: Bere'sheet Ballet

Introduction

A bit of guilt hits me in the chest as I put pen to paper, but a battleship full of happiness covers my sin. If I live another fifty years I will not stop thinking, in wonderment, about the events of the last few months. Anne and I have been friends forever, yet in such a short time, we've lived through some of the most frightening, daring, sexy, and life-changing events, that even a brilliant mind like Anne couldn't conjure up. This is a ride down the steepest jagged crag with monsters waiting at the bottom and rose petals and clover at the top.

Anne Cooke and I are forever changed.

Suzanne (Suzie) Larsen

Chapter 1

Anne Cooke, my very best friend, is in trouble. Her life may be endangered, but some little switch in her brain has malfunctioned and I can't seem to reach her. She is teetering on the edge of an abyss, unusual for her. A retired, astute businesswoman, is about to tumble into an irretrievable hole being dug for her; I don't think she even cares. Should I call the FBI? The CIA? Dr. Phil? This is going to be a problem.

Words are her passion. Anne loves to write, and play word games, so when online word games became popular, she was elated and has played every day for twelve years. Playing with people from all over the world makes it even more interesting. She rarely accepts a game challenge from men because they have mistakenly made it a dating site and she's not into that.

Anne posted her profile picture on the game which clearly shows she's a senior, yet she gets hit on by men half her age. Since her retirement, her obsession with the game hasn't been a concern until now. She's smart, savvy, and well-aware of scam artists. She needed something to challenge herself and though she's been in a loving relationship for ten years with Mark, his ability to meet Anne on her level just isn't there. She's more adventurous, while Mark's routine is mundane.

Traveling has lost its appeal since the Covid Pandemic, so I understand her interest as her friend. I had no worries when she began telling me about Troy, her online game-playing buddy. It doesn't take her long to ferret out men who can't behave themselves. She curses them and hits delete.

She'd been playing with Troy for a week or so and he had not sent her a single message which was fine with her; refreshing. She was only there for good, clean competition. His profile, extremely limited, said he was a male from Australia and had been playing for only a month and there was no picture of him. From my point of view, I didn't see any cause for concern. Anne frequently visited with people from around the globe.

Anne called, "Hey, Suzie. How about meeting for lunch tomorrow?"

I love spending time with her so, of course, I agreed. She is the sister I never had. We've been friends for so long that neither of us can remember how or where we met. I'm two years older so I've always felt I had to look out for her. She is capable, can take care of herself and she's experienced many hurdles in her life most of us wouldn't have survived. She's always come out the other side of hell with a positive attitude. She never complains about her life and has always bounced back from whatever tragedy befell her. I truly love that gal.

She told me more than once, "When I look back, I realize everything happens for a reason. Sometimes the reason is I was stupid and made bad choices." We laughed. "I hope I'm wiser and don't make the same mistakes again. At my age, I'm not sure I'd survive some of the pitfalls I did earlier in life." She's genuinely a nice person with a "don't push me too far or you'll regret it" persona. I've never seen that side of her, though she tells me it's there.

Entering our favorite Italian restaurant where there's Chianti on the table, a bottle of amazing olive oil and herbs awaiting the warm, crusty bread, Anne is already there at our usual table. She's always early.

Hugs are in order; I love spending time with her. She's always doing something I wouldn't be gutsy enough to try, so to say she's entertaining would be an understatement.

"I think I'll have the light chicken Alfredo if there really is such a thing, and a glass of Riesling," Anne laughed.

"Hmmm, sounds good but I'll have a cup of your soup du jour and a salad, oh, and don't forget that warm crusty bread of yours, and I'll have the table wine. So there went all my good intentions once I smelled the bread," I said.

"Suzie, none of us are getting out of here alive so we might as well enjoy some guilty pleasures while we're still here."

She has such a way of taking my guilt and throwing it away like a used napkin. The wine and fresh bread arrived with aromas warming my soul. Nothing beats fresh-baked bread and lunch with my best friend, so I'm all in. Anne didn't waste any time dipping a piece of the warm manna into the herbed olive oil.

"Whatcha been up to, kid?" I asked knowing we might as well get to the juicy stuff sooner rather than later.

"Well," Anne answered. "I started teaching my new ukulele class since the pandemic. I'm hesitant because hell, we're not as young as we used to be and I don't want to catch that crud, but I can't stop living entirely," she said as she sipped her wine. "You should come, Suzie. It's so much fun."

"It's fun for you; I'm sorry it holds no interest for me, but I respect you for learning a new skill at your age. I did start ordering some winter bulbs so I'll have new tulips next spring. It won't be long till winter will be howling if you call fifty degrees winter. You know how I love gardening so I'll be ready for warm weather."

"I know," she pouted. "Different folks, different strokes."

"Boy, that saying really dates us, doesn't it?"

"Yeah, kids nowadays wouldn't know what we're talking about," we giggled. "I think I'll write a letter to my grandkids in cursive. They won't be able to read it but they'll think I've learned a new language."

Dipping her bread and biting off a hunk, Anne said, "I know you're not into ukulele but after all these years playing my word games, in our chats, no one ever comments when I talk about my ukulele passion. Of course, men are the only ones who chat, so big surprise. It's a worldwide phenomenon and it's enjoying a completely new renaissance."

I respect her ability to reinvent herself. There's always something new going on and I love hearing about her escapades, although I wonder if, sometimes, she exaggerates a bit to make things more interesting. If she does, I'd never question it because I think I live my life through her and that vivid imagination. That's why I'm in favor of her newest passion of writing novels. I can't wait to read one but she won't let me touch her manuscript until it's an actual book. I'm dying to know what's up her sleeve.

"Okay, Anne, so ukulele is amazing; we've established that so what's that got to do with anything?"

"This Australian guy I'm playing with genuinely seems interested in things I'm doing," she said with a satisfied smile on her lips and a nod of her head.

"Tell me what's going on."

"Remember me telling you about Troy, right?"

"Sure, I remember; you said he doesn't message you. So, what's the big deal about someone who doesn't talk?" I asked.

"He sent me a message a couple weeks ago and it was different- not the usual, "send me your underwear" type, or the new standard line, 'Do you live alone'? That's so creepy. He talked about the game, that he was new to it, but since he was quarantined, he needed a diversion. It was refreshing. He was very complimentary about the ukulele but thought his hands were too big to play one. He loves to play harmonica. I told him, 'Don't you LET me win this game'. I need to win fairly."

"And…what happened?"

He said, "I want you to win. It's good for the spirit, but you have to fight me for it. I'm a nice guy but not that nice."

"I smiled, Suzie. Then he said Happy New Year and asked if I did anything special. I told him I did a little writing, working on my third book."

"You're a writer?" he asked. "Wow, I love reading. There's nothing more beautiful than the papaya-colored sunrise over the mountains and the written word. Words on paper take me to outer space, inside someone's mind, on a magic carpet ride, or on an adventure down the Amazon. I love it. What genre do you write?"

"Of course, there's more to this, right, Anne?" I could tell she was excited, though trying to downplay it.

"He seems intelligent, articulate, not totally self-centered or just a sexual worm," she said.

"Sexual worm? Where did that come from?" We laughed and clinked our glasses in a toast. "So, what did you tell him?"

"I told him I'd written lots of short stories, had a few published. I don't know if I have a genre, but the book I finished is following the life of a young woman whose mother is the leader of a religious cult."

"Did he respond?" I asked.

"Not about the cult but he said, 'that's great, Anne. I imagine it must be like having children. You should be very proud of yourself. Well done. I hope you end up famous.' You know me, Suze, I don't respond well to flattery but this seemed different- sincere."

"Just be careful, Anne. The world is so different than when we were young. You don't know if he has an agenda or is just being nice. Seems most everyone is looking to take advantage or get something for nothing."

"You're such a skeptic, Suze. I think you're more negative than you used to be. You must be watching Dr. Phil too much. This is nothing but a fun conversation, that's it." We laughed.

"Okay, so do you want to fill me in on the rest of it? Just remember girlfriend, the world is a dangerous place nowadays."

She had a questionable look on her face when she said, "This is where it gets interesting. Of course, it's probably bullshit but I'm intrigued."

"Don't leave me hangin," I said.

"I told him thanks for his kind words but I don't care to be famous. I've had some moments and it didn't thrill me much."

He said, "Yeah, but if you get famous, it would mean I know someone famous, instead of people like Idi Amin and Robert Mugabe, old mongrels that they were."

"Ooh, that sends a chill up my spine. Do you think he's just blowing smoke?" I asked.

Anne said, "Probably, then I wrote back and said, my, my, strange bedfellows. I wasn't sure I wanted to open that can of worms, and you know I'm not into history so I was just going to let it go. I couldn't intelligently comment without Googling and I wouldn't even know what to look up."

"And? And?" I questioned her.

"He told me he'd done a few interesting things in his life that he wished he could forget but those are indelible. Idi Amin oozed evilness; it was evident the moment he knew you could be trusted. He said you couldn't pick it out so easily of Mugabe, but you soon got to know it. Most people don't understand the underworld…the REAL world; the world that makes things happen just the way they're planned and nothing is left to chance. You buy WHO you want and the rest falls into place."

"Anne, this is scaring me. You should let this go. Don't dig, delete. Those men were two of the most brutal dictators to ever live. Did he work for them? What did he do? Was he a killer? Please, honey, stop this now. There are lots of other people to play games with."

"Suze, he's half a world away. He doesn't know where I am and he knows I'm harmless. Anyway, I asked him if he actually knew them."

"Yes," he replied. "I worked for both of them, at one time or another." Then he posted a tearful sad emoji.

"Anne, listen to me. This is not something to play with. What if he gets obsessed with you? He probably has connections and you could be in danger. Please stop," I pleaded. "I know how you are. Type A personality, a fixer, a doer, always trying to help but I'm really fearful for you."

"Don't be silly, Suze. It's just a conversation- nothing more. Don't worry," she said.

"Is that the end of it, I can only hope?"

"Oh, hell no! It's just getting interesting," she said with a glint in her eye. "I have a feeling I'm pregnant with a book!"

"You should stop telling me this. I don't want to be a target, too if he comes after you."

"Gee, thanks, friend. But he's so damn interesting, I find it hard to quit."

"Okay, a little more, Anne, and then I'm done. I don't want to hear anymore after lunch. I want to forget it and hope you're smart enough to forget it, too."

"I've got to tell someone and you're my best friend. So anyway, I asked him if I should say sorry. You know, for the sad emoji. His comment stopped me." Troy said, "No, I have nothing to hide anymore except myself, keeping a low profile, but I have a saying. It goes like this: I am not the man that, with Jesus' help I could be, and I'm not the man with the Lord's help, I should be, but thank God, I'm not the man I once was."

Shaking my head, I said, "Okay Anne, lunch is officially over. I don't want to know or hear anything else. I don't know where this is going, but I've got a bad feeling. Why don't you just delete it and go play dominoes or ukulele, something safe?"

She laughed. We said our usual goodbyes, finished with a hug and I drove home. I couldn't get my mind off of it; I was concerned about my friend, but she was smart. She would do the right thing- I could only hope.

****

Anne couldn't clear Troy from her mind. He was the last thing she thought of before falling into a fitful sleep and the first thing in the morning. She could barely wait to brew her coffee to open the app to see if there was a message from him. She was intrigued and excited about conversing with him. Was she having a virtual affair? Being catfished?

Opening the game again, she picked up where they left off. She asked, "Do you feel you need to forgive yourself? Sorry, that's probably too personal. I have regrets but it seems human nature tries to justify the bad choices we've made which is sometimes impossible." Trying to relieve the situation, she texted, "On to happier things."

He answered her question. "I can't forgive myself, but I'm trying to earn some forgiveness. There's been a lot of water and so many bridges in my life. I sometimes wish I could have been carried away by those torrents of raging, black water that thrashed me around most of my life."

She wanted to ask what he was doing to earn forgiveness but she wasn't sure she wanted to know. He seemed deeply troubled.

"Troy, I somewhat understand, but we can't know the depth of God's forgiveness and love. His mercy endures forever. Have you ever tried writing about some of it? Not for anyone to read but maybe to purge your conscience?"

"It's all written up, my dear, sealed in my safe," he said. "It's my confession, to be read when I'm gone." He posted another sad emoji. "I can't talk about it in this life. It's too dreadful and no one would trust me ever again."

She typed, "Should I be worried for my safety?" inserting a scary face.

Anne had the kind of demeanor that seemed to be a magnet for others' troubles. Every place she went, in line at the grocery store, in the restroom at a concert, she was usually corralled by someone pouring her broken heart out. Was there a tattoo on her forehead that said, Tell me your troubles?

Now there's this person, probably a man, who seems to want to unburden himself of his past sins. Anne's imagination went on hiatus as she thought of possibilities about the life of this man. When someone leads into such a subject, it's easy to wonder what heinous crimes they may have committed. Was he a killer? A child molester? A sex trafficker? A drug dealer? A secret agent? The possibilities were endless and the more secretive he was, the more curious Anne became.

She didn't want to ask too many questions because she knew he would then ask things of her. For her security, she thought that might not be wise. She still had some sensibility and waited for him to divulge tidbits that she could piece together to determine what kind of man this was. Perhaps he hadn't done bad things, but was instead, just sensitive and took his transgressions more seriously than most; maybe it was all just a yarn. He was probably some skinny, geeky little guy with black horn-rim glasses, getting his jollies off pretending to be Spiderman or some other superhero. He could be her neighbor for all she knew. Things are different now. That would be a story to tell. Words began clicking in her brain. This could be a good story.

Each time she opened the game, knowing he'd written her, she fought her instinct to open it, trying to break the cycle. I pleaded with her several times to delete this thread causing her such curiosity, and refrain from this man a world away. At least I hoped he was far away.

She told me, "It's like trying to quit smoking; you can't just quit a little bit. You have to quit cold turkey and Lord knows, that's hard." All she had to do was not open his profile...but her excuse was, "I love word games." She opened his latest message.

"Hey lady! Where have you been? I was getting worried that I had offended you. I would never want to do that."

"No worries," she quipped wondering if he'd notice her attempt at an Aussie expression. "Just been busy, read your comment about your confession and hope you're not in a rush to leave this world. Life is precious to me because I don't know what's on the other side. It may be worse than what we endure here, so…I'm good."

Smiley face. "Ha! You may have read between the lines; very astute of you, but please don't judge me too harshly. There are times when depression buries me; but I have done some good things in my life, too. I've been in counseling for many years now to convince myself to keep on breathing."

Attempting to lighten things up, she said, "I have skeletons in my closet, too. I take Mr. Bones out every Halloween! We're never too old to change and never too bad to be forgiven as long as our repentance is sincere. Just my opinion."

Crazy face emoji- "Ha! My skeletons would eat yours for lunch! You need to remember that."

Chapter 2

Anne didn't hear from him for days. She checked the app several times a day, almost desperately, but there was nothing from him. She began to rethink the situation and realized this was becoming an obsession; more than a game of words. She's not prone to depression, but she didn't seem as perky as usual. I knew it was bothering her and I felt she was more attached than she was letting on.

She felt like she had been dumped. You know that feeling when you were in high school, went to the homecoming dance with the captain of the football team, kissed him your very best kisses and then he never speaks to you again? Yeah, it was that feeling.

After four days, Anne decided she would delete the game and Troy. It was ridiculous. She was somewhat satisfied in her relationship with her partner Mark and didn't want that to change, yet she was nearly breathless over someone she didn't know. Was he old? Young? Black or white? Ugly or handsome? Disabled or athletic? Was he that geeky guy or her neighbor? What did it matter? She would never see him or talk to him. This was just a game that gave Anne a little excitement. She thought about those stupid older women on Dr. Phil who had been duped by phantom scammers and had sent them money. She wasn't one of those women. No one would ever take advantage of her. Being her closest friend, I couldn't get it off my mind.

Opening the game, Anne clicked on the conversation tab to a message. "You sound like a very wise person Anne, and quite pleasant as well. Thank you for your words. You're intuitive and sensitive. Somehow, you comfort me; make me feel like I'm worthy to wake up tomorrow."

She fought the urge to respond but closed the game without answering. He made her wait, so turn-about was fair play. It seemed Anne was being penetrated like a worm boring a hole in an apple. I know, not a pretty thought, but I was worried as hell about Anne and I wasn't shy about voicing my opinion. "Please, Anne, delete him. You don't need this stress in your life. A game is supposed to be fun and it sounds like you're taking it too seriously."

"I know you're right, Suze, but I've been writing about him and his stories and that's the most fun of all. I'm trying to get enough information for a good story. Who knows what might happen?"

"Yes, Anne, that's what's making me crazy. We have no idea what might happen. He might know everything about you; he could be stalking your every move." Anne laughed at my concern and said, "Gee, Suze, maybe you should be writing the book! Your take is probably more interesting than mine."

Two days later, she opened up the tab again. "G'day, Anne. How's your day going?"

What the hell? It's only a conversation. "It was good. I started teaching my newest ukulele class. Not many people, but good. People are being Covid conscious. What did you do?"

"I went for a ride on my new Harley around the countryside. I love the solitude and beauty of spring. The foliage, the sun on my skin. It's heaven. But what about you, lady? Ukulele, aye? Girl of many talents. Well done." He inserts a thumbs up. "You must be pretty good if you're a teacher. I'd be a very attentive student if you teach me." Oh, here we go. Men thinking with their "other" head. Cliché, I know, but it fits. I shouldn't stereotype, but damnit!

"We had a conversation about my ukulele life. Have you so soon forgotten? I know you have so many other women on the line, it's hard to keep us all straight." She inserted a crazy face.

"Oh Anne, I hope you don't really believe that. I do play with other people but I am not attracted to anyone like I am you. You're clever, witty, understanding, and empathetic. I couldn't ask for a better game buddy." He sent a red heart.

He sounded sensitive - not sexual, but romantic. There is a difference and she liked that about a man. She'd never known many truthful, sincere men. They don't really pay attention; if they ask you what's wrong and you say, nothing, they *will* believe you. Their brain is attached to a thread between their legs which only takes a tiny amount of stimuli to activate; that's when their true colors show. Their sensitive side is only a facade. She was stereotyping but years of experience had taught her all about that phenomenon. The perfect man is like the unicorns. They missed the ark in Noah's flood.

After that personal rant, she felt she should comment on his motorcycle.

"Good for you! I'm glad the weather cooperated. By the way, I used to ride motorcycles about a hundred years ago!" Anne typed, inserting a laughing emoji.

Sometimes she felt as if she'd lived many lives. She'd done so much, had several careers, many heartaches, and wondered how she'd managed to fit so much in. She was better at telling her story on paper than talking. She loved to write and tell slightly embellished stories about her life. She called it poetic license. I always like reading her short stories. It gives me an insight into that busy brain of hers. She should create some far-fetched tales to tell Troy, but then her truths were stranger than fiction.

"Don't tell me you were a wild child, Anne?"

"No, not really, but competitive. Riding motocross was my deal."

"Gee," he wrote. "You're like a female James Bond International lady of mystery."

She was impressed that he actually read what she wrote. Most men just skim over words waiting to insert their own sexual innuendos. This was fun.

"LOL, you're hilarious!" she commented and inserted a crazy laughing emoji. "Maybe your next career could be stand-up comedy."

"Or... you could teach me how to play the ukulele. I haven't got a bad voice ya know. I could accompany myself, hey?"

They all have their agenda, their pick-up line so he'll use the ukulele to soften her up. She knew it couldn't last forever. He'll turn into the sexual fiend she was hoping he wasn't. She turned the game off and went to bed.

The next morning, she opened the game and hesitated to hit Troy's game. What the hell! Let's just see where this is going although she was sure she already knew. He had played a word worth 106 points, hard to ignore. She liked intelligent men. Even his spelling in their chats was perfect so she assumed he'd been well educated.

"Wow! Nice play! You're making me work for this, aren't you?"

He said, "If you like the competition, then yes, but I don't want to stress you out."

"Ha! Don't do me any favors. I work best under pressure," she said.

"Funny you should say that because my life is one crisis after another that I have to work through. If you only knew. I've been through enough to have lived four lives."

"Yeah, you and me both. Tell me about it, Bad Boy Troy!"

She needed to stop this line and lighten things up. She'd had enough trauma in her life and didn't need anymore. She wanted to keep things light.

"Let's talk about food, Troy. What are some of your favorite choices?"

"I can always talk about food. I love to cook; I love smoking meat and seafood. I'm crazy for any kind of pasta, home-baked bread, and hand-churned ice cream. Fresh oysters, when they're in season are one of my favorites and mushrooms I glean from my woods. How's that? What do you think?"

"Sounds delicious to me. Now you've made me hungry! You didn't say anything about vegetables."

"Oh Anne, I have a vegetable garden year-round. Certain things only grow at the right temperatures but I've come to be quite the gardener; I love most all vegetables, do you?"

"If it's food, I like it. Now I don't go for anything funky but regular food, yes."

"I gotta tell ya, Anne, I've decided I like you. You are very easy to talk to, and that is a good thing. I find it hard to talk to people at times. I think it is because I frighten them; you have to get to know me usually, and that is not an easy thing to do. That's why I think this is a good platform for me. I can chat without scaring you. You might wonder, what is so scary about me? I can only say that my face is a well-written page; time, pain, and loneliness were the pen....so thank you for your time and chats. It means a lot to me. Somehow you have helped lighten my depression and you treat me like a human being. Thank you. I'll have to find some way to repay you."

Chapter 3

Who is this man? Is his face weather-beaten from the elements or something more sinister? He said he worked for two of the most brutal killers known to man. Perhaps his face was disfigured from his association with those regimes. It seemed he carried a lot of guilt. Anne was feeling more anxious, not knowing what, or how much to believe. She had her secrets, too, but his seemed much darker. He didn't ask much of her; she wondered about that. He didn't ask if she was married, had a family, or had a career. I told Anne it was probably because he had her investigated and knew all he cared to know.

"Who's the James Bond now, Suzie?" Anne laughed. "Why would anyone go to that much trouble? I'm a nobody, playing a game, that's it. Your imagination is getting the best of you, girlfriend."

Anne continued to check the game but there was nothing for two days. She wouldn't contact him first. That's not the game she played. Finally, on the third day, there was a notification that he had played. She opened the message tab and read:

"Oh Anne, I need to tell someone that my donkey, Ivor has died. Sometime through the night, he was bitten by a tiger snake; the vet couldn't save him. He was such a gentle soul and I am devastated. I can handle the death of people, no problem, but not my animals. He was a rescue and he loved me as much as I loved him; I feel responsible. I should have checked on him sooner, but I've been a bit lazy lately and I think maybe it's God's way of punishing me for my evil deeds. I have to think that, otherwise, it makes no sense to me."

That seemed like a strange comment; death of people is no problem? What kind of man says that? A man without a conscience? Evil deeds? Anne's curiosity kept her coming back. She'd never talked to anyone like this before. Even if he wasn't at all what he seemed, the talks would still make an interesting story if she continued to write it.

"What evil deeds? Do you think God is keeping score and your evil deeds unforgivable?"

"Anne, I can't share that with anyone. It's all locked in my safe so someday, my family will understand the hell I've gone through and the things I've done."

"Okay, Troy. I'm trying to understand, but maybe you're just overly sensitive. There is always forgiveness. You're being very hard on yourself. I see there are many sides to you. I'm sure you aren't as bad as you say. Are you still working? Have a job?"

"Listen, Anne," he wrote, "I'll tell you something that breaks me into crushed glass every time I think of it and rarely talk about it. This is the first I've ever written of it, but here goes. I don't celebrate my birthday, not since 2000. You see my mum came to visit me in jail for attempted murder. While at the jail, she had a stroke and never regained consciousness. I went to her funeral, on my birthday in handcuffs and leg manacles. I know I broke her heart, more times than I can admit, and I blame myself for her death. When my birthday comes around, I'm lucky to even drag myself out of bed, from the depression that covers me like a black fog."

"That's a truly tragic story, Troy, but there comes a time when we must accept the fact that we can't turn back time and we have to move on. No amount of mourning and blaming ourselves will change the past."

"I know but I keep trying to make retribution. I celebrate each birthday in my family by giving them $5000. It doesn't matter their age; everyone gets the same on every birthday."

"That's incredibly generous of you. You have a large family, right?"

"Yes, we could start our own settlement!" (Inserts happy faces) "Money is really no object. I like to make them happy."

"Are you trying to tell me you're wealthy?" she asked.

"No, I am *telling* you, I'm rich- *very rich*. I have more wealth than I could ever spend, at least at this time of my life. It pleases me to help others with the gifts I have."

"Oh," she typed. "You must have had a good job." Anne could only hope his claim of wealth was true. That would make this whole endeavor worthwhile.

"Let's just say I had many opportunities that allowed my wealth to grow to massive amounts," he answered. "You may think I'm bragging but, trust me, I would never lie to you. To answer your question, no, I don't need to work so I'll say I'm retired, although I'm still a very active person. Much of my wealth is in the form of Krugerrand gold coins from Africa. I could tell you about my coins and let you do the math but then I might think you were talking to me because of my prosperity and that would not be a good outcome for you."

He continued, "My nephew is Covid positive and I spent some time with him over the weekend, but so far, I have tested negative but I have to lock down and test daily for ten days, so it is a bit stifling. That's just the state the world is in now and we have to live with it. Thank you for listening and for your patience. I truly do appreciate your time, although I feel that I've stolen it from you. There is nobody else I can talk to. You have become my stranger at the bus stop- I hope you don't mind, but if you do, I'll stop."

Anne chewed on his words and felt some of what he said might be a fabrication. However, if he truly was that wealthy, she was barking up the right tree. When the last game was over, she challenged him to a new game but the computer said, "this player has too many games to accept a new one." She thought about confronting him but thought it was best to let it go. She was certainly not the only one he was playing with. She knew this was more than a word game, for both of them.

She wrote back. "Wow, I feel like I just ate a huge meal of truth and it sits heavily in my gut. I'm so sorry about Ivor and the guilt you carry about your mum. I wish I could comfort you somehow."

"There's really nothing anyone can say or do- just something I have to deal with in my own way. I think that's why my animals are my world now," he said.

"It's amazing, so special, the bond that happens between humans and our faithful friends. They never lie or deceive us," Anne said, wondering how much of what Troy said was true. "They dish out comfort and unconditional affection. I find our talks almost too interesting to believe. Are you sure you're not a novelist? If not, you should be. Thank you, by the way, for being respectful to me. That's rare. Sometimes I blame God when unfortunate things happen including heartbreak, that brings me to my knees, but that's probably the point, right?"

"Thank you for your beautiful words and your patience, Anne. It means a lot to me and is comforting. Good night, sweetie."

There's a red flag, Anne thought. Perhaps "sweetie" is just a term of endearment as friends. That's what Anne chose to believe.

Chapter 4

"Good morning/night, Anne. It's 5:00 AM here. Hope you're doing well," he began.

"Hello, Troy. It's 1:00 PM here on January 5th."

"Well, it's January 6th here so that means you're in the Northern hemisphere. How's your day so far?"

"Unexpected. Our little dog is in pain so we took her to the vet. She's such a sweet girl, it hurts me. Waiting for some test results. Not knowing is exasperating."

"I understand," he wrote. "I hate it when my animals are in pain. I go straight into panic mode. It affects me more than when people are suffering. I do hope it's nothing serious with your baby. And how is that novel going?"

He had no way of knowing she was writing a story about him. Even if he wasn't being truthful, it was a good storyline. Now and then she let worry speak to her, but their distance gave her comfort. Besides, she wasn't writing anything defamatory – just words that he had said.

"My current project is in its infancy. How would you feel if it was about you and our conversations?"

"I was thinking the same thing- might be interesting. You can be the captain of the ship and you have my permission to take liberties as most authors do," he wrote with many laughing emojis. "I have a couple requests, though. Make me six-foot two with a rock-hard body and a chiseled physique, please." He inserted several laughing emojis.

"I can do that, since I'm the captain of the ship. HA! I don't know if it will be a short story to add to my collection or something more. I'm not good at fiction, I'm too realistic to make things up, so I'll have to rely on you to fill in some of the blanks. What other animals do you have?" Anne asked.

"A little terrier mix named Maggie, one horse, (Dobbin), and a pig named John. I may check on another donkey. I enjoyed Ivor so much."

Anne wanted to know more about him, but he was careful about what he said, although there were a few nuggets she found interesting.

"You must live in a rural area. I live in a big city now, but when I was a girl, one of my favorite pets was a 400-pound sow named Bessie. She loved to swim with me."

"Yeah, pigs are funny animals. John adores me." Happy face. "You won that game! Nicely done. Up for another?"

"Sure, I love playing games- all kinds, and, you know I love to win! It's been a few days since we talked. Do you have any Covid symptoms?" Anne asked.

"No, feeling fine. I don't get out that much. LOL. I keep a low profile if you know what I mean. What about you,

Anne? Are you well? I hope you had a good sleep. Welcome back to our game."

"Thanks," inserting three happy faces. "I'm wondering how you're handling the loss of Ivor. Are you able to sleep?"

"It's 2:30 AM and yes, it's difficult. I can't get to sleep; my sorrow is eating me up," he typed.

Anne was curious about the stranger. She hoped he would open up to her but it had only been a few days. What was his life like? Who was he and why did he carry so much guilt? His callousness about human life was unsettling but perhaps it was a pretense. She would carefully try to gain his trust so she could better understand him, and then there was his bank account.

"Sorry, Troy. Being unable to sleep is the worst. Sleep is usually my escape. I'm well, thanks. Looking forward to my writing class- love the instructor. Do you have any hobbies or special interests?" she asked. "I don't want to keep you awake if there's a chance you might drift off."

"No, it's fine. I have a few interests, but my favorites are music, most any kind of game, the written word, and of course, I love animals. I do have a preference for country music."

Surprisingly, Anne hadn't kept up with current music so when he began telling her of artists he liked, she was curious, his choices good. She understood the genre but when she listened to his favorite songs, they were all sad and dark. She felt compassion for him. It seemed he was grieving from within and she wished she knew why. He was a mystery.

Over the next couple of weeks, their conversations were minimal and he seemed to shut down a bit. She hoped he felt he could trust her but he didn't talk about anything personal. They continued to play the game and Anne seemed to win consistently.

"Troy, are you LETTING me win?"

"You must be kidding. I would never insult you like that, plus I'm just too competitive to do that! You know Anne, you are absolutely the sweetest person I've ever <u>not</u> met. It's a pleasure playing with you. Well done on another win, but I'll get you sooner or later."

She wasn't sure what context he was talking about, but her imagination led her astray. She hoped his statement was regarding the game, but there was a certain feeling that intrigued her, maybe even excited her, but she wasn't going there. "I'm not so sweet," she said. "I'm grumpy- just letting you think I'm nice."

"I don't believe that for one minute."

She wasn't sure she should have said that, but she wanted to seem mysterious, too. Maybe he wouldn't think she was a predictable assumption.

"Look, Anne, if I talk too much, you can tell me to piss off, but you have to let me come back. Is that alright with you? I promise I will never disrespect you. You've got to believe me."

"I enjoy our conversations. As long as we continue to respect each other, I'm good," she said. "It's sometimes hard to believe a man's word when so much of it has brought me pain. I don't think I'm naïve but perhaps I am."

"Do I detect tragedy? I hope not; that would hurt me."

"I'm great, although I've had my share of heartbreak; everyone suffers in their own way. It doesn't make me special. Now I enjoy my uke and writing, but feel like I waste lots of time."

Chapter 5

"Oh delight, Anne's back. I'm very happy now. If writing makes you happy, then you must write. Life is short," he reminded her.

"Thanks. How's your day going? Are you busy today?"

"Well, this will probably gross you out, but Ivor and John were very good friends. John knows his buddy is underground and has been very naughty trying to dig him up. I've been dealing with that. I've had to pen him up to keep him away from the burial site. I'll probably have to move Ivor to the back of my property."

"I'm sure that's difficult for you. Off the subject, I'd like to ask a question. What was your motivation to start playing this game? I see you haven't been playing very long."

He answered, "Honestly, I'm lonely, but I did not think I would get to know people like you. I didn't even know I could send messages until someone told me, so it's a nice bonus."

Anne felt she needed to establish some guidelines although she was hesitant to tell him too much. She said, "Troy, I know we haven't shared much personal info, your friendship is gratifying, however, I'm not interested in any sort of romantic relationship."

"God forbid. I would never try to do that. I just am the way I am. Always been very open about some things, others are better left buried, no pun intended, but I would never ever disrespect you."

Anne sighed, feeling his response about their friendship was appropriate. However, his 'buried' comment left her unsettled. She didn't know where this might be going but, she hoped he would never try to find her. After all, she didn't even know how old he was or even if he was in Australia as he said. She was curious about his life and continued writing about their conversations, sensing there was some interesting stuff in his life that might make a good thriller. She just didn't want to be the subject of his criminal life, if, in fact, he was that person. Anne smiled thinking he was probably that skinny little computer geek with glasses and weighed about 110 pounds, instead of the macho tough guy he was portraying. She'd heard of people doing that as a game in itself. Quite imaginative, if that's his game.

"Thanks, Troy, I think you're a good man. How's John doing being penned up? He probably misses his freedom. That's probably how quarantined people feel, huh?" LOL

"John, the pig isn't happy but when you break the rules, there are consequences to pay. *No one gets away without paying the piper, in my world anyway.* This is his retribution. I'm dealing with hay fever right now. Happens every year for a while so I'm not doing much except sniffling. Tell me what the young Anne was like."

She answered off the cuff. "Married young, had babies, lost a husband, lost a lover, lost my mind. Life had things in store for me and threw me some curve balls, but complaining won't change a thing."

"Are you sure you don't want to talk about it?" he asked. He seemed sincere but there was no sense in digging up the stink she'd made of her life.

"No, life is complicated enough."

"Oh Anne, I'm so sorry. Here I am, dumping my problems, my grief on you when I should show more concern for you. You're such an incredible person, I find you so easy to talk to."

"Troy, please, you know I love our conversations and I feel honored that you trust me with some of the things you feel."

The next few conversations were about music, which artists and songs he liked. He was much more knowledgeable than she was, even though she was a music teacher, of sorts. She was more interested in Troy and his life than famous singers, hoping to pick up more fodder for her story but she didn't dare be too pushy to make him suspicious of her and her ultimate goal.

Days came and went with mundane chit-chat that didn't amount to much although Anne felt she was getting a better feel about the stranger. She imagined there was more to him than she had heard. She just needed to ferret it out. One morning he wrote:

"Anne, I had the most amazing night. I slept on my verandah and enjoyed the most incredible thunderstorms I've ever seen; hundreds of lightning strikes danced everywhere and thunder rolled on and on. It was so beautiful; I lay there for hours just absorbing it. I daydreamed about you during the storm so please, tell me where you have lived or something interesting about the Anne I'm learning about."

She didn't know how to answer so she let it lie. Finally, she said, "Grew up on a beautiful island, moved to a different island, now live in a big dirty city and hate it."

"You have an island? How wonderful. Tell me more." (Happy face)

"No, not anymore. I spent every summer there as a kid. When my parents died, it was left to me but an evil man stole it from me in a lawsuit lasting 12 years. I still grieve."

"Hmm, do you want me to kick his face in, because I will, just need a name? I won't say much but I have resources to eliminate problems like they never existed. Calling in a small favor like that would be nothing for me."

Anne cringed but felt elated at the same time. Now they were getting somewhere. "I wish I'd had that offer years ago, but it's too late now. Some people are born evil and I have to let it go. I wonder why they get to breathe," Anne felt that sorrow she hadn't allowed herself to admit for a long time.

She didn't hear from Troy for a full day and that made her anxious. She was enjoying their chats and intrigue. This was going to be a good story. When he played the next time, she felt relief.

When he answered he said, "They breathe because they don't live in a land of real men. They exist in a small world. The only way they can feel superior is by making others feel inferior. He was an oxygen thief. A man like me would never have treated you like that. There is a reckoning; that's why I pray for forgiveness. I know I must humble myself before God, but that man will be judged. You must believe this."

Anne responded, "If you only knew the suffering he has caused, including killing innocent people, abusing children, mind control. Just thinking of it turns my stomach. His heinous deeds are beyond believable."

Troy responded, "Vengeance is coming, so he will suffer. Forget the dog and comfort yourself with the thought, that he will suffer God's retribution."

"You know what I find curious? The townspeople, where this evil man lives, are completely up in arms, going after him after all these years. It reminds me of the movie Frankenstein where they were trying to kill the monster. Facebook lights up every day with more about him and the abuse he's committed over the years. You may have hit on something. Maybe this is the beginning of his retribution. I pray for that every day."

Chapter 6

Anne was comforted by his words and snuggled into a sound, peaceful sleep, except for light storms during the night. When morning came, a message awaited her.

"Hello sweetie. How are you feeling today? Hope you had good sleep and sweet dreams, very important for the soul."

"Hey! We had thunderstorms during the night which causes our terrified little pup to breathe in my face. Not the most pleasant, although I adore her."

"You may not get much out of me today, Anne. I got very, very drunk last night and I'm not at my best."

"I had a bit too much bourbon myself last night so, take a break. We'll talk when you're feeling better."

Several hours later he sent her a message. "I'm so sorry, sweetie. I feel like I'm neglecting you, but I'm really hungover. Don't you dare give me sympathy; this is self-inflicted and does not deserve any pity. I'm very naughty."

She noticed he was getting freer with his use of 'sweetie'. She couldn't let it get out of hand. "My question Troy is, who were you partying with and I hope the fun you had, was worth the misery."

"It was a very old friend, one I had not seen in years, actually thought he was dead. We saved each other more than once. He's staying over for the week; we just got into it like gluttons remembering the horror and good times, but now I must pay the piper. What's this I hear about you and bourbon? Have you been holding out on me?"

Anne felt this was a good bit of information. She hoped she could coax a bit more out of him. Her instinct told her there was a story here; she needed to figure out how to loosen him up. "Can't beat a good bourbon, Troy. Did you literally save each other? How so? Unless you're not comfortable saying."

"They're long and violent stories, but I will tell you, he once carried me twenty miles and I was full of holes at the time."

Anne sucked in a breath, not knowing how, or if, to answer. This could get very interesting if she could convince him to trust her with his secrets.

****

<u>Suzie</u>

I hadn't talked to Anne since our lunch, a quick text here or there, but I couldn't get her "project" off my mind. I hoped she wasn't crawling toward quicksand.

"Hey Anne, we haven't talked in a couple weeks so I'm just checkin' in," Suzie said. "What's going on? Anything exciting?" I was almost afraid to hear the answer.

"Hi, Suzie. You caught me at a good time. Just relaxing a bit before going back to the computer to write. I've been trying to discipline myself to do it every day."

"I'm not sure why you torture yourself, put that pressure on your life. Not saying you're not good at it, but what do you hope to accomplish? I know you've always wanted to have a book published, even though you've never submitted one," I laughed. I felt her smile. "Anyway, at our age, even if you did write a bestseller, what's the point?

"Hmm, good question. I'm not sure, except for the satisfaction of knowing I kept at it until it happened. I would feel like I left a legacy for my family."

"You've done so many things, they have plenty of memories, why this? You managed a theatre in New York, got a degree, played and sang in a band, became a commercial fisherman, earned high accolades in the insurance game, owned several businesses...did I miss anything?"

"Yeah, married three men, buried two, live with one who calls himself Henry the Eight! The old fart! I did have some exciting flings as well, but maybe that's better left unsaid."

"Don't forget about teaching ukulele to yourself and several hundred others. That's quite an accomplishment right there, girlfriend. Then you wrote a short story about that and were published, right? That's pretty damn good."

"I know, but the writing fever has a grip on me. My cells tingle when I begin, and now talking with this Troy guy from Australia, I'm thinking maybe I can make something out of these conversations."

I was hoping she had moved beyond that. The bits of information she shared with me gave me cause to worry. What if he was a terrorist? A sniper? A mass murderer? What if he could make a call and have my friend snubbed out? It was a fearful thought but I knew the more I tried to convince her to delete this person, whoever he was, the more determined she'd be to keep it going. That's just who she was. If someone told her she couldn't do something, that's when a team of horses couldn't hold her back. She'd lived her whole life that way and I've seen it in action a hundred times. It's probably better not to talk about it; maybe it will burn itself out before he finds her, figures out what she's up to and all that's left is her funeral, which I agreed to officiate if she goes before me; not a pleasant thought.

****

A new message from Troy startled her. "Just took a close look at your profile pic, Anne. I swear, before God, you must have been absolutely delightful in your youth. You still shine very brightly, and no I'm not trying to charm you, just being myself, a man who means what he says and says what he means. Please do not take it the wrong way. You delight me,

Anne. I look forward to every word we share." He waited for her to answer and became a bit nervous. "Either we have a very delayed connection or you're being elusive so, which is it?" Why are you not chatting with me?"

"I am chatting with you, why so impatient? I'm sure you have better things to do than sit there talking to me. About the picture, God has a terrible sense of humor. After we suffer as humans, we get old, wrinkly and ugly; then we die. That's not even funny."

"Anne, you will never be ugly. I don't even like that word. You're beautiful to me. Nothing could be further from the truth," he wrote. "You have helped lift me from my depression and sad state that I've been in for a while. I thank you for that. I'm not even paying you for the counseling you're giving me. You have a lovely, kind face. I like that."

Anne chuckled. You may not be paying yet, but you will if I continue to work my magic, she thought. You don't know how clever I am and how I can manipulate men. She wasn't being egotistical; her experience was proof enough. If Suzie knew the truth about me, she'd probably dump me and call me a skank. It's probably true, but it's who I've become and it's exciting.

"I'm just enjoying our talks. I find you interesting and attentive. Seems like you're a detail guy. So, you said you're a Patsy Cline fan. That's "CRAZY". She inserted a crazy 'stink-eye' emoji.

"See, you have this way about you. That crazy comment made me laugh so hard my ribs hurt!"

"I'd love to see you laugh," she said "The sound of your laughter would fill my soul." Anne knew she was beginning to swim in dangerous shark-filled waters.

"No Anne, you wouldn't love to see me laugh. I told you I would scare you. I just want to be your friend. Please don't expect to ever see me."

"I'm so sorry, Troy. I didn't mean to offend you. Do I have to think about every word I say before I do?"

"I hope you're not trying to upset me. That would not be a good thing and you would see a side of me that few live to see," he said.

"No, I would never want to upset you; just idle conversation. I would never tease a gorilla unless he's 10,000 miles away. (Happy face) Can you tell me one of your favorite childhood memories?"

"No offense taken, Anne. Forgive me, please. I still laugh when I think about my mum, and some of the things she used to say. For example, I'd ask what's for dinner? Her reply was usually 'shit and sugar sandwiches', son. I'll put some extra sugar on yours to keep you sweet, but you'll still be eating shit. She was priceless and I loved her so much, but I know that what I became, hurt her deeply."

"That's a cute story but it leads me to wonder what a man like you could have become that would hurt a mother? In all our chats, you seem gentle and sincere."

"I can't share that with you, Anne. If I did, I'd have to kill you and that's not just a figure of speech. Please, don't push me."

"I hope you're kidding," she typed, as she noticed her hands shaking a bit.

Chapter 7

There was no answer for a long time and it was her bedtime. She thrashed, going over bits of their talks, wondering how much she could believe although he hadn't really said much. He did, however, portray himself as a badass.

Anne started doing some reading about Uganda and Zimbabwe since he said he worked for dictators of those two countries in Africa. Searches don't usually divulge the real horror of things that happened, especially several years ago before the internet was so present. She tried to find some mention of someone with his name but was quite sure it was an alias at best. She didn't know how long he had been retired but he could have worked for the Mugabe regime as recently as 2017. She hoped he had been a janitor in his palace or a gardener and nothing more heinous but, her instincts weighed heavily on her. Perhaps he was telling her stories to make himself sound more interesting. That would be a good thing and still make for a good story. If that was the case, he was imaginative. She had so many questions she wanted to ask but didn't want him to pull away.

In an attempt to relax him, she said, "Troy, when we were talking about music, I didn't tell you one of my favorite artists is Gordon Lightfoot. Wow, love his music. My favorite is Song for Winter's Night. It has such meaning to me that I wrote a short story about it. When I was young, I was in love with a sophisticated young man who taught me more about love than I needed to know at my age. Then he disappeared and I didn't hear from him for forty years. We then wrote a book together about losing love and coping with the mistakes we made. I played that song a hundred times one night as I wrote him of my heartbreak."

"Wow, that's quite a story!" he responded. "Is it true or are you catfishing me? Sorry, I shouldn't have said that, but, in my line of work, it is impossible for me to trust anyone completely." Trying to change the subject, he said, "I love Gordon Lightfoot, too. I think you and I have a lot in common."

Not wanting to let that comment simmer, Anne asked, "Catfishing? I had to Google it to even know what that is! You have nothing I need…except friendship." Anne could only hope he wasn't getting suspicious of her. She was interested in his life, his feelings, the grief he seemed to carry, but she had 'Writer's Brain' in full force and found it hard to quell. She hoped to gain his full trust by the lovely words she carefully sent to him. And there was his bank account. Was she catfishing? Whatever it was called, she hoped it was lucrative…for her.

"There's something I need from you," he wrote. "I need to see you walking into my big, beautiful kitchen, sleepy-eyed and sexy with the sun on your face, while I cook you an amazing breakfast."

When Anne read that comment, her knees nearly gave way. She wasn't sure if it was from excitement or fear. It doesn't take much for ladies like us to get riled up. This is where it was starting to get sketchy. She laughed and kept her answer generic. The little minx.

"That paints a pretty picture, Troy, but you know that's not going to happen for a million reasons. Nice of you to think of me, but too complicated."

"A man has to have dreams Anne, and you have released some dreams in me that I thought were shot to hell, literally. Have you ever been to Australia? I just woke up, so give me 5 minutes to have a quick dip in the pool, then we'll have a nice chat. Sorry I've been neglecting you."

"No, I've never been there and probably won't. Don't like those long international flights. I'm four years older than you so it would take a toll on an old broad like me. Have you ever been to the USA?"

"Please don't demean yourself like that, Anne. You're beautiful to me, in every way."

"No, I've never been to the US," he responded. "They won't let me in."

Anne didn't know if she should ask but, what the heck? This had become her mission. "Why won't they let you in? Sounds crazy to me."

"I might tell you someday but I'm not ready to go there yet. I hope you'll trust me. Let's just say it had something to do with my gardening practices." (Happy face)

****

<u>Suzie</u>

The next time Anne and I got together over coffee at Starbucks, she seemed even more excited than before. I detected a little hesitation as she told me more about their communication.

"Well Suzie, we're still talking and playing the game. I'm not really sure if he thinks we have a relationship. I've made it abundantly clear to him that I'm looking only for friendship."

"What makes you think that, Anne?" I wasn't sure I wanted to know the answer.

"He said his dream was to see me walk into his kitchen, sleepy-eyed, sun on my face while he made me a delicious breakfast."

"Whoa! That sounds a little too risky for me. You know the longer you keep this up, the more complicated it will become," I said shaking my head.

50

"He asked if I was catfishing him? That shook me because I thought he might be doing the same to me. He could be someone around the corner just pretending to be this guy."

"Anne, this is scaring me. I wonder how many times he's told these stories to how many women? What's his end game? Has he said anything else inappropriate?"

"No, he's been a gentleman and I really didn't take offense at his comment but I couldn't let it go. I had to stifle it right away."

He told Anne he was a native Aussie but had moved away for several years. He bought his property seven years earlier and had done major renovations. Sitting on 300 acres, he claims to have taken a five-bedroom home, removed walls, changed the floorplan, and now had a home with two massive bedrooms. He gardens, grows herbs, the world's greatest garlic, according to Mr. Wonderful, and loves to cook. He claims to have built all his furniture from wood he has gathered from the 'bush'. He has a new Harley, gardening equipment, and a pool next to his home. Anne said he's so descriptive about it, she can envision it. He tells the story as any good writer would. This makes me wonder if he is writing a story, just like my friend Anne.

Chapter 8

Three days later, after his '5- minute dip in the pool', she got a message from him. "Anne, I'm so sorry. So much has happened since we spoke. First, my phone had some kind of glitch, then the neighbor was giving his 16-year-old daughter driving lessons, and crashed into my fence, then John, my pig, got loose and I spent hours looking for him. Finally, two days ago, I got stung by a hornet in the neck. It's been a rough week."

"So sorry for your troubles," Anne said. "How's your neck? Did you have any reaction to it?"

"Yes, that's one reason I've been absent from our chats. I went to the hospital three times before they actually gave me something that helped. I felt like I was on fire. It was bad. I hate hornets; it was huge."

"Maybe she was just kissing you!" trying to add some humor. "Now that you're feeling better, just wondering if you can fly yet?"

"FLY? Whatever do you mean?"

"I thought maybe you'd turn into "The Green Hornet" superhero. Bzzzzzz!" (Laughing happy face)

Troy inserted a grumpy face. "Were you a cruel mother?"

"What do you think?" Anne asked.

"You look so sweet and kind."

"Things aren't always as they appear. I'm sure you know that," she said. "FYI, Hornet one, Troy zero."

"Have you no shame, Anne? I thought you were my comfort, my hug when I have trouble, but here you are, playing a game with a hornet at my expense. You never really know someone until push comes to shove," he said. "Like my friend Dave. I thought he was here to catch up, and reminisce about old times, but no, he had an agenda. I hate people who want to use others instead of just being forthright about their purpose. You're different, Anne. Chatting with you has become the highlight of my day and I know I can trust you, my little catfish."

Anne gulped a burst of air and didn't know what to say. Was he wise to her? Her heart beat a bit faster and she really began thinking about what she was doing. Maybe she should just tell him she's writing about him and their "relationship". They had discussed her book so she was more concerned that he was suspicious of her, hoping to tap into his bankroll. That would be the end of their chats, maybe even the end of her life if he was as ruthless as he was leading her to believe. She didn't like that; still found him intriguing. In her mind, this was mostly a game and she thought it was the same for him.

Two days later Troy messaged her. "G'day, Anne, how are you today? Sleep well? I hope so. I'm much better today than yesterday. I might even do some work today."

"Hi ya, Troy! Glad you're feeling better. Happy Monday."

"You won't guess what I just did Anne. I put a profile picture on our game page, so now you know what I look like," inserting a toothy, silly emoji. "What do you think? I'm not pretty, am I?"

Anne was hesitant to open the picture and wondered why he did it since he said she would never see his face. Maybe it wasn't really him- just some random guy. She was shocked when she saw it. He looked nothing like she envisioned, younger than his sixty-two years, as he said. He looked chiseled and muscular, built tough like a Ford truck. His hair and long beard were deep copper, slightly unruly and curly, with eyes that looked like delicate lavender orchids. Perhaps this was an old picture because she couldn't imagine he had done all the things he said, if he was as young as his picture. He was definitely a big man and above the contour of the beard, she could see considerable scarring that looked like burn scars. She choked back a gasp. She had to be careful how she responded. If he had relented to post the picture, she wanted to commend him for his bravery. Thinking carefully, she wrote:

"Wow! What a great beard! Friendship isn't about being pretty. I'm happy to see you, finally. It's funny how we create images in our minds. You're much prettier than I pictured you," she said.

"So, you like the beard?"

"I'm not typically a fan, but if that's who you are, then yes, I like it!" she said.

"That's very kind of you. I was not a fan of beards either but they do grow on you!" he joked. "Besides, it covers up some of the battle scars."

"You're on a roll, Troy. Beards don't grow on me, thank goodness! Is that your natural hair color?

"Why? Does it look weird? I was hoping you'd think I look so young for my sixty-two years, so no, that was taken several years ago before my hair and beard turned into the silver fox. Just wanted you to be impressed. I'll post a recent picture, but don't say I look like Santa."

"I'm always impressed with you. Why did you say your face was scary?"

"Apparently, it's my eyes. People say that they seem to look into them and they feel like I know all their secrets. I look into their eyes, don't blink, and cannot pretend to like someone if I don't like what's in their eyes. I have been known to severely beat people just because I didn't like what I saw in their eyes. Thing is, I don't remember ever being wrong about how I felt about someone's character. Sort of a 6th sense."

Anne drew in a breath. "Hmmm, interesting. Do you have a bad temper? Let me get this straight. You have attacked people, unprovoked, because you didn't like their eyes? Is that who you are now? I think I'll call you 'Bad Boy Troy' from now on." She didn't know how far she could take this conversation.

"Yes, I have a bad temper, fierce," he wrote. "It's why I don't have/make friends. It's why I don't leave my house much. You see, people are the reason I love animals, never ever has an animal let me down. Their love has no conditions and their eyes are innocent."

"Maybe you should mellow out a bit. Do you ever feel you overreacted, that you should have walked away? Does your reaction have anything to do with the work you did?" she asked cautiously.

"I truly hope I have not offended you, Anne, but I won't lie to make myself look better, (well except for the old picture). I cannot abide a liar and I do usually give warning signs, but some people ignore the signs."

"No offense taken, Troy. You are you, and I'm not trying to change you- just like to know you better."

"I have mellowed a lot, but it's always lurking just below the surface and yes, I think my work is part of the problem, but it's also that I have seen the worst that man has to offer, and it's not good or nice. I often wonder who the real animals are."

Fear was gripping Anne to the point she was having trouble sleeping. Yet, she couldn't let it go. She was so intrigued by this man, wondering if he really was the man he said he was. What was his real story? He did bring up catfishing so he's savvier than he wanted her to believe. He seemed dangerous in a sensitive sort of way. If he can't come to the US, Anne felt cautiously safe, even if he did find out she was using him as a subject for her book. I'm fearful for Anne. I think she's messing with fire but is so far in now, that she's thrown reality to the wind. It's like she, herself, is reading a thriller novel. Weird that she can be reading it *and* writing it.

"I'm no judge, so no worries from my part of the world," she said. "What are your plans for the day, friend?"

"Work, work, work, and then more work. I find keeping myself busy helps to soothe my conscience for a bit."

Anne responded, "You have lots of property, so the upkeep must be huge."

"No, Anne, I can afford to employ workers to do what needs doing, but I do most of it for my sanity. I like creating things; it sort of makes up for the destruction of my past, I think."

Every positive thing he said, he stripped from his character. He couldn't accept anything good that he did. A good honest day of work shouldn't have to make up for the 'destruction of his past'.

Anne found his comments shook her, made her shudder and she knew she should be cautious.

"I hope you can find some peace, Troy, and moments of happiness. I've found happiness is transient."

"Yes, I think you're right, Anne, and just when you find a bit of happiness, there is always some bastard that wants to take it from you. I will tell you a story in a bit, but I have to think about it. I don't want to offend you."

"Troy," Anne said, "I'm so sorry your life has been tragic, but there comes a time when you have to put it to rest. That's what you told me when I mentioned how that evil man took my island, my dreams, and separated me from my family. If your advice is good for me, chew on it for a while. You might like it. I'm going to cut out early tonight. A girl needs her beauty sleep and don't you dare laugh. It's a real thing! I hope our friendship continues. Good night." She inserted one red heart.

Chapter 9

Anne woke several times wondering if his story would be worthy of putting on paper. She was excited but also apprehensive. Her writing coach called her the romance novelist. When one of her classmates had to write a romantic scene, they asked Anne for help. If she was writing a book about this, there would be no romance in this story. That's not where she was going with this. She wasn't sure how much she wanted to know, just in case he was as vile as he said. When she opened the computer the next morning, a story was waiting for her. How much she could believe was up for grabs.

"About ten years ago, I ran into an old school friend who I had not seen in years. We were having lunch at a local pub, having a grand old time when, all of a sudden, he said, "Look at the tits on that." I turned to look and there was a young girl, probably 18. I said to him, "John, if you say that again, I will break your legs." He thought he would test me and said it again. Within 7 seconds, I had broken both his legs. He still can't walk properly. He overstepped the mark. When I worked in Africa, the black guards had a special name for me that meant Quick Fist."

Anne found herself doing lots of heavy breathing and she knew it was a combination of excitement and fear. Can a person be so ruthless? So violent? There was a pause in his text, then he continued.

"I wish I had not told you that. I don't know what possessed me, please just ignore it, but that's me. It's how I am. There are times when the broken me, surfaces and it's not good. I couldn't bear to lose your friendship. The date January 1, 2022, is permanently a part of me, tattooed in my heart. That's the first contact I had with you, sweet Anne.

"Listen, Troy, you don't have to be sorry. Who am I to judge you or anyone? FYI, there's no need to close the gate AFTER the horses escape." She inserted some silly laughing emojis. "You can talk to me. Sometimes unburdening our souls, helps. I almost drown a man and I wouldn't have had any regret. In fact, I regret not doing it. So, you see, we are all capable, given the right circumstance. You know the old saying, 'until you walk a mile in my shoes…' I know you get it."

He didn't respond so Anne went about her day. She and her partner Mark had been invited to some friends' house for the afternoon and early-bird dinner. (That's what it's called when you get our age!) Anne and her two former students played some ukulele together, had good laughs and good food. It was uplifting to get the weight of writing about Troy off her shoulders and anxiously waiting for him to share some other interesting tidbit. Maybe she was having an online affair as her daughter suggested. That's ridiculous, Anne thought, but her excuse was 'research' in hope of writing a best-selling novel before her ashes were blown by the wind into the Gulf of Mexico.

When she got home, Troy had sent her a message. It seemed he was more willing to share darker things from his past. Perhaps he was writing his own book based on their conversations. Wouldn't that be the ultimate switch? He was articulate, his writing interesting, his stories nearly unbelievable, but impossible not to read. What would his novel be called?

"Greetings Anne. How are you today? It's a beautiful morning here. I was up as the glory of the sun was rising over the ridge. I love that time of day when the mist sparkles off the wildflowers, the sky retreats from honeydew melon to colors of majestic purple, and the world comes to life."

These are the kind of words that made Anne more curious about the rough, violent man. He seemed too sophisticated to be a killer. She found herself shaking her head more than ever.

"Troy, can you tell me a bit about the area you call home?"

"Sure, Anne. It's beautiful here. I'm very near the mid-Eastern coast in an area considered sub-tropical. My property is surrounded by lush mountains, rolling hills, and many vineyards. I live about twenty minutes from the nearest town of 77,000 in New South Wales right near the coast. I can garden all year; the perfect area for me. I sometimes miss the company of good friends, but my animals are a godsend. They make me laugh; never a dull moment. I stay away from people as much as I can. I don't have much tolerance for their nonsense." (Inserting a snorting bull emoji)

She responded, "You make me laugh but I also nearly cry about your life and what you must have suffered."

"It is what it is and no one can change the past. We can only try not to repeat our past transgressions." He continued, "I've got a funny story for you, friend. I could tell you about the time I accidentally splashed urine on Idi Amin's shoes and was publicly flogged for it."

"That doesn't sound funny to me, Troy. You have a strange sense of humor. I was hoping your association with that evil regime was a long, tall tale."

"Believe me, it was not funny at the time, but thinking back on it, I have to laugh. The flabbergasted look on his face was priceless. I was urinating off his palace balcony. The only reason he didn't have me killed was that I was drunk and he was the one who supplied the alcohol."

"Oh my! Do I want to know why you were there?" searching for more information without sounding too obvious. "Publicly flogged? Seriously?" He didn't respond to her question so she let the sleeping dog lie. "Hey, did you just win that last game?" she asked. "You were distracting me with that awful story. I've decided your game-playing tactic is, 'it's not how you play the game as long as you win'. Quite a strategy, Troy."

"Flogged you, mate! You haven't been too kind in our games lately. You've scored better than me too often," he wrote.

"Too much flogging going on; just trying to impress you," Anne said.

"Oh yeah, well you have succeeded brilliantly," Troy said. "Off the subject, but something has been bothering me, and I'd like to talk about it to clear the air. Remember when I asked if you were catfishing me? I've heard the term and thought I'd sound more current. You have become the highlight of my day, every day, and I don't want anything to come between us. I would be very unhappy without you."

She hoped his comment was figurative. There was no real relationship in their future. She didn't want to lead him on, yet she needed to keep him on the hook to keep him talking. Shit! Maybe she was a catfish. She was hoping to get her hands on some of his wealth but a plan had not been completely born.

While he was still typing, she replied. "Troy, no need for an apology. I had to look it up myself. I can't, for a minute, think you would do that."

He continued. "Who or what kind of human would do something like that? Pretending to be someone they are not, in order to take advantage of a woman, is a terrible offense. I've never been a fan of technology, so this offends me even more. I was just lonely. Please believe me, that thought never occurred to me. Anne, if you ever need money, I would give you whatever you need, just ask me. I have more than enough for my needs."

"I actually believe you, but I will admit, you frighten me a bit with some of the things you say. I'm not sure who you really are."

"Anne, I feel sick now just thinking about it. I don't know what to say," inserting a tearful face.

"Let's just forget we had this conversation and move on. I love our chats; you challenge me with the game and make it fun," she assured him.

Troy said, "This does not change anything between us, but I am just not capable of even thinking about anything, at the moment. It's like I'm stunned; I keep trying to think but I can't. I'm mentally blocked!"

"As you know, better than I, people can be downright evil, preying on the vulnerable with no thought for the agony they create. That's not us, thank God, and no, I want nothing from you," she wrote, that being one of the biggest lies she ever told.

"I never wanted a phone so when I started to play this word game, I didn't know I could message anyone. Someone told me about it and I just wanted some company. That's why I picked you. I looked at your profile and I thought, she looks safe. I never gave a thought about how people would perceive me and now I feel ashamed of myself and yet I've done nothing wrong. Anne, it's not you. I didn't think of that side of it. I wonder if other people think I'm a catfish."

She answered, "You seem genuine to me. Please don't let this affect your ability to have online friends. Not everyone is bad, but beware, someone might catfish you."

"Thank you for your lovely words; they mean a lot to me. I think it's more the shock of it, like my integrity has been questioned. I know it was never your intention, but I wonder what others think of me now."

"Wow, you surprise me, not at all what I would expect from you, Bad Boy Troy. You are much more sensitive than I imagined, not the bully you pretend to be. I like this side of you." She wished there was an emoji with a tearfully sad face holding a pitchfork. No such luck.

"It's why I stopped my career, my work. I can't tell you about it, but I thought I was the good guy, and then one day

I realized I was fighting for the wrong causes and that I was, in fact, the devil to some people. I couldn't do it anymore."

"Bless your heart, Troy. We all have regrets but you are beautiful to me. I hope you don't distrust me."

"Never. You are my dear friend and I will only ever have good and decent thoughts about you, I promise. Good night, sweetheart."

Chapter 10

<u>**Suzie**</u>

It was time to get caught up with my friend Anne. She had been distant for the last two weeks. I needed to know what was going on. I could only hope she wasn't still carrying on with that Australian guy. We ordered our wine, truly one of our vices, and dipped our warm crusty bread.

"Okay Anne, what's going on? I haven't heard from you. It's like you dropped off the earth. Spill it, girlfriend."

"Suzie, I know you think I'm crazy but I finally have something exciting to write about. I don't know, maybe he's catfishing me, gaining my trust, but he seems so sincere."

"Isn't that what a catfish is all about? Gaining trust then making the hit?"

"I don't know. I've never been catfished. I enjoy our conversations; it's like having a brother. He's very respectful and fun. He's a good game player, a good conversationalist and it's giving me lots to write about," she winked.

"What can I do to make you stop this? I've never known you to be so careless. This is how unsuspecting women get taken to the cleaners."

"Okay Debbie Downer, what could possibly happen?" taking a sip of her lovely red wine. "There are a couple of things that make me wonder a tad."

"Now we're getting to it. Tell me. Maybe we can make some sense of it."

"Well, it's nothing major, silly stuff actually, but I can't quite stop thinking about it. Remember when President Bill Clinton was getting grilled about his affair with Monica?"

Suzie laughed, "You mean like fifty years ago? Yeah, I remember. So…?"

"Clinton kept saying, 'I _did not_ have sex with that woman'. Many behavioral specialists claimed that when someone said every word and didn't use contractions, it often indicated a lie. Well, Troy rarely uses a contraction. I thought maybe it was easier to type the whole word rather than apostrophes, but I'm not so sure."

"Anne, as much as I don't want to defend this guy, that seems like quite a stretch to me. Maybe that's how they talk in Australia."

"Geez Suze, you actually said something positive," crunching on another piece of bread.

"Is that all you've got, girlfriend? Anything I can throw a flag on the field for?"

"Well," Anne said, "he was describing his homestead to me in detail, of which he is very proud. When I asked him how big his man cave/workshop is, he answered in feet. That threw me because they use the metric system. It just seemed weird to me. He's using _sweetie_ more often and sending emoji kisses. I don't really care but I don't want it to get out of hand. Then we had this whole conversation about catfishing. He was very defensive about it, sensitive like I've never heard him before. It seemed out of character for him. He comes off as a badass and then I felt like he was going to cry about our catfish segment."

"It's a tough call, Anne. I don't know what to say," I said. "You are the most loving, giving person I know, and I don't want to see you get hurt. You always see the best in people and would never do anything wrong. Just be careful. I don't know how many times or ways I can say it. Will you listen to me and take it seriously?"

Anne dabbed her mouth, took a sip of wine, and said, "Of course, Suze. I didn't know you considered me so innocent and naïve. There's nothing to worry about. He's harmless and it's just a diversion for me, AND if he gets funky, I assure you, he'll regret it," she laughed and growled. "The fucker won't know what hit him."

Dipping my head, and avoiding eye contact with my friend, I admit I was shocked at the kind of loathing that came out of her mouth. I'd never heard Anne sound so fierce. She'd been through so much in her life, so much heartache, maybe she's just in self-protection mode; that would be a good thing. I know she really isn't capable of anything hateful. It's probably her second glass of glorious red wine talking.

We hugged and said goodbye knowing we would see each other soon. My very best friend was the gal I knew I could trust with any secret or sorrow and I hoped she knew she could count on me. We'd shared love and loss, triumph and tragedy, life and finally death when it comes down to it.

Anne couldn't get this man off her mind. Hoping it was only the excitement of writing a book she might finally get published, but it was more than that invading her thoughts. When she didn't hear from him, she worried. The longer his silence continued, the more she panicked. It had been two days since there was any word from him, even though she had messaged him several times. She had to stop seeming so "needy."

"I'm so sorry I've been out of touch, Anne. I had some chest pains during the night so I called an ambulance. Since I live twenty miles from the hospital, they are in no rush to service my area. I waited nearly five hours. By the time they arrived, I was so angry I could have killed them with my bare hands. I sent them away and finally drove myself to the clinic. I waited in the emergency for three hours and left without seeing a doctor."

"Oh my," Anne said. "That's nothing to mess with. Do you have a history of heart problems? Now I'm really concerned."

"I knew you would be, sweetie, but I had a lot on my mind and couldn't be fair to our conversations while I was wallowing in my self-pity. Please understand."

Anne sighed, feeling sorry if his story was true, but he tells incredulous stories so she took it like a bad pill. Maybe he was a prison inmate and had limited computer time. Offering a spoonful of sugar to make the medicine go down she said, "Troy, you must take care of yourself. Were you thinking of your previous life while you wondered if you would survive? God forgives. Please remember that."

"I've had two stents put in my heart a while ago and have been fine since then, so I'm not sure what the problem was. I have an appointment in three weeks to see the doctor. Socialized medicine is wonderful. That's a good example of being cheeky, in case you're wondering." HA!

"Where are you now, Troy? Safe and feeling okay, I hope."

"I'm lying in my pool, naked as the day I was born with the brilliant morning sun filling me with hope for another day. Don't worry about me. I am a man who walks, cannot die and I am a true phantom- invincible.

"That's a stretch to believe, Troy. Don't rely too heavily on that assumption. It could be the death of you." (Crazy face emoji)

Troy and Anne played a couple of games and then he became silent again. He always had a great excuse and Anne was becoming more doubtful about the real truth of this man. He rarely asked about her, except the usual, 'how are you doing?' Few questions about her life, her marital status, her children, or where she lived; he only talked about himself after Anne asked questions. She wondered what the conversations might be like if she didn't ask. Anne began thinking this behavior seemed suspicious. He probably had fifteen other women on the hook. He was charismatic. Perhaps all he wanted was a book written about him.

She wondered if he really cared, but then again, his previous contacts may have allowed him to garner all the information he needed about her. It's easy to do. She was becoming wary. Maybe he didn't care to know anything about her since he was just going to make some kind of move on her later in the game. She wondered if he would ask her for money, like so many scam artists today. Some doubt about his honesty crept in like a thief in the night. She needed to up her game and not get sucked in. Maybe she should suggest they talk to each other on one of the free apps. Many times, a person's voice and demeanor tell a more honest story.

Another few days went by without a word. She wasn't sure she would answer, if and when, he contacted her again. Her laptop dinged and it was him. She debated, finally opening the message.

"Anne, hi! I'm so sorry. I know you must have been concerned about me. I wouldn't want you to be worried but I did have some trouble. I've been in police cells for two days."

Ah ha, she almost squealed; maybe she called it right. "Naw, why would I be concerned? You're a big bad boy, aren't you? What did you do this time?" Did your temper get you in trouble?"

"It wasn't my fault, from my point of view. When I first got my new Harley, the police took note and watched me, jealousy maybe. She's a beauty. Anyway, I had it a week when they pulled me over for speeding- not that fast, but they were showing their authority. So, a couple days ago, I took her out for a spin and wanted to see what she'd do. I was in the countryside, I opened her up and the police were watching. They clocked me at 140 mph in a 60 zone. They took my bike- really pissed me off so I said some not-so-nice words and one of the cops laughed at me. I warned him not to laugh but he continued. I sucker-punched him in the throat. Bet he's not laughing now. He's still in the hospital. I'm laughing now. I win!"

"I don't know what to say," but she continued anyway. "You need a good talking to, young man. It's time you grow up and control yourself, for your own good. If I was your mum, I'd give you severe time out and face you in a corner, at the very least. I have an idea. How do you feel about using one of those apps where we can converse, and share photos and things? It's free no matter where we live."

"That would be amazing!" he said. "Let's do it…NOW! Maybe I could call you tonight if we get it set up."

Anne was excited but also hesitant. At this point, she didn't know what it could hurt. She was already in deep. She made quite an investment with the time she put into writing the book, so perhaps talking to him would give her more insight into the mystery man. She signed up and downloaded the app. Away we go!

10:00 PM, Anne's time. She grabbed her phone and went to her office. Her heart racing like a cheetah, she hesitantly answered his call. "Hello?"

"Anne?"

"Yes, Troy?"

"It can't be you. I've waited so long to hear your voice but I didn't want to be the one to suggest it. I can't believe I'm talking to the most important woman in my life."

"That's so kind of you, Troy. I've been hoping to hear your voice as well. You've got an amazing accent," she said.

"I don't have an accent," he said as he laughed. "You have an accent, but to be honest, I thought you'd sound a little more southern belle."

If he wants 'southern belle', that's what he'll get. She was good at speaking with different accents. "Well, darlin," she drawled. "I can be whatever it is your fantasy has become."

"I don't think you'd be comfortable in my fantasy, Anne. I'm 100 percent man and you are the woman of my dreams. We've only met too late, but that doesn't stop me from dreaming about you."

Here we go, she thought. This is probably going to get sexual and she couldn't do that. "I'm not a prude, but I appreciate the respect. I have been around the block a few times, ya'll."

"I'd love to take you around the block a dozen times, Anne, at whatever pace you prefer," he said. "If you like it slow and steady or fast and furious, that's what I'll give you."

"Troy, you know I can't have this kind of talk with you. Sorry. As long as I am in my relationship with Mark, I can't compromise that. It wouldn't be fair to him…or you for that matter."

"I know. I apologize but I'm so excited to hear your sweet, sexy voice. You sound so young and vibrant. Now I understand why people say, age is just a number."

"I believe women are more sensitive to age than men are. We're judged more harshly as we age but men get more distinguished. That's a crock if you ask me. That's why women are more hesitant to have a relationship with a significantly younger man. Of course, there are exceptions. Age doesn't mean we love less intently or our sex drive diminishes. It simply means we have more wrinkles and lots more experience; most men think that's a good thing."

"Croc? Do you want to hear about crocs here? They're big and ferocious man-eaters. Oh, I should leave that for another day," he said. "They are a real danger here so I'm always vigilant when I'm around the water, but I'll give you a lesson about crocodiles when you arrive. I can't wait to see those wrinkles and enjoy your experience."

"What?" Listening to his voice, she was giddy, even a bit turned on. He did sound sexy. "You know I will never come to Australia. Why do you tease me like that?"

"There's no tease to that, Anne. I'll make it happen, if you'll accept."

"Sorry, Troy. It's not in my budget or my lifestyle. I can't just pick up and go halfway around the world on a whim. By the way, when are you going to post a more recent picture of yourself? I want to see that silver fox."

"I'll do it. I hope you won't delete me when you see the real me."

"I told you before, Troy. It's not about looks; it's about what's in your heart."

"Anne, you make me miss my mum so much. The things you say to me remind me of her and I cry because of the things I did that broke her heart. I would never hurt you that way. Sometimes I wish I had a second chance to make it up to my mum. Anyway, the police proceeded to trash my new motorcycle and someone's going to pay. Sometimes I just can't let things go. I have to stand up for myself and, as I said before, human life doesn't mean much to me. They're jealous because I'm considered wealthy here, have a big beautiful home, and lots of toys and they've got nothing but their pissy little attitudes. Sorry, but that's just the way I feel. I didn't intend to bring our first conversation down. Forgive me."

Well, that was quite a mouthful and it tasted bitter in Anne's mouth. "It's okay, Troy. Friends can unload on each other. That's what friends do."

Their conversation continued for over an hour, sometimes a bit uncomfortable, funny, and heartfelt, leaving her with a feeling she needed him in her life, though she would never admit that. His voice was soft and comforting, soothing, delicious, intoxicating.

"Troy, I'm going to have to go now. This has been delightful. Just knowing you really do exist, not just on an internet game, has meant so much to me. Thank you."

"Anne, you have no idea how you've made me feel. I almost want to wake up tomorrow and spend another day on this planet. I know that sounds dramatic, but I'm isolated here and rarely interact with anyone other than occasional family. To know that someone thinks I'm worth spending time on has lifted me to heights I don't know if I've ever been. Can we talk again soon, please?"

Anne couldn't sleep, her mind taking her to places she had no business going, like into his arms and bed.

Chapter 11

Before she went any further with this nonsense, it was time to do some digging and find out who this man really is.

She looked up the area where he said he lived and it was amazing. Of course, it didn't mean he lived there, but his area code was correct. He probably lived in a penitentiary. She called the police station and asked if he was there. They didn't divulge much but they knew him and had recently had an altercation with him. Putting her suspicions away about prison, she paid an online service to do some criminal investigation. She researched the Idi Amin regime to see if there was anything there about him. She contacted two other agencies and paid for their services to find any information pertinent to him. She couldn't be too careful.

When the information began coming back, she carefully combed through all of it. It seemed his stories were quite accurate. He hadn't been convicted of any serious crimes in Australia. He had lived in Uganda and Zimbabwe but there were no formal charges listed during his stay there. There was no information about his education or profession. He had been married once, he was one of ten children and listed no children of his own. He was the owner of the property where he currently lived and there was no mortgage, but several bank accounts with undisclosed balances. Several satellite views of his property showed the beauty of the area.

Surprisingly most of what he told her seemed to be true. She couldn't confirm that he actually had worked for the dictators he named, but it seemed like a reasonable assumption since the pieces appeared to be coming together. There were, however, several articles about a sharp-shooter assassin who was unnamed. The stories about his ability were fascinating but no one was able to identify him, although it was believed he was from Australia. He supposedly carried out the murderous orders barked out by Idi Amin. Many stories related to high-ranking officials who had challenged the dictator, disappeared without a trace. Unexplained deaths were investigated with no conclusion as to who was responsible for this reign of terror. The articles Anne read indicated the sniper was clever, never being seen, but extremely ruthless. No target was safe. Confirming many of his statements, she hoped he was as respectful to women as he seemed, or she might be in trouble.

The information, or lack of it, spurred Anne on. She felt more confident about his stories, but also shaken to think a man who seemed so kind to her, could be a murderer for hire. He seemed to have a certain respect for women that caused her to reflect on a conversation they had recently.

Troy said, "Anne, did I tell you about the big Russian woman, the only woman I have ever hit? Now that was a fine fight. She very nearly killed me; stabbed me three times."

"Oh my!" (adding scary emojis) "You are a great storyteller. That's not really true? Seriously?"

"Seriously," he said. "She was a brut, tall, muscular, not an ounce of fat with fire-red hair. I'm a sucker for redheads. She was crazy and mean as a caged viper. She was a friend, a cohort. She was bragging about Brezhnev and I mouthed off. I told her if she mentioned him once more, I would go to Russia and root him. We were very, very drunk. She stabbed me 3 times and nearly killed me. She continued her attack; I kicked her in the pudendum as hard as I could with steel-toed boots. I lost almost half my blood. It was truly a life-or-death situation. The craziest thing was, that I bedded her while bleeding out. Go figure, I'm just a nice, forgiving guy. Love me those redheads!" (A dozen crazy emojis laughing)

"That's a frightening story. Not sure I want to hear more."

"Anne, if I can forgive a Russian minx who stabbed me, I can forgive anything you might toss my way."

Anne felt beads of sweat collecting on her forehead. She may be in over her head. Sharks, cannibals, venomous snakes, scorpions, crocodiles, and Troy; she wasn't sure which she feared the most.

"I've got you pegged, Troy. You're trying to distract me from our games with your stories so you can win. I feel that competitive need coming from you. You'll do anything to win…but don't underestimate me!" She hoped his mind stayed focused on her comment and not her real purpose.

"Ha!" he wrote. "I know you're withholding secrets from me. You're very coy and wicked. You never offer me anything unless I ask and then you are cagey; but I'm such a gentleman, I'm going to forgive you."

"Don't scare me, Bad Boy Troy."

"Now come on sweetie, I would never, ever do anything to hurt my precious Anne. You are officially my new best friend, actually my only friend at the moment and probably the only one I need. You're like my surrogate mum. I'll bet you were a redhead when you were young. If you were a sexy ginger, you would have had trouble getting rid of me. Tell me the truth, sweet thing."

Those comments were too close for comfort and she felt something was building in the air. She wondered if he was as lonely as he wrote or if it was all a ploy. Most everyone has an agenda; two can play that game.

"Actually Troy, I was an auburn, freckle-face girl a million years ago. If we had met back then the only thing that would have appealed to you was my red hair. I would not have been your love interest. At this point, we can be friends and share stories with each other, no commitment, no worries."

"Don't be so sure. I am the phantom; I am relentless. I relate to older women. Oh, I didn't tell you. I'm getting a new donkey; it's a Jenny and I'm going to name her Dolores Claiborne. She's a beautiful creamy color with dark rings around her eyes. She looks unusual. At seventeen years old, she has been badly mistreated, but she'll do fine here. She can move straight into Ivor's bedroom and I'm sure she'll be happy. What do you think?"

"Dolores Claiborne? That gives me chills. That movie, Misery, portrayed her as one badass psycho, but okay, it's your call. It seems you have a thing for redheads, older and evil women. I think it's wonderful that you have a soft spot in your heart for abused animals and I'm sure she'll fall in love with you. I wish I could meet her one day; of course, I know that will never happen," Anne interjected a sad face emoji.

Troy answered immediately, "I see no reason why you can't meet her anytime you'd like, do you?"

"That's a very nice thought, and if that's an invite, I appreciate it, but it just can't happen. I'm going through some things that I can't talk about right now, but thank you, sweet man."

"What?! Have you been holding out on me? What can I do to make it better? I'm here for whatever you need."

"Oh no," Anne said. "I'm not one to ask for favors or rescuing. I'll be fine; it will just take a while to sort through things." If he had a plan, she had a better one and it was clearly in motion.

"Please, don't make me worry. I care so deeply for you and I will do anything to help. You just have to let me know. I'm quite a wealthy man so if it's money issues, though I know you wouldn't ask, I've got you covered and then some." Hearts and roses emojis.

Anne had a feeling her plan was working and she was proud of her finesse. He won't know what hit him until it happens. She needed to protect herself, but she'd come this far, and like a good mystery novel, it was reading well.

****

<u>Suzie</u>

It seems Anne has been more distant to me than usual, no texts or calls unless I initiate them. I'm not sure what it is, but if she's having trouble with something, I'd never let her down. I just have to dig a bit deeper to find the problem. I texted.

"Come over for lunch on Friday, okay? I'll make that California Pie you love so much," I said, inserting a happy tongue-licking face.

84

"That sounds fun. I can tell you what's going on with Troy".

"There shouldn't be anything going on with some mystery man, but I still want to see you. Noon, okay"?

"Noon is good but don't be a stick in the mud. I've got some great stories."

"Oh, okay, stop. See you Friday".

I fidgeted for two days letting my imagination run wild. Anne wasn't the kind of person to get carried away with such silliness. I'd known her for over forty years and she's acting like the teenager she was when we met.

My house smelled as delicious as any five-star restaurant; sautéed vegetables, roasted turkey, and fresh herbs tucked inside handmade pie crust with a thick layer of melted Havarti Dill cheese, and fresh-baked bread. If the food didn't loosen her tongue, maybe the Long Island Iced Tea would.

Our afternoon began with our customary hug and, of course, she brought a lovely bouquet of flowers for the table. Anne knows no limit to showing her appreciation for any kindness. She's an amazing woman.

Slicing the warm bread and pouring our tea, I gave her an inquisitive quirky smile. "Okay Anne, spill the beans. What's going on with you? I won't let you eat until you tell me what you've been up to."

A devious-sounding giggle escaped, "Whatever are you talking about?"

Making a face in jest that said, tell me now or you'll be sorry.

Anne grinned again before holding up her hands, "uncle, uncle. I'll tell you anything you want to know. Want the combination to my safe? My jewelry?"

"You know damn well what I want, girlfriend. Now give!" as I smacked my hand on the kitchen island. "Tell me what's going on with that Australian crocodile hunter. Hopefully, you're not still messing with him."

"Okay, okay, but there's not that much to tell," she said.

"Then why are you being so coy about it? I am your best friend, right?"

"Of course, Suze. Look, Troy and I have some interesting conversations. He's been involved in some incredible situations- almost unbelievable stuff. Sometimes I think maybe he wants a book written about his life and he's chosen me to give it a shot. He could just be making it all up as we go along.

"That would be clever of him but where would that leave you? Does he know you're writing about him?"

"Yes, I put the hook out there, and he bit. I have his permission to write and be the 'captain of the ship' as he said. I also have his permission to dream about him every night.

He's pushing the sexual innuendos a bit too far for me, but sometimes a girl has to do what a girl has to do."

"Oh Anne, I was going to say you're playing with fire, but you're playing with an atomic bomb!"

"It's just a cat and mouse game. He's ten thousand miles away and can't come to the USA, so what's the problem? It's fun. Besides, we talked on the phone and he's got a beautiful voice, so sexy. Oops, did I say that?"

I grimaced, "the world is smaller than we think; he was probably sitting there with a butcher knife in his hand, thinking about how good you would taste! And who's to say he doesn't know people here if he wants to get to you?"

"Look Suze, I've got nothing he wants. Romantically, I'm much too old, he's not looking for a wife, he's a loner. No worries, as he says," Anne laughed.

After Anne left in the Uber, I paced the floor. Something's not right with this. Damn internet. If she puts all this time and money into writing this book and then he comes after her about rights to the book, that would suck. Not only am I worried about her physical and emotional safety, but her financial safety as well. What if he is a catfish? I don't understand what her end game is, but I know it can't be anything questionable. That's not who Anne is.

Chapter 12

Anne got home at 3:00 PM, the time she usually hooked up with Troy online. She signed into the game; he had played and sent her a morning greeting. She responded, excited to hear from him.

"Hi, Troy. What are you doing today? You're up a little earlier than usual, aren't you?"

"Why are you always so concerned about me? You always remind me of mum. She's the only one who ever treated me the way you do. I didn't sleep well. I was miserable all night from a sunburn. I was working in the yard yesterday so now I'm lying in my pool as naked as the day I was born. Maybe this cool water will take some of the sting out of the burn. I'll probably blister since I used to be a redhead."

"I think I should scold you for not being more responsible and caring for yourself, but lying in the pool sounds like a good thing."

"I made my morning tea so I'll get out soon, sit under a tree and give the neighbor lady a cheap thrill in a bit."

"What are you talking about?" Anne questioned.

"I don't know if I told you this, but I like to walk around naked. I swim naked, drive my tractor naked, and work around my property and in my gardens naked. I love it. It's very private but there is an old girl who lives in a house about 350m away on a hill overlooking my space. I have felt for a while someone was watching me and yesterday, I caught her red-handed with a pair of binoculars. Remember, I might be 62 but I am in pretty good nick. Please don't be offended by what I am about to say, but the fact is, I am hung like a Jerusalem donkey. I always try to put on a good show for her. She's never called the police so I think she enjoys it. Yep, there she is now, binoculars and all."

The vision in Anne's mind was raw and unfiltered; she wondered if he was trying to break down the barriers of sexual adventure by throwing suggestive ideas at her. She answered his story. "I guess you have a right to be naked assuming you're not offending anyone. This sounds a bit like a 'fish story'. The one that got away was always the biggest; if you're generously endowed as you said, why did she need the binoculars?" Oops, she shouldn't have said that but she hit send before she censored. She went back with some laughing emojis. Men are sensitive about size.

Troy didn't miss a lick. He came right back with, "I said like a mule, not a tree trunk! I did not intend to sound like I was bragging but it is a funny story, don't you agree? Please don't be offended, not my intent."

"I might be old, Troy but I'm not dead! I've had my share of encounters, too."

"Right then, since we're on this delicate subject, when I was 14 years of age, Miss Carson was my science teacher. She was 38 years old, looked about 19, and had the most luxurious red hair. I'm a sucker for redheads, you know. I'm quite sure I had a major crush on Miss Carson. I was rather a well-developed young man at 14 years.

One day Miss Carson asked me if I would like a job tidying up her gardens. I agreed. Came the weekend, I arrived bright and early, knowing I had a big job ahead of me. It was sweltering hot and before long the only thing I was wearing was my boots and a pair of tight cut-off jeans. At lunchtime, she called out to come in and eat. She had prepared a nice meal and I was hungry. She commented on what big shoulders I had. I told her I played sports and worked out but they were aching right then from the hard work. Miss Carson stood and began giving me a massage. Little did I know, the next four months would be the happiest and sexiest of my life.

She most certainly educated me on the art of Tantric lovemaking, which is something I have put to good use over the years. Our sexual relationship came crashing to a screaming halt when a teacher walked in whilst we were flagrant. I can't tell you what an effect this had on me but it changed the course of my life. If you want to know how it molded me, let me know."

Anne shook her head as she read, knowing this would be child abuse today; she wasn't sure how she should respond. "I don't know what to say. It's nearly taken my breath away to think about how she violated you. If it fashioned your life, of course, I would be interested in chapter 2, whenever you're ready but I don't approve of what she did to you."

Troy answered, "I hope you're not upset with me, Anne, but there are very few people who know anything about this and I feel so close to you, I felt safe."

"I'm sorry for what you went through but I have to say, your stories intrigue me and spur me on to continue to write, (of course with poetic license) about your life. If telling me helps you unburden your soul, please don't hold back. I hope we can look at this as a pleasurable experience that allowed us to create a judgment-free friendship and end someday with only the highest regard for each other."

There was complete silence while they played an entire online game. Neither of them knew where to go after Troy revealed that very personal story. Two hours later, Troy wrote, "Sorry I've been silent. I had to regroup. Sometimes when I think of my life, I get very depressed. You really don't know much about me and the vicious man who lives inside me. Some things I cannot tell you or you might become vulnerable; better to leave some things unsaid. I must always look over my shoulder."

"You're scaring me, Troy. Do I need to worry for my safety?"

"No Anne, I feel a kinship with you- like you are family. I will only protect you. However, what I find strange is I can punch, kick, and kill a fellow human being, but I could never hurt an animal. Isn't that strange? I guess that's what comes from seeing the worst in mankind, and I have seen the worst man can do, believe me!"

Anne rubbed her hands across her face, more fear creeping into her. "Troy, perhaps that's who you were at one time, but I don't believe that's who you are now. You're so respectful, even playful; I believe you have changed."

"See, that's what I love about you, Anne. Did I just say that? Sorry but I have to confess I have constant thoughts of you. You're the highlight of my days. I open the game the minute I open my eyes. It's you who brings out the best in me. Here's a hypothetical, if we had met 35 years ago, do you think you would have liked me? Would you have followed me on my adventures and would you have looked after me when I got hurt? Or would you have hated me with a vengeance? Would you have given me a darling little red-haired princess? I am absolutely fixated on you. I can't stop thinking about you. I think I might be in love with the idea of you. I have a vision of what you might be like and if my vision is correct, I don't know what to do. My mind wanders where you are concerned. I wonder if you could be my new Miss Carson. I'm sorry if I offend you."

After absorbing his words, she wrote, "Whew Troy! That's a lot of conjecture and since we can't turn back time, we can only guess what might have happened. I really know so little about you and you know almost nothing about me, it's impossible to say. I shouldn't say this, but I've got a few talents of my own that perhaps even Miss Carson didn't know. However, I'm four years older than you so we just need to agree that I'll be your pretend mum or your favorite auntie. Any ideas we might have for a future together is a moot point."

"Well, I can dream, can't I?" he said. "If we had met thirty years ago, make no mistake, you would be mine now, guaranteed. You have to admit, I don't suffer from a lack of confidence. By the way, I've just posted a recent picture of myself. Now you will see the real me. I'm still a handsome devil, despite the years."

She was anxious to see his new picture. He was tanned to golden bronze color, sitting shirtless in front of the camera. His shoulders were broad and thick, with his silver hair and silky beard flowing onto his chest. She was even more attracted to his current look than his younger self. She'd like to touch that beard and put her fingers around the loose curls in his hair. She couldn't allow herself to go there but she wasn't sure she could stop it; it was fun to let her imagination take a little trip. She needed to stay with her plan and her pen.

"I'm in awe of your shameless confidence. I assure you; I wouldn't let you outbrag me," she said. They enjoyed friendly banter. "I like the new picture. I'm not sure why you didn't want me to see you."

"I do want you to see me," Troy said, "but here, in person, on my turf."

"I can't tell you what to do, think, or feel, but I have too much baggage for you to think of me that way. My troubles are ongoing but I'm not going to burden you with them. I got myself into this mess; I'll have to find a way to get myself out."

"WHAT? I can't stand knowing you hurt. Please share with me. I'll do whatever you need to help you. I really will," he pleaded.

With a slightly evil glint in her eye, Anne gleefully rubbed her hands together. She knew her plan was working. "Troy, this story is more about you than me; there are certain things I can't share with you. I know you understand that."

"I'm going to keep asking. I have connections all around the globe and I can handle things almost anywhere if you get my drift."

****

Anne had a feeling if they were actually talking, he would have whispered that statement. She felt her skin crawl and feared she might be playing out of her league. She needed to rethink her strategy; this had worked for her in the past, but she had to tweak her approach.

Heading toward her office, she reached for a wine glass. On second thought, a vodka martini would better fit her mood. She needed a good swift kick in the ass to get her plan rolling. She twirled her pen around her fingers several times thinking about her successes. She wasn't sure why she had become so elated and obsessed about victimizing men; perhaps it was because she had been abused and crushed so many times in her past. Maybe it was to prove that, even though her youth had faded, she still had something that men wanted. At her age she wasn't worried about spending time in jail if she was ever caught; she just didn't want one of her quests to retaliate and torture her. She wasn't a fan of pain. She knew she had to play her cards just right with Bad Boy Troy.

Sipping her martini and savoring her olives, she always liked two, she thought about Harry, a recent pursuit. He was so very rich, a man of his own making, yet he fell under her spell so easily. That was a beautiful transaction, a feather in her cap. When she saw his mansion in the Hamptons, she was all in and he was doomed. She gleaned him of enough to feed her passion for Gucci and then some. A few diamonds, some Saks Fifth Avenue threads, and endless baubles, a total success. Anne smiled with satisfaction. It was like shoplifting, only better.

David, ah, sweet David. She almost had a moment of regret thinking about her relationship with him. It wasn't about the money, he had plenty to share; it was the heartache she left him with when she admitted she couldn't stay. He was so vulnerable; she felt a tinge of remorse, but she warned him that she was gasoline to his fire. Poor David. After all, Anne loved games.

Troy was going to be more difficult although her confidence soared each time he made confessions about his feelings for her. She wouldn't be playing on her home turf, a disadvantage for sure. Laying out the plan to have him willingly and gladly put a couple hundred thousand dollars in her hand, made Anne giddy. She wondered how Suzie would react if she knew the naughty game she was playing. Suze thought Anne was a woman of complete honesty and integrity, however, she didn't have a clue how smart and devious she was. Anne hoped Troy was as rich as he appeared. It needed to be worthwhile to follow through.

Chapter 13

It had been over a day since Anne heard from Troy. Their messages were getting longer, more frequent, and personal so she was surprised that he hadn't contacted her. She didn't want to be the chaser so she needed to make certain he was still infatuated with her. "Hey, Bad Boy, hope you're okay. You're not in jail again, are you? LOL"

A few seconds later he answered, "I'm really busy. Can't talk. Problems."

Whatever it was, she hoped it wouldn't mess up her plans. She knew dealing with this man was dangerous, but the challenge was irresistible. Don't tell her she can't do something because she would prove you wrong. She was a 'go big or go home' kind of gal.

A few hours later, a ping notified her of a message. "Hello sweetie. I'm sorry I've been neglecting you, but things have been difficult here for me."

"Troy, I'm so sorry. I was beginning to think you had dumped me for one of your other girlfriends!"

"Don't be ridiculous, Anne. You're the light of my life. You can't get rid of me that easily. I've had some big problems and no, I'm not in jail…yet anyway."

"I won't ask but if you want to share anything with me, you know I'm here for you."

"You're so sweet. Where have you been all my life? If I had known you years ago, I'm sure my life would have been much different. You bring out the best in me…if there is a best side."

"Listen, Buddy, no one is all good or all bad. Given the right circumstances, any of us can turn into a creature we can't recognize. I think you've just been dealt a lot of crap that's influenced you."

"See, that is something else I love about you. You have a mother's heart and you always try to soothe this savage beast."

"I don't believe for one minute you're a beast- misguided maybe," she said.

"Okay, I have to vent and you are a wonderful listener. Australia is the driest continent on the planet so it is rare that we get any substantial rain. It started raining three days ago and it is still raining. I was loving it, freshening everything up, giving my gardens and 110 rosebushes welcoming water. Then it happened. I have a creek that runs near my home and workshop. It began to overflow and was rising quickly. My animals were getting nervous with the water invading their pens. I brought them closer to the house and tied them until I made sure they were safe, but the water kept coming.

Soon, my huge shop had nearly two feet of water inside. All my tools, tractors, ATV, mowers, and pool equipment were getting flooded as the water gushed closer to the house. I had no choice but to bring the animals inside. I know it sounds gross and unsanitary but I could not let harm come to them. I knew something was wrong to cause this flood. It had to be more than the rain. I got into my truck and followed the flow of the creek to a dickhead neighbor three properties away. HA! There was the problem. He had dammed the creek to get more water on his garden and that caused the flood."

"Wow! I'm sorry you're dealing with that. Once the neighbor understands the problem he caused you, he will remedy it," Anne said. "What is the situation now?"

"Now? Let me see… the rain is nearly done and the son-of-a-bitch fixed the problem with his end loader while I watched. He's lucky to still have a head on his shoulders. His jaw and eyes will be sore for a while, but I do not think he will give me any more issues. Done and done."

Anne sucked in a hard breath wondering if this guy was for real. His stories left her disbelieving that anyone could be that ruthless with no concern for the human factor.

"What's the condition of the animals, Troy?"

"They are just fine. We did have a couple issues with poop on the floor but to be expected. My floors are all slate so that's easy cleanup. Dolores Claiborne is the sweetest little donkey you have ever seen. She is tiny as donkeys go.

She is laying on a sheepskin rug in my guest bedroom at the moment. I think she's smiling. LOL!"

Aha! This was the perfect time to cast her net. "Nice for Dolores, but where would I sleep if I come to visit you?"

"What?! Would you consider coming to visit me? I would be overwhelmed with joy. You could always sleep with me," he inserted a little devil emoji.

"You know I can't do that but…nice try. We're just friends, remember. I'm like your mum or your favorite auntie."

She liked his reaction and knew she hadn't lost her touch. Her plan to get her hands on Troy's money was working like reading a playbill. She was concerned that maybe he wouldn't like her in person but that was a gamble she was willing to take.

"Right, but you are the first person in many years who has treated me as a worthy human being and I can't help but fantasize. If you insist, I will settle for some big kangaroo hugs!"

"It's fun for me to fantasize about you, too, but everything I have is tied up at the moment. I couldn't even afford a ticket. I've always been independent but, somehow, I let my guard down, and now I have a major problem. It would be nice to get away, just to take a breath of Australian air," and you, she thought.

"Anne, money should not even be considered. It is no problem for me. I will pay for your ticket and treat you like a queen. Please tell me you'll come and I will start making arrangements," he nearly pleaded. "I want to see you, eat breakfast with you, have a cocktail, show you what I have built here. You would be impressed. You might decide you like it, and me, you might not want to leave."

This was the reaction Anne hoped for. She just had to remain careful to keep her real purpose from him. "That's so very kind of you, Troy. You're as sweet as I thought you were. I might be able to come for a bit but couldn't stay long or I stand the chance of losing everything I've worked for all my life."

"I can hardly breathe, Anne. The very thought of you walking across my CLEAN slate floors has me in a dither. When can you come? I will set everything up."

"Troy, don't jump the gun. I have lots of things to check before I can decide. I'm not sure I can leave the country with a pending lawsuit; I have to try to secure my assets as best I can and then, most importantly, I'd have to figure out what to wear!"

"HA! You are so funny. I haven't laughed so much in years since I met you. What can I do to make this happen for us?"

"Don't get excited yet. I'll let you know after I've checked everything out here on my end. You have to assure me you'll treat me with respect."

"Of course," he answered. "Nothing but complete respect, always throwing in some kangaroo hugs."

"Are kangaroo hugs like bear hugs here?" she added some crazy eye emojis.

"They are EXACTLY like bear hugs."

"Troy, I meant to ask you how your visit was with your old friend Dave. You said he had done something that disappointed you but you never mentioned it again. You don't have to say if it's too personal."

"No Anne, I don't mind you asking. It's just sad. He was in the same business as me, and his agenda was money. I gave him $75,000. I will never miss that small amount of money but it was hurtful really; I do owe him my life, so I did not mind too much. Just wish he was here to see me, and not my money."

"I'm so sorry, Troy. I shouldn't have brought it up. I don't know what to say. I can tell it's painful for you and that is not my goal."

"I just gave it to him as a gift. Saving my life at his own peril was worth a small gift, but I hoped he was here to see me. Friendship doesn't mean to others what it means to me,

I guess. Don't you dare feel bad about asking. I'll tell you anything you want to know."

Anne started feeling nervous about her plans for Troy. After all, he owed her nothing and since they didn't really know each other, she wondered how far she could push. Maybe he knew more about her than she suspected if he had contacts around the world, as he said. He wouldn't really have any reason to investigate her. Nothing she said or did would warrant suspicion. She would continue with her plan but no one must know. She was just little old Anne. He was probably a bigger scam than she was, a more ruthless catfish.

Thinking about her 'relationship' with Troy, she gloated a bit. Her first idea was to write a book based on his stories and their conversations. It was fun to talk with a stranger and build a real character from someone she never met. What was even better was that her writing was good enough to make this stranger fall in love with her, with nothing but her words. Maybe this would be a best seller. The rest of this story remains to be seen. She had never been so bold as to travel halfway around the world to pull off one of her little scams. She was, after all, a tiny fish in a very big pond. Hoping she would be successful and come back home alive, without damage, though scary, was exciting. What the hell did she have to lose? She wasn't getting any younger, so why not take some risks?

Later that day, Troy started a new game. "Hey, my darling Anne. Hope you're doing well. I'm sitting here with a new book and wondered how your book is coming along. I guess I'll become a legacy…at least in my own mind," (inserting four smiley faces).

"Hi, Troy. I've been working on the book but I don't know if you'll like it, if you ever read it, that is. It's partly your stories and mine with some flavorful fiction thrown in. Gotta keep those readers engaged!"

"I hear you. Have we kissed yet or made love? I'll be excited to hear how that goes."

"Troy, WE haven't kissed or made love, not in the book or ever. The characters are getting better acquainted but they haven't even met in person. You know this is all a fantasy, right?"

"Yeah, I get it but I can't help but think of you that way. I'm sorry. I believe the written word is the most beautiful of things. I can escape to faraway places, paradises, into someone else's mind, into space. I can smell the aroma of foods, feel the sun and breeze on my face, from words someone puts on paper. It's a magical thing. I don't know what I would do without books. When I don't have a book, I read labels on cans."

"Gee, Troy, that's poetic and beautiful. Are you sure you're not a writer trying to get ideas from me?"

"No, I'm too honest to do something like that, but it's a nice compliment. I'm a lot of things that are less than good, but honesty is the motto I live by. Oh, by the way, you asked if I smoke. Yes, I do but I'm not a heavy smoker. I love having a joint now and then, especially when I'm feeling sorry for myself. It helps relax me. How's that for honesty?"

"I'm impressed and I love that you have no problem talking to me, a total stranger."

"Anne, you're no stranger to me. I look into your soul and see nothing but good. I feel like we've known each other forever. Do you feel the same?"

"Yes, it's odd how we can have such a connection without seeing each other and only hearing our voices, yet I feel the same about you. I will admit, you scare me a bit; that temper of yours worries me."

"I would NEVER EVER hurt you, Anne. You have become part of me. You've become as precious as my animals and I've never said that about another human being."

Sighing deeply, wishing she had one of those joints he was talking about, maybe it would help her nerves, too. She wondered if she should rethink her plans and not mess with this man. He seemed like a loose cannon, unpredictable, ruthless, yet loving….and rich.

"That's quite a compliment coming from someone who puts no stock in the human race. You never cease to amaze me," Anne wrote.

"Thanks, my dear sweet Anne. It's 1:00 AM and I need to catch some sleep but I will dream of you. You've changed my life. I love you, Anne. Goodnight," (inserting hearts and kisses)

Chapter 14

Pouring herself a glass of wine, Anne sat in her near-dark house. Thinking this was moving entirely too fast, she was pleased with the progress she had made in a few short weeks. How much time did she want to invest in her 'project'? The sooner she could complete her plan, the better. There was some hesitation festering inside. She was feeling something for him. Perhaps it was sorrow, empathy, excitement at knowing her words could change a man, ignite emotions he hadn't felt in years. She'd come this far; she saw no real reason she shouldn't continue. Game ON! Anne was going to Australia and Troy was going to pay her to come. He just didn't know it yet.

****

Suzie

Startled by the ringing of her phone, Anne reached for the light in the kitchen and answered Suzie's call. "Hey, girlfriend! How are you? I was just going to call you," a little white lie.

"I'm good but I'm curious about you. It's been over a week and complete silence. Cat got your tongue?"

Anne laughed. "I don't have a cat, silly. Busy with stuff; you know how it is."

"Yea, I think I know how it is. You're too busy playing with your Australian boyfriend. What gives?"

"Well…" wondering how much she should tell Suze, "He's not my boyfriend but I am going to Australia."

Before she could get all the words out, Suzie was screaming over the phone. "No! No! Have you lost your ever-lovin' fucking mind? What the hell is wrong with you? You can't go around the world to meet some psychopath. Tell me it's not true, Anne, please!"

Anne laughed, a slight quiver in her voice. She'd like to have her best friend's nod of approval but it wasn't a deal-breaker if it didn't happen.

"Suzie, calm down, please. First, it's only halfway around the world and…

"Stop it, Anne! This is serious. This is no time to joke. Have you lost your senior marbles? Should we have you committed?"

That comment tickled Anne and she giggled. "Listen to me, Suze, and don't interrupt until I've finished; then you can say whatever you want. Okay?"

I stood shaking my head and pounding my fist on the other end of the phone, but agreed to listen to this craziness. "Go for it, Anne."

"You, of all people, know the crap I've been through. I've given until my heart is raw. I have no more to give. I've always been the subject of someone's ideals and orders for my life; always doing the right thing, even if wasn't right for me. I don't have much more time when I can travel and do something for myself. If anything happens to me, at least, I did it and I'd have no regrets. I'm making plans to cover my bases and I'm sure I'll be safe. As far as Troy goes, I can't imagine he would have any desire to harm me in any way. That's my story and I'm stickin' to it!"

"Anne, Anne, Anne. What can I do to make you understand? Think about your daughters, and your granddaughters. How would they feel if they knew you were playing with fire like this? I have this vision of you standing on the edge of a volcanic inferno, ready to take a leap into the center of it."

"You know, Suze, I think they'd be damn proud of me for stepping out of the mold everyone has poured me into. I'm finally thinking for myself and following through, even if it seems crazy. We know we're not going to live forever so…I think I deserve to actually LIVE a little."

"Okay, Anne. I've known you long enough to figure out I can't change your mind. Will you do me a favor?" Not waiting for a response, I continued, "Please get your affairs in order before you go. You know, make sure you have a will and how things are supposed to be dealt with. I know it's terrible to ask you to do this, but it's good preparation, even if you do make it home safe and sound."

"You're quite the drama queen, Suze. I'm sure everything will be fine but, just in case, I've already taken care of it. Gotta run, hon. Talk to you soon. Love you. Bye."

My friend hung up the phone so quickly I didn't have a chance to respond. I think she didn't want to hear any more of my opinion, but damn, I'm worried about her.

****

Because of the time differences between the USA and Australia, Troy and Anne didn't have much time to communicate before one or the other had to go to bed. Just before Anne was turning in, Troy messaged her.

"I've been thinking about you coming to visit and I'm so excited. There are so many things I want to show you. I think you'd love my home and gardens, and of course, Dolores. She is so sweet. I just picked up my brand, spanking new Toyota Land Cruiser V8 diesel, with every possible bell and whistle you can think of. Now I'm waiting on my new boat that should be here in about three weeks. With my new vehicle, I'll be able to tow the boat if I choose and stay on the water for days at a time. It's got sleeping facilities, a galley, a head, and ample deck space. I'll probably lease a space at the marina on the lake so the dockmaster can have it ready in a short. That makes more sense to me."

"Wow, that sounds amazing!" You're talking my love language now. Anything with water, boats, fishing, cooking, and eating. I am an Aquarius after all!"

"Anne, wouldn't it be nice? I could take you to my favorite fishing spot, guaranteed to catch fish. I can't catch a cold in freezing weather but women are luckier than men. We could put out crab pots and go down to a little spot where the best oysters grow straight off the rocks. Doesn't get any better. I can't wait. Love you, sweetie. Please think about it seriously."

"It sounds amazing, Troy. I have kicked it around but I don't know if I could swing it right now."

"I decided it's time I spend some of my hard-earned money. I can't take it with me so I might as well enjoy it while I can. I didn't *need* the new boat or Harley but boy did I want them, but I NEED you! Whatever it takes to get you here, and have you in my life, I'm willing to do without a thought.

"I can understand. We should all try to enjoy the things that bring us some happiness before it's our time," she said. "Tell me where you plan to launch the boat, you know what the area is like."

"My favorite place to fish is Lake Macquarie. It's beautiful. Look it up on the internet. If you love it as much as I do, when you spend some time there with me, I would even buy you a house right on the water. Let me know when I can buy that first-class plane ticket for you." (Kissy face) "I also think we should get a houseboat, always wanted one. What do you think?"

"Believe it or not, a houseboat has always been a dream of mine. I've thought about renting one for a while to see if it's as lovely as I imagined."

Anne was overwhelmed by his offer. If he was for real, she hit the jackpot. If he was a bigger catfish than she, this was going to be a great story to tell. She wasn't sure what he wanted from her. He hadn't asked for money; he hadn't been overly sexually suggestive; he's a man so she had to expect some of that. Overall, he seemed genuine. There has to be a hook somewhere that he's hoping she'll bite. The way things were going, it wouldn't take long to figure out his angle.

"Troy, you need to be careful. There are too many women who would love to take advantage of you. Your offers are much too generous for someone you don't even know."

"I do know you, Anne. I've become closer to you in the two months we've been talking than I've been to anyone in years. There's no one else I want to share my time with or care for. I love you, sweetie, not in a lustful way, but in a caring way, in the kind of way that if something happened to you, I would be devastated. You have become a very important part of my life. You need to know that. I could never do anything to hurt you, but I would do anything to protect you; if I had to, I would kill or die for you…remember that."

Anne had to clear her head. This was too much to comprehend. It had to be a gimmick. No one can fall in love with a total stranger by the words she has written. What came to mind was the tale of Cyrano de Bergerac. He was a talented poet and swordsman with an extremely large nose, which he thought made him unlovable. He fell in love with a beautiful woman and wrote poetry for her, but had a handsome man deliver his sonnets because he felt she would never accept him. Turns out, it was his words she fell in love with, not the other man, and his nose was of no consequence. Anne became more confident in her ability to create a story of significant impact.

If this was all real and Troy was actually so taken by Anne, she was flattered and more confident that her book would be a hit. This entire situation was becoming out of hand. While she was contemplating ending the pseudo-relationship, he wrote:

"Are you napping, Anne? Your silence is deafening. I don't want to offend you but you need to know how amazing I think you are."

Anne wrote back, "I don't know how to respond. You are lovely, though rough and tough, you are lovely. The way you express your feelings impresses me. Few men can expose their emotions the way you do."

He responded immediately, "We never know when our time is up. You have brought life back to my dead heart and I'd like the opportunity to pay you back in some way. I may not be the Phantom, man who cannot die, that I brag about. I'm quite certain I have an expiration date, so I want to live my life to its fullest with someone I care about. That person is you, Anne."

Teasingly Anne said, "What if Australia won't let me in? I hear they're pretty fussy." (Silly laughing emoji)

"That's the difference between you and me, Anne. You're letting your head rule your decision, while I am ruled by my heart; there's always a way around every situation, except maybe death. If you ever need anything, just ask Bad Boy Troy and I'll make it happen!"

Bantering between them was fun. The word game and the app for talking were their only contact points. Seemed he had a great sense of humor. She always reminded him her heart was open to any secrets he wanted to share with her. She needed more to create a memorable and notable book. She so hoped that would happen. She couldn't help but wonder if he knew anything about her at all. She had shared only a few things with him. He knew because of the time difference, that she was in the Northern Hemisphere, that she was four years older than him, that she had daughters, had owned a riverboat, and played the ukulele. How in the hell could that be enough information to cause a man to act the way he is?

Anne knew she was being erratic, maybe even out of her mind as I had told her, but I couldn't talk any sense into her. She was determined to follow through with her trip to Australia, can't stop the outgoing tide. I knew she was writing about their conversations, hoping to write a best seller but I can't imagine that would be enough to make her jump off the mountain and into a river of lava. What was she thinking? I came to the conclusion that she wasn't thinking.

"Hi Honey. Just woke up and of course, my thoughts are immediately on you. I hope your sleep was peaceful, except when you dreamed about me," Troy texted. " HA! HA! I'm quite sure you feel the same about me as I do you; you're just not giving in to your instincts, that "head" thinking again, instead of your heart. Anyway, I was thinking about your trip, wondering if you could wait until my boat comes in so I'm ready for you. What do you think?"

"Ha! That's a good one, Troy! Made me laugh out loud, and nearly peed my pants! Waiting for your ship to come in, huh? SPOILER ALERT! I AM NOT YOUR SHIP!"

A half-hour later, he answered. "I had to think about what you said. Google told me about your American saying and that's not at all what I meant. I pray you meant that only in jest; that's just not who I am."

"I'm sorry, Troy. I couldn't resist. That saying is a long-standing reference to waiting for a windfall and it hit me right in the gut! You're funnier than you think you are!"

"You had me worried that I had upset you. I guess I wear my heart on my sleeve more than I thought, even though I rarely wear a shirt, LOL! What do you think about waiting a couple weeks?"

"I'm not sure I can come yet, so waiting is no problem. I told you I have things to take care of here before I can even consider a trip that far from home."

"I have a suggestion. Why don't you wrap up all your affairs, as if you're not going back to America? I'm not saying you won't go back, but I plan to make you feel so special and loved that your affection for "home" would mean nothing. You have no idea what I will do for you. Of course, you can leave anytime you choose, but I think you will soon want to call this home. Just sayin."

Anne wasn't sure how to take that comment. She flinched. "I have my wonderful family here; I couldn't bear to leave them and not see them again."

"Ah, a feeble and unwarranted excuse. We have technology so you can FaceTime them anytime you like, AND we have airplanes! Imagine that! I told you money is no object for me, so I will fly any, and all of them here, anytime they want to come. Free vacation to Australia? Who wouldn't want that?"

"It's hard to believe you are so generous. Not saying I don't believe you, but you have to admit this is an unusual situation. FYI, I wouldn't be good as a drug smuggler, I'm too old and fat to be sold into sex trafficking, so I'm not sure what I'd be good for. LOL! Can I get your offer in writing?"

"Now you made me laugh until the tears are rolling down my cheeks! Maybe we should take our comedy show on the road! I'll give you anything you ask me for, no worries, sweet Anne. The only thing I want from you is the joy of your company for as long as I can."

Chapter 15

Anne made her decision to leave the life she knew and take a big trip. She tidied up her financial affairs so if something happened to her, there would be no loose ends. She found herself changing her mind a dozen times a day. "Yes, I'll go. No, I won't, yes, I'll go." She had no idea what she was walking into but hoped it wasn't a trap. If he was as easy as he seemed, this should be a piece of cake to fleece him of some of that money he cared so little about. The challenge was exciting but the fear was real, too.

They continued their word game-playing and banter. He was a tease like she imagined a big brother would be. Who was she kidding? Her feelings were not brotherly love feelings. Recalling his violent stories, if they were true, she couldn't quite match the violence to his comedic, romantic nature.

Suddenly, Troy didn't play the game. There were no messages from him. This had happened several times; she wondered what caused him to 'disappear' on a regular basis. Was he involved in something sinister where he couldn't communicate? Did he have health issues? She had earlier ruled out that he was in prison unless he was recently incarcerated. Four days came and went and Anne wondered if this entire thing was a fluke- a pipe dream. Of course, it was, and she was probably better off if she never heard from him again, but it was fun while it lasted.

****

<u>Suzie</u>

I kept texting and calling Anne, but she hadn't responded in a couple days. I hoped she hadn't hopped on a plane to Australia but she was acting differently than I'd ever known her to be. I decided to call again.

Anne picked up on the second ring. "Hi, Suze! How are you? What's going on?'

"No, no, you don't get to ask me first. I've been trying to reach you and you've been ignoring me. What gives, girlfriend?" I asked.

"I was going to call but I've had issues with my phone. Sorry about that."

"I'm not going to let you off that easy, but nice try!" I laughed. "I need to know what's going on. You've never kept me in the dark like this all the years we've known each other."

"Okay, okay. There's really nothing to tell. I had fun playing the game with that Troy guy but he has bit the dust, I guess. I haven't heard from him in days, so I'm not going to Australia. It was fun while it lasted. I'm going to continue with the book; I'll just have to make up an ending."

119

"Oh my God, Anne! I'm so relieved. I'm not much of a prayer person but I've been praying that you'd get your sense back. I'm so thankful."

"You make me laugh. I had you worried, huh? I wouldn't have really gone. It was just a fun little fantasy."

"You've made my whole life better, Anne. Why don't we have lunch?"

"Okay, but I can't for a couple days. I've got some appointments that I can't get out of, but I'll call you when I'm free so we can get together," Anne said.

I had the feeling she wasn't being straight up with me, but I didn't want to push her. I'll give her two days.

****

On the fifth day of not hearing from Troy, Anne got a message. She wasn't sure she wanted to open it. She was disappointed that he had left her hanging for so long. Actually, she was just plain pissed so maybe she'd just make him wait…and wonder. She loved games but not when someone played a game on her.

Her curiosity got the best of her and she opened his message.

"Hi, sweet Anne. Sorry, it's been so long since talking with you but I've had issues with my phone."

That really brought things back around for Anne. What a lame excuse, but the same one she used on Suzie.

"Really? That doesn't really work for me. Can't you come up with a better excuse? I'm tired of that one."

"Okay, Anne. Remember me telling you about the neighbor who had dammed up the creek? Well, they issued a warrant for my arrest for beating his face in. Of course, I think he deserved it but he didn't agree. They took my phone and personal effects from me. I knew you'd be worried. They locked me up for two and a half days before we got an audience with the judge. When my attorney was able to tell my side of the story, the judge threw it out of court, in my favor. I was so exhausted, that I just wanted to sleep until I got my brain and body rested. Please try to understand. It was nothing about you. I promise."

His explanation made sense since he had told her about his encounter with the neighbor but his stories were incredulous; her cautiousness of him was renewed with a vengeance.

"I figured you were either dead, in jail, or in the hospital. I gave up trying to figure you out. You're an amazing storyteller, I wonder if everything you say to me is part of the story *you* are writing."

"You've just broken my heart. I can't believe you would think of me that way, but I don't blame you. My stories probably seem bizarre, nevertheless, true. I got a call just before I messaged you that my big, beautiful boat is coming in tomorrow. What do you think about that?"

"I think you're a big dreamer. Having dreams is good but not at the expense of an unsuspecting senior woman. We have laws against that here," she wrote with her teeth clenched.

"Please, Anne. Let me prove it all to you. I want you to come so badly. I will be a total gentleman. I want the privilege of your company. Let's exchange emails."

"How do you plan to prove it to me, Troy?"

"Well, give me your email and I'll send you pictures of everything. Please."

Anne wanted to believe him and giving her email address wasn't a big deal. She agreed.

Over the next few days, the pictures inundated her email. There were pictures of his house, his gardens, his roses, his workshop, the creek that flooded, his brand-new SUV, and even Dolores Claiborne sleeping on the furry rug. Someone took a picture of Troy standing beside his massive boat, hooked to his new vehicle in his yard. It all seemed legit. Anne tried to stay neutral but she was excited; no doubt about it.

Anne and Troy seemed to be more open with each other and that worried the hell out of me. Anne and I have known each other most of our adult lives and I've never seen her act like this. I still think there's something wrong with this whole picture. I can't talk any sense into her. It's like she's a different person.

A few days later, Troy emailed Anne. "Hey, Anne! I hope you got my emails. I'm so happy we can communicate and talk. Love the word game and don't want to stop but being able to hear your sweet voice is a comfort to me. Oh, by the way, I sent you something via FedEx so be on the lookout for it. Get Ready!"

"What?! Wait! How could you send me something? I never gave you my address."

"Oh, about that. I told you I have contacts all over so you weren't too hard to find. I don't think you'll mind once you see what's inside. Don't get mad, okay?"

"I can't guarantee I won't get mad. I'm more cautious of you now and I'm not sure what you're up to. You scare me and I don't want to blindly trust a potential psycho that may have evil things in store for me."

"I'm sorry you're distrusting of me. I can promise you, no ill harm will come to you. I will care for you with my life. I'm not saying I don't have evil thoughts about you. I'm a guy, remember? They're not murderous evil thoughts; they're loving, tender, gentle, hard as a bat, thoughts. I know I shouldn't have said that, but I will never force myself on you or make you uncomfortable in any way. I will treat you like the lady you are…unless you want to be a bad girl," he teased.

"I'll let you know. I've got to go now. Bye."

Walking in circles, not even knowing what she was thinking, she grabbed a martini glass and made herself a nice Grey Goose vodka martini with two olives, and headed to her patio. The weather was perfect, her pool glistening and her cocktail delicious. Thinking about the situation, she was second-guessing her infatuation with Troy. She didn't understand how this had happened. She was happy with her situation; she had been with Mark for years; he was constant, loving, and protective of her. She had a lovely home, debt-free. Her family was all nearby and she lived her life to enjoy them. How could she possibly think of leaving that all behind? Perhaps Suze was right and she really had lost her mind. Dementia? She lived for games though, and this seemed like the ultimate competitive challenge. She needed to see it through. She laughed out loud just thinking about the possible reward. She was lucid, cognizant, and of sound mind, just excited about the potential of pulling this one-off.

Chapter 16

The next morning at 9:00 AM her doorbell rang with a FedEx driver awaiting her signature. She accepted it but was hesitant to open it. What if it had poison inside or a letter bomb? She wondered if Troy was that crazy.

"It's now or never," she said as she pulled the zip tab on the package. She sighed when it didn't explode. Carefully peeking inside and taking a sniff, she didn't see white powder and she didn't fall to the ground foaming at the mouth. She'd seen entirely too many movies. She laughed at herself.

Inside was a single sheet of paper with a hand-written note, and two envelopes.

My Dearest Anne, I truly hope I'm not being presumptuous. All I've promised you is true and I can't wait to see you and give you one of those kangaroo hugs.

Love, Bad Boy Troy.

She reached for the two envelopes inside. One was thicker than the other so she chose that one first. Opening it, she shrieked. A bundle of US currency was secured in thousand-dollar stacks. There was $8,000 in cash. What the hell? Tearing at the second envelope, she gasped. A first-class ticket to Australia, leaving in a week, made her heart race. She must be dreaming.

She paced like a circus tiger. "Be cool, Anne," talking to herself. Pouring a cup of fresh coffee, she needed to think. "Lord, help me make the right decision." She went to her patio with her coffee and inhaled it without even remembering it. "What do I have to do to get ready for my big trip? I can always come back anytime if I don't like it. Let's see, I'll take some of that money to buy some new clothes. A girl can't go on vacation without new clothes and shoes. She had her jewelry covered; she loved her bling. Next, she'll have a few Botox injections, get her teeth whitened, and get her hair dyed red. He told her more than once he was a sucker for redheads. Thanks for the incentive, sweet boy Troy.

Anne asked Troy for all his contact information in case of emergency, like him cutting her throat. Maybe she could do a bit more investigation before she got on that plane. She paid for an online service but nothing disturbing came up.

Two days before she was to leave for Australia, one short email came in; it was Troy.

Don't come yet. Drama here. Will take care of everything. No worries. I'll be in touch.

Love, Troy

"Damnit, I should have known. He's a fake, a phony," she said slapping her thigh in disgust and anger. "Now he's got me talking to myself. Maybe I am losing it. That's it! I'm done!"

Angrily she stomped to her bedroom and began tearing things out of her packed luggage. "There! Take that, asshole! I don't know how I could have been so foolish."

She picked up her phone, threatening to throw it against the wall. Taking a deep breath, she dialed the number Troy had given her a few days before. The call went straight to voicemail. The message said, 'this caller is not taking calls at this time'.

Anne had to vent to someone or get falling-down drunk and that was too painful. "Siri, call Suzie." Before Suzie could even start talking, Anne started ranting. The rant went to cursing; the cursing to tears. "Suze, I'm such a blubbering idiot! You were right all along. I should have listened to you," she said through her sobs.

"Anne, please honey. Try to calm down and tell me what's happened."

"I don't even know, honestly. Troy sent me a first-class ticket to Australia plus $8000 to use to prepare for the trip. I was supposed to leave on Saturday and I just got a message not to come! Can you believe the ass would do this to me?" sniffling her nose. He said, "**Drama**" and he'll take care of everything. No explanation, only two days before I was supposed to leave. He just left me hanging like a bunch of bananas on a tree.”

“I’m so sorry, Anne. I’m sure there’s a logical explanation. Do you want me to come over?”

“That’s sweet, but I just need to wallow in my puddle of stupidity,” Anne sobbed.

“Okay, honey, but you know I’ll be there for you if you need me. You’ve always been here for me.”

Anne poured herself three fingers of Wild Turkey Bourbon with a splash of Seven-up. It probably wouldn’t help her feelings of rejection and anger, but it was a good start to help her sleep and forget her miserable state for a while. Sleep, though fitful, finally came.

The following morning, she had to get back to some normalcy in her life and she damn sure didn’t want to write about the Australian Arse! She’d had enough, even though she thought it was a good story. Being dumped is probably an even better one, but she couldn’t go there right away.

She dressed, grabbed her ukulele, started her Mercedes, and headed for the rec center where a group of friends was meeting for a jam session. Playing seemed to lift her spirits and she certainly needed that. She greeted everyone and played for an hour, with her head pounding like a bass drum and strumming sounded like cymbals in her ears, from the bourbon she drank the night before.

She needed to get back on track and stop licking her wounds. Life is tough, then you die. She wasn't ready for the grave just yet so she busied herself with projects around the house, lunch with her daughters, and babysitting two of her grandchildren. She was being such a brat about the whole situation. It wasn't like someone she loved had died. Pity party over!

****

A week after her canceled flight, as she was looking up a recipe on the internet, her phone rang. Oh, no! Troy was calling. She didn't accept. It rang again and again. She was just getting her life back together and now here he was trying to squeeze himself back in. Three minutes later, her phone pinged with a voicemail. Of course, it was Troy, followed shortly by a text. She printed her recipes for oatmeal raisin cookies, silenced her phone, and put it in a kitchen drawer with her towels. She wanted no part of him.

She made the cookies and prepared chicken Caprese like a pro. She was a good cook after owning a large elegant restaurant for several years. She served Mark a great meal with a special pecan apple salad paired with a bottle of sweet German Riesling wine. As they visited over dinner, guilt began to twist a spike into her heart; she knew she had

129

treated Mark unfairly, but he waited patiently, wondering what would happen. He didn't ask, just hoped she wouldn't leave him. They had a great ten-year run but he sensed she was unsettled lately. He didn't judge, didn't ask, just waited. What kind of man would be so forgiving? What kind of woman could be so foolish? At bedtime, he gently put his arms around her and leaned in for a kiss. She turned away. It just wasn't the same. Her heart was someplace else, but not here and Anne's reaction confirmed what Mark had been feeling.

The next morning after Mark left to play a round of golf, Anne lifted her phone out of the kitchen drawer and took it, and her coffee, to the patio. She had no intention of reading his text; of course, she did but it was hard to admit she was so vulnerable. Her curiosity got the best of her.

"Hello, sweet Anne. Please read this before you delete me from your life. I'm so sorry. I will do anything to make this up to you, but first I need to tell you what happened. You must believe me; it's the absolute truth. Eight days ago, I went to spend the night with my brother Keith. He's not well and he's alone. He only has one eye and ten percent sight in the other. He's nearly deaf so he's defenseless. A couple weeks before, the inside of his house was robbed when he was there. They took thousands of dollars' worth of treasures he had collected over his lifetime. He didn't see or hear them, but it was on camera.

At 12:30 in the morning, I stepped out on the patio to have a smoke when I saw a light flickering in the work shed. I went to investigate and lo and behold, what do I find but some junkie arsehole ransacking his shed. I apprehended him and called the police. The problem is that somehow, he received a punctured lung, a ruptured kidney, and two dislocated shoulders. I was charged with assault.

Occasioning grievous bodily harm, they refused me bail. It took my solicitor six days to get me released, but I'm not worried. He will drag it out and by the time it gets to court, I probably won't be around. I know it sounds like a far-fetched tale, but believe me, it's just who I am. I've had a fuckin' gut full of it and the junkie dog is lucky the neighbor heard him screaming or he would be buried in the mountains at the back of my property next to Ivor. I am angry with myself that I didn't handle the task quietly. These thugs are oxygen thieves that breathe air that should be for decent people. They prey on the weak, and the elderly; I feel it's my job to rid as many of them as I can.

I've always been this way. What they don't realize, is there are animals like me in the jungle who hunt them. When they run into a big bad wolf like me, they're done. I told you when we first started chatting, Anne, that I've done terrible things in my life but I've never laid a finger on an innocent, decent person. When the weak are hurt, a red fog descends on me and I can't stop it. Please forgive me for doing this to you. I'm so very sorry." (followed by hearts, flowers, kisses, and tear faces) "This, in no way, changes my plans to have you come for a visit, and I promise, I'll be on my best behavior. You are so important to me but I had to defend my brother. It's what I do."

In all of Anne's years, she had never known anyone whose stories could suck the air out of her lungs like Troy's. Again, though fearful that it might be true, her fascination couldn't be quelled. During their many conversations, he seemed so sensitive and caring to her, with a great sense of humor; it was hard for her to believe he was a true-life Jekyll and Hyde. He had so many endearing qualities. Her heart had melted into strawberries and chocolate for Bad Boy Troy. All she needed was the champagne to go with it.

Chapter 17

Two days later, Anne fastened her seat belt inside the first-class sleeping pod on the luxury airliner. She felt pampered and spoiled. Troy had come through in a big way and she was excited to finally meet him and perhaps experience a kangaroo hug. She had only seen his pictures on her email, so the real proof was yet to be seen. She reclined slightly, in the wide leather seat, sipping her Grey Goose martini with her usual two olives, as the engines roared to life. A long eighteen-hour flight was ahead but she would be well cared for. Troy had taken care of all the minor details including some of her favorite snacks, a massage halfway through, and warmed blankets.

Two hours later, the massive plane had leveled off at 38,000 feet, heading for the land down under. She was served a gourmet meal of tender filet mignon and succulent lobster tail. It was like a five-star restaurant. She could get used to this lifestyle. Troy had sent some books to the airline to be delivered directly to her on board. She closed the door on her pod, warm and cozy, opening the first book by Henry Lawson. He had specifically marked a story called Double Buggy at Lahey's Creek. As she began to read, it was revealing an insight into Troy that she hadn't comprehended in full. The story was about a couple in the early 1900's.

They were in love and the wife wanted a buggy. The story continues about the husband's many efforts to fulfill her wish, but in the end, it was the wife's ingenuity that did the trick. It was very thoughtful of Troy to leave no details to chance.

She soon drifted to sleep; nightmares began. She was on Troy's property. There were snakes all around her feet, climbing her legs. Suddenly, Dolores Claiborne, the donkey began chasing her. She charged Anne, braying, and kicking. Her lips curled in fury as she snapped and bit at Anne in a violent attack. Anne tried desperately to outrun her, bleeding from the bites. Anne jumped into the swimming pool to save herself as Troy stood laughing at Anne's terror.

Someone was gently shaking her and whispering her name. A flight attendant asked, "Are you okay, ma'am? You were thrashing and screaming. Are you in pain?"

"No, no," Anne replied with beads of sweat on her forehead. "I must have been having a dream. I'm so sorry if I disturbed anyone. Please don't hesitate to wake me if it happens again."

Anne was embarrassed but couldn't shake the dream. She wondered if it was an omen of things to come; or if she was to become a victim of his sick sense of humor…or torture. What had she signed up for? When her heart stopped thumping hard against her chest, she tried to relax and sleep.

Each time she began to doze off, the horrible scene flashed behind her eyes; it was like she was living this nightmare. It was too late to turn back now. She had made her bed and it might not be as pleasant as she planned. She could only hope this was the result of some pent-up fear and hesitation about the phantom of New South Wales. Obviously, his stories had infiltrated her brain much deeper than she realized.

An hour before arrival time, the flight crew was preparing for landing. Anne had her morning coffee, a refreshing steamy towel, and an amazing croissant filled with raspberry sauce. Freshening her makeup, brushing her teeth, and fluffing her newly-dyed red hair, she was apprehensively ready to meet the mystery man.

Stretching her legs, waiting for the circulation to return, she made her way to baggage claim. She turned the corner and, as usual, there were livery people with signs, looking for their customers. She gasped; there was a man that looked like Crocodile Dundee wearing a black hat as big as a bucket, a snakeskin belt, and holding a pink heart. In bold letters it read: **WELCOME MS. ANNE COOKE** This man didn't look anything like the pictures she'd seen of Troy and the man she envisioned she'd been talking to for months. This man was tall and thin with a nice smile, in his early thirties. She wasn't sure what options she had if she didn't introduce herself. She was 10,000 miles from home, on a foreign continent, didn't know a soul, and no return ticket back home. She didn't have a choice but to say hello.

"Hi, I'm Anne Cooke," she said trying to sound confident and sure of herself. "Are you Troy?"

He threw his head back and laughed. "No ma'am. I'm Steve; I help Mr. Kent out from time to time, like today."

"Where is he? I was expecting him to meet me here."

"He sends his deepest regrets, but he had an emergency last evening and he's still trying to sort it out. I am to assure you he'll get everything worked out and will see you soon."

"Oh," Anne's eyes shifted around, and a deep sigh escaped her. "Another emergency, huh? Seems like he has lots of those. So, what am I to do?"

"He's very sorry, Miss Anne, but he is quite a busy man. He sent me to retrieve you. It's a nice relaxing drive and I can give you a bit of tourist information on the way. Let me take your bag and we'll be on our way," Steve said.

Hesitant, but left without options, she followed him to a new Land Rover. "Miss Anne, would you care to ride in the front or back?"

"Ah, the front will be fine, thanks." She climbed into the luxurious vehicle as he loaded her luggage in the back. Driving away from the airport in Sydney, she hoped she would live to see this place again on her return trip…if there was a return trip.

Traffic was heavy nearing lunchtime so he began his tour guide rhetoric. They drove past the famous Sydney Opera House so at least she knew she was in the right country. It wasn't long until the traffic thinned and they exited the freeway onto a two-lane road. She could sense they were heading north and east, which seemed to be right according to the map she had looked at.

"This is a vast nation, Miss Anne. There are so many things to see and do. We have the Blue Mountains, the Watagan Mountains, Lake Macquarie, beautiful state parks, walking trails, biking trails, and amazing weather changes depending on where you go. The vineyards in Mr. Kent's area are a sight to behold and wineries so plentiful you could visit a different one every day for a year," he said.

"It sounds fascinating," she said, noticing there were fewer houses and more dense forests. She became more concerned as the road seemed deserted. After two hours of driving, Steve turned right, down a dirt road.

"Where are we going, Steve?" she asked in a panic.

"We're almost there, Miss Anne. You're going to love it. Everything is fine," he said with a sing-song voice. It seemed he was enjoying the mystery and the note of fear he detected in Anne's voice.

Driving about a mile with thick foliage hanging over the road creating a canopy, she saw a clearing ahead. A small well-kept cabin stood in the middle of a groomed lawn with flowers in full bloom. It looked inviting but nothing like Troy had described to her many times, or the pictures he'd sent. Steve pulled around the circle driveway and put the vehicle in park. He walked to the back and pulled Anne's luggage from the vehicle. "You can get out now, Miss Anne," he said in a commanding voice.

"Where am I? Is Troy here? What should I do?" Tears flooding her face, her heart galloping in her chest. "Please, No! Please don't leave me!"

"No worries, Matey." He smiled, tipped his big black hat, and left Anne standing in a cloud of dust in the stifling heat.

****

She felt like her head would explode. What had she gotten herself into? She desperately dug in her purse for her phone. No service. "Oh, God! What am I going to do?" She had made a terrible mistake.

She dragged her luggage toward the cabin and hoped it was unlocked. She turned the handle but it didn't open. Panic magnified, she gave the door a kick with her high-heeled Jimmy Choo shoes, and magically, it opened. The cool air rushed toward her as a sigh of relief escaped her parched throat. Taking in her surroundings, it was nicely appointed and clean as her feet after a pedicure. The fridge was stocked with wine, beer, her favorite vodka and olives, water, soda, and food. She grabbed a cold bottle of water and guzzled half of it in one gulp. At least she wouldn't starve to death. On the counter, she noticed a hand-written note.

"My dear, sweet Anne, I'm so glad you finally arrived. I hope you're as excited as I am. I'm sure you'll find this strange but our relationship has been based on game-playing. I know how you love it, as do I, so I've arranged games for you to play. The first one is like the game we've been playing online, so we'll play the ultimate Scrabble game. Hidden inside the cabin are 102 tiles. You are to find them. Once you have located them all, if you arrange them correctly, you will find me. You get to play Scrabble, a scavenger hunt, and hide and seek. There is a total of twenty-three words to guide you to my home and my heart. This is so much fun and hopefully my arms will give you one of those kangaroo hugs soon. The better you play, the sooner we will be together. Your Move, good luck. Love, Bad Boy Troy"

Sputtering and fuming mad, Anne stomped her feet and beat her fist on the counter. "What a total dick he is. He's got a sick sense of humor. This is not looking good for me. Oh Lord, what am I going to do?"

Trying to calm herself, she pulled off her blouse, reached behind her back, and unsnapped her bra. After wearing it for 24 hours, she did a little shimmy to let the girls feel some freedom. Walking through the cabin, she checked closets, the toilet for snakes, and under the bed for any monsters that might be lurking there. The bed looked comfortable so she hoped she could sleep after all the hours on the plane. She was wishing she had not been so foolish to come. She should have given Suzie the address where she was. Hell, she didn't even know where she was. She was in big trouble. Troy was probably a psycho and she'd end up buried in the mountains behind his house like the others and his dead donkey Ivor. She could only hope that was a tall tale.

She pulled her luggage into the bedroom and grabbed her bag of toiletries. She needed a shower and a big glass of wine. If he thought this was the proper way to start a relationship, he was dead wrong. She was just plain pissed. Taking the rest of her clothes off, she walked toward the kitchen. Rubbing her face, and shaking her hair, she felt stupid, vulnerable, and captive. She had to ramp up her strength. She flexed her muscles, did some stretches, and made some sexy moves with her hips. She wouldn't let this man steal her confidence.

She grabbed a bottle of Moscato and corkscrew, threw her head back, and managed a loud scream to release some tension. Suddenly, she was drawn to the TV mounted high on the wall and just above it, was a surveillance camera that was motion-activated, to catch her every move. Grabbing her boobs with her hands, she looked at the camera. "SHIT!" she roared. "You will not win! I'm a better game player than you!" She rolled her blouse into a ball and threw it over the camera. "Ha! There you go, asshole. So much for your peeping Tom scheme!"

The shower was a gift, the water soft and warm. Fluffy white towels were neatly stacked on the shelf. She grabbed a luxurious, fragrant towel as a piece of paper drifted to the floor.

"Hi Anne. You will need a compass or a good sense of direction. Troy"

"What the hell?" she stomped. "This is ridiculous. I have made a complete fool of myself. Live and learn, I guess. I hope I get to live a bit longer, but who knows with this psycho?"

As she dried herself off, she looked around the bathroom. She checked above the light fixture, in the vanity, in the linen closet, in the wastebasket, but no compass. She lifted the heavy porcelain lid on the back of the toilet and taped inside was a small compass. Maddening, but clever. This must be a clue.

Dressing in her soft cotton lounger, she poured herself another glass of chilled wine, sat on a stool at the counter, admiring the landscaping and beautiful flowers out the front window. At least Troy had some class. She hadn't figured out his game yet, but if he thought she was a foregone conclusion, he was dead wrong.

Carrying her wine, she slowly walked around the small cabin looking for tiles. There were some taped inside a lampshade, some in a flower pot, and some lying on a jigsaw puzzle in progress. As desperate as she was to actually meet Troy, her eyes were heavy with sleep. This game would have to wait until tomorrow.

She was so exhausted, not only from the trip but from this trauma Troy was putting her through. She wondered how long she would have to play these stupid games before someone would rescue her. She snuggled into the soft down bed with crisp white sheets and fell asleep so quickly she didn't even remember closing her eyes. As the morning sun was peeking in her window, she stretched, feeling rested and refreshed. Actually, this would be fun, under different circumstances. But since she hadn't even met him yet, frustration was overtaking her. She could feel anger rising to her face. Suddenly, she heard knocking on the door. She quickly wrapped her robe around her and looked through the peephole. It was Steve with a large white box in his arms. She opened the door; he stepped in. "Mr. Troy wanted you to have a delicious breakfast. Enjoy." Before she could respond, he was out the door.

Opening the box, there were beautiful roses of every color. She took them out and found a vase to put them in. The fragrance was hypnotic. He must have cut them from his rose bushes. Looking through the box, there was a thermal container of coffee, fresh cream and sugar. Fresh-squeezed orange juice tempted her taste buds. Opening the largest container was a breakfast fit for a queen. Nothing was left to chance. An omelet filled with fresh vegetables, probably from his garden, warm croissants and fresh honey and butter. She was impressed. The food looked incredible but his thoughtfulness was amazing. Now if he was as lovely as the food, she could get used to this.

Breakfast tasted even better than it looked. Somehow food always tasted better when someone else cooked it. As she was savoring each bite, a thought hit her in the face like a sledge hammer. What if Steve was actually Troy? Anyone could post a fake picture online. She had no way of knowing what he looked like, even what ethnicity he might be. It really wouldn't matter; it was his words and the means he supposedly had, that she fell for. Afterall, she was here for one reason…his bank account. Maybe she should be nicer to Steve just in case he's Bad Boy Troy.

As she was crumpling up the paper lining the box, it stuck a bit. She pulled it up and there was an envelope with a note inside.

"Good morning, Anne. Welcome to the third day of your journey. I hope it hasn't been too stressful for you. I'm waiting patiently for you to finish your challenge so we can meet face to face. I trust you enjoyed your breakfast. Maybe tomorrow morning you'll join me for breakfast, all sleepy-eyed and sexy from a peaceful night's sleep. Good luck finding the tiles and solving the puzzle. Isn't this fun? Love Troy."

She couldn't let this get out of hand. She wasn't here for a relationship; she had a life in the USA and she wasn't about to leave it all behind. She still wasn't sure what kind of game he was playing, but she knew it wasn't just a word game or scavenger hunt; she had to be shrewder, and savvy. After her morning routine, she began her search in earnest for the tiles. She needed to solve the damn puzzle. Time was wasting and she wanted to get this over so she could go home. His games were messing up her plans which was exactly what he wanted. He was having fun, totally at her expense; the competitive clown. She had to up her game.

By noon she had located eighty-three tiles but felt like she had exhausted every possible location. Frustration began to set in; she felt like crying but she wasn't going to give in to that especially feeling he may have more cameras watching. She smiled, did a little dance, and gave Troy the finger hoping he was spying. This was more like imprisonment, not a fun game. Maybe some music would help. She stood on her tip-toes to turn the stereo on and her fingers touched three more tiles. Now she just had to find the remaining tiles. She carefully combed each room from top to bottom, turning all the furniture upside down to make sure she hadn't missed anything. She only had five more to complete the tile count.

At 6:00 PM, she was getting hungry. She went to investigate the food in the fridge. Inside was a large bowl with a lid. Picking it up, taped to the back were the last five remaining tiles and a note. "Enjoy these fresh, delicious oysters, picked just for you." How the hell did he know what she would eat, what she would drink, what her routine was? It seemed he knew more about her than she knew. She placed all the tiles she had found on the bar and began moving them around, as she savored the deliciousness of the oysters.

At 1:00 AM, nearly cross-eyed, she gave it up for sleep. She wasn't going to be sleeping in Troy's house tonight. The puzzle was ridiculously hard. The few clues he gave her were beginning to help. The compass told her there must be directions. She started with North, South, East and West. The rest would have to wait till tomorrow. She slept comfortably and woke refreshed but wanted this game of his to end.

Chapter 18

Anne loved solitude but not so much in a foreign country, not knowing where she was and this man, or monster, playing his stupid games. This had gone on too long. She sat for hours deciphering the puzzle and finally at 4:00 PM, she was going for it, right or wrong. He couldn't be far away. The puzzle read:

NORTH THIRTY PACES, WEST EIGHTEEN PACES, GATE, KEY IN HYDRANGEA, WATCH FOR SNAKES AND EMUS, SOUTH FORTY PACES, GATE, LOOK FOR DOLORES, WEST.

Anne had completely lost her patience with this whole scene. She quickly packed her bag, put on her Sketchers and slammed the door on her way out. Dragging her luggage, reading the directions, she found the gate. SNAKES? SHIT! "I hate snakes. Why did he have to say that? Emus? Who knew they were dangerous?"

She found a stick to beat around the hydrangea to announce her presence to any snakes that might be lurking for her, she located the key to the gate. Once through the gate, there was a flagstone walkway, with pampas grass and tropical flowers lining both sides. She followed it until she came to the second gate. The latch was open, so she walked through, spotting the donkey Dolores, lying in the sun under a shade tree. She had recently attacked poor John the pig and nearly killed him with her bites. Anne wanted no part of that especially after the nightmare she'd had on the plane.

She turned to the west as the directions instructed and there, beside a Poinciana tree, stood Bad Boy Troy, exactly as she had pictured him. She felt stupid that it took her so long to find him when he was so damn close. Shaking his head in disbelief, a smile as big as the moon, he opened his large muscular arms and wrapped them gently around her. Relief swelled inside her; she couldn't hold back the tears. His voice was soft and comforting. "My sweet Anne. I'm overwhelmed to see you," as he placed a sweet kiss on her forehead the way a father would. He smelled like a fresh spring rain; shoulders as broad as two normal men. His silky beard brushed against her cheek wisping as soft as spun cotton. His clothes were stylishly appropriate and made of the finest linen. He wasn't a handsome man but very well put together.

By this time, Anne was sobbing. What had come over her? She was letting this emotion show instead of being strong. "Please don't cry, sweetheart. Say something. I want to hear your voice."

She wiped her tears on the back of her hand, pounded her fists against his thick manly chest, and screamed, "You're a son-of-a-bitch!"

His laughter boomed. "There's the feisty, cheeky Anne I've come to know and love!"

"Wait a minute," she said. "How did you know I was coming from the cabin?"

"Steve put a GPS on your luggage when he picked you up at the airport. I didn't want to take a chance that you might get lost; I knew you wouldn't leave without your bag," he smiled.

"Well, aren't you clever, Mr. Kent? You thought of everything. I think you're a pro. How many women have played your little game?"

"Now, sweet girl, don't get testy. I tried to think of things to challenge you, care for you, stimulate your imagination and, most of all, make you more excited to meet me. How'd I do?"

"If I wasn't at your total mercy and, if I didn't have to pee, I'd tell you! Point me in the right direction."

He laughed whole-heartedly as he grabbed her luggage, and her hand, and led the way to his house.

Anne was in awe of the grounds; a magnificent rose garden scented the breeze with the delicate fragrance only roses possess. There was bougainvillea in every imaginable color, hydrangeas the size of a man's hand, fringe-leafed banana trees, and an abundant vegetable garden. The exterior architecture and the magnificence of the home were all, and more than Troy had said.

Inside, he gave her a short tour but she wanted more. She had been an interior designer most of her life, so she was enthralled with his good taste. It was a minimal design, masculine and woodsy. The appointments were mostly natural with native species of woods. He had created beautiful tables, benches, and cabinets, created from his own imagination; crafted with his own hands. He used soft grey wood stains with some accents of deep-greenish grey. She could spend a long time taking it all in.

He took her to the kitchen and mixed her a Grey Goose martini with two olives as the clock chimed five. He laughed. "Perfect timing, huh?"

Was the Grey Goose martini with two olives just a lucky guess? There was too much to think about. Anne was dizzy before she even drank her martini.

He poured himself a shot of home-distilled Slivovitz over ice. He raised a toast, clinked glasses with Anne, and said, "Here's to the most beautiful soul I've ever met. I want you in my life until I draw my last breath."

"That's a nice sentiment, Troy, but you know I have a home and family waiting for me. Unless you plan to die in the next ten days, your wish will go unfulfilled." She couldn't read the disappointment forming on his face. She hoped that's what it was and not something sinister.

He grabbed a beautiful fruit and cheese platter from the huge refrigerator. "Let's go sit on the verandah since the sun is behind the trees now," he said as he turned to lead the way.

The sparkling pool looked inviting but then she remembered he always swam naked. She hoped he would spare her. She couldn't tolerate that. This wasn't what this trip was about. She would make her agenda known soon enough but she had to allow him time to trust her. The view was spectacular. Rolling hills began in his back yard climbing their way up higher and higher. The details of the landscape became obscure in the elevations. She studied their beauty and the blue haze surrounding them.

"I hope I'm not going to sound stupid, but I assume the blue haze I see around the mountain range is why they're named The Blue Mountains?" she asked.

He winked and gave a little snort. "I didn't know American girls were so smart!"

"Are you making fun of me?"

"Of course not. I know how cheeky you are so I never know when you're teasing me."

"Okay, good. I want to keep you guessing. So where is the old lady's house with the binoculars that spies on your body? I'm not sure I believe that story."

"I'm crushed," Troy pouted. "How could you doubt me? I have been completely honest with you. The old lady is not always peeking at me, but I think when she hears my tractor, that seems to be the trigger."

"I'm curious to see that," Anne grinned.

"Oh! So, you want me to get naked and start up my tractor? Okay then."

"No, not naked!" Anne nearly shouted.

"I don't want to disappoint the old gal if she goes to the trouble of pulling her binoculars," he said with a frisky look in his eye.

"Spare me, please. I wouldn't want to go blind. Keep some clothes on. I would die of embarrassment. By the way, you didn't allow me much privacy and you saw me naked. That's perverted. Those cameras were totally unacceptable, you know. Shame on you."

"Hmmm, if you die of embarrassment, then I would bury you in the foothills and you would be here forever with me. The cameras? Clever, wasn't I? I drew first blood, so to speak."

An ominous chill crawled down Anne's back at that comment. She knew she couldn't completely trust him. He had told her stories about his disregard for human life. She hoped he wasn't planning to kill her. She was going to be very careful not to set off the red fog that he says falls on him before he kills.

He pointed toward the east and Anne noticed a small cabin perched at the top of a tall hill overlooking Troy's property. "You can't see her until she comes outside to spy on me. Wait here and keep looking up there. We'll see if she's got her hearing aids in."

"No, no, it's okay. I was only kidding," Anne nearly begged.

"I need you to trust me and all I've told you so, here we go!"

Before Anne could protest again, Troy walked to his shed which looked as big as a football field. A minute later, she heard the engine roar to life. He gunned the accelerator until it stopped sputtering and began to run smoothly. He put it in gear and slowly pulled out of the shed. Anne was afraid to look. She didn't want to see his naked body. She kept her eyes fixated on the old lady's cabin. Troy putted around the yard, shifting gears.

"I'll be damned," Anne said out loud to herself. There was the woman, with her binoculars, pointed right at Troy. He put the tractor in neutral, set the brake, turned the engine off, and stood. Anne was afraid to look, but when the old woman turned away, Anne stole a quick glance. He still had his shorts on but without his shirt.

Relieved, as he stepped down and walked toward Anne, she said, "I guess I'll have to believe that story. Does Santa Claus and the Easter Bunny reside here? You tell such outlandish stories, at this point, I'll believe just about anything."

He laughed and patted Anne's arm. "I would never lie to you, Anne. I'm not that man. Oh, by the way, there's a few leprechauns and the tooth fairy who lives in the barn!"

Chapter 19

They laughed together as he offered her his arm, walking back to the house.

Back on the verandah, he ignited the grill. "I think we should start some dinner."

"Sounds good," Anne said. "I'm starving," rubbing her tummy. "What are we having?"

"You'll know soon enough," Troy said. "Have a little patience, girl."

"It's not something gross, is it? Like snake or lizard?"

A slight smirk showed on his face, "No, I'm saving those delicacies for tomorrow."

She hoped he was teasing as she felt her stomach turn in disgust. He went to the fridge and pulled out a glass bowl with grouper filets soaking in milk. Next was a tray of huge shrimp. She hadn't seen shrimp that large since she had traveled to the Far East some years before. They looked like small lobsters. She wouldn't have any trouble enjoying this meal, for sure.

Troy grilled the seafood to perfection along with a generous serving of asparagus. Anne set the table. Finding everything was easy; the cabinets didn't have doors. They were more like open shelves. She dished the delightful food onto pure white porcelain plates and found a bottle of Pinot Grigio, a perfect pairing with the seafood.

Their conversation was comfortable with no strain between them. He seemed the perfect gentleman, courteous, thoughtful, and knew how to use his flatware. That was a treat for Anne since she grew up in a household where table etiquette was as important as bathing. Anne's father was reared in a wealthy household, and though he squandered his inheritance on women and gambling, his upbringing was evident at the dinner table. Following dinner, Troy lit some tiki torches around the verandah as they enjoyed after-dinner drinks. The time spent with Troy was totally delightful so far. She hoped she wasn't judging the situation too soon.

At 11:00 PM, she found herself nodding, not having caught up from the trip and time change. "Anne, why don't you get ready for sleep? Everything is prepared for you but if you need something, please ask. I usually stay up later, as you know from playing games with me all these months. Sleep as long as you want in the morning. I'll have your coffee ready when your beautiful hazel eyes open."

"Thank you, Troy. I am still catching up from the trip, not to mention what you put me through with your games. I hope it was more fun for you than it was for me! I was extremely frustrated that you put me through that. Why did you do it?"

"Aww, as you look back on it, you'll realize how clever I was and you'll see how much you appreciated it. You'll come around and be impressed knowing it was all about making you more anxious to see me, and I think it worked. We both love to play competitive games. That's how this whole wonderful relationship started. You'll come around to appreciate it.

"I hope you're right because now, I'm still pissed at you."

"You'll get over it, Anne. Sweet dreams until I get to see your beautiful face in the morning. You have permission to dream about me, but you must leave my clothes on in your slumber."

"No guarantees," she said, a little embarrassed that had slipped out of her mouth. He liked the sound of that as most men would. They're so predictable.

As she stood, he escorted her to the huge guest room, turned the comforter down then extended his arms toward her. "May I give you a hug?"

"Of course," she answered. Leaning into his strong body, she somehow felt safe, secure, and satisfied. His hug felt intimate, not sexual but so completely heartfelt. Anne felt she could tell a lot from the way a person hugged. She snuggled in and her sleep was restful and welcomed. She was surprised she felt no fear of this man who admitted to being violent and questionable.

Suddenly, during the night, something woke Anne. She sat up in bed, letting her eyes adjust to the tiny bit of light beyond her door. It had been closed when she went to sleep, but not now. She saw the black silhouette of this big man Troy, standing in the doorway. She gasped, not only at seeing him looking at her, but she was sure, in the dim light, she caught a glimpse of an ax he held at his side. Afraid to speak, looking for someplace to run, or jump out a window, she threw her feet out of the bed and stood. He softly spoke, "it's okay, Anne. I just wanted to check on you to make sure you were comfortable."

"I *was* comfortable until you startled me to death, stalking me in my sleep, holding an ax. What the hell?"

She could see his white teeth glimmer slightly as he smiled. "You don't think I would hurt you, do you?"

A bit embarrassed, she said, "How would I know what you're capable of? Maybe you're a cannibal and want to try some fresh fatty meat from the US."

"Wow, your imagination is incredible. I like that, however, untrue. I always keep some kind of weapon handy in case we have an intruder. It's just my thing. You'll get used to me soon."

Anne had a hard time calming down to go back to sleep. She thought it was unacceptable to invade her privacy like he had when she was sleeping. Slumber finally overtook her.

As the morning sun crept into her room, she smelled coffee brewing and bacon. Who doesn't love bacon? She slipped her light cotton robe on, quickly fluffed her hair, brushed her teeth, and went to the kitchen. As she entered, Troy looked up from his cooking. "Anne, you have just fulfilled my dream of you since we first began talking. I told you I wanted to see you in my kitchen sleepy-eyed, looking all sexy, while I was making you a good breakfast…and here you are. Sometimes I'm amazed at the blessings I am granted, despite the troll that I am."

"Nice of you to say, Troy, but it wasn't totally your idea, you know. I wanted to come, needed to get away from my troubles and you made it easy for me…. well except for your stupid game that lasted a day and a half. That was brutal."

"Now, now. You know you loved it and it wouldn't have taken so long if you had applied yourself. You probably took too many naps to finish sooner."

Anne was used to his napping comment and it always grated against her. First of all, she wasn't a napper, and secondly, he could go for days without contacting her but if she didn't respond in five minutes, he was all over it. She wasn't going to allow him to get the best of her over a ridiculous game. "I'll get even with you. Just you wait, big boy!"

"Oh, I'm so scared. I can't wait for you to get even. Don't threaten me like that, unless you mean it. I may have to take you over my knee and spank your arse."

"Cold day in hell, Buddy!" she quipped. It seemed strange that she didn't feel intimidated by this burly man who claimed to be an animal. There was no feeling of an age difference even though he was four years younger. It seemed like a very natural friendship. She felt as though she had known him all her life. What was even better is that he made her feel young again. She hadn't felt anything in a long time but now there was excitement, anticipation, and pleasure just being in his company.

Chapter 20

<u>Suzie</u>

Dialing Mark's number, I hoped he would answer. "Hello?"

"Hi Mark, this is Suzie. How are you?"

"Hi, Suzie. I'm okay, a little lonely since Anne's been gone" he said.

"That's what I want to talk to you about. Do you have a minute?"

"Sure. I've been thinking about calling you, too but I didn't know what to say. I feel like I've been hung out to dry, if you know what I mean."

"I'm so sorry," I said. "Let's start from the beginning. First of all, do you know where she is? I've been in a total panic for nearly a week. Anne's phone goes straight to voicemail and she's not answered my emails."

"Same here," Mark answered, sounding dejected. "I came home, her car was in the garage and her Louie Vuitton luggage was missing. I didn't think much of it; she's done lots of traveling with her design business and, more recently for research for the books she writes. What I found strange is that she's never left without telling me where she's going or when she plans to be back. She's been preoccupied lately, but that's not unusual."

"She has always told me about her trips as well. Did she mention anything about some Australian guy she's been playing an online game with for a few months now?"

"Yeah, I think she told me something about it, but I didn't pay much attention. Didn't seem like a big deal to me. You don't think she's gone to meet him somewhere, do you?" His voice had a note of panic.

I tipped my head and raised my eyebrows. "It wouldn't surprise me a bit, Mark. She's been talking about him for a while now, plus she's writing a book about their conversations. She's almost giddy about it, very excited. A couple weeks ago she told me she was planning to go to Australia and then they had some sort of falling out. She assured me it was over, but now she's gone."

"She wouldn't just take off and go half way around the world without telling someone where she was going, would she?"

"I don't know but, if she didn't tell you, and she didn't tell me, my guess is that's exactly where she's gone. The biggest problem is the WHO she's gone to meet. She calls him Bad Boy Troy and from what he's told her, he's a mean ruthless man, maybe even a killer."

"What? You can't be serious? Why would someone like that fascinate her so much that she would take this risk? Do you think her life might be in danger, Suzie?"

"Look Mark, I'm really worried. The last time we talked, she seemed devastated and said she was not communicating with him anymore. I'm not sure why, but she said it had something to do with his being arrested, put in jail for nearly murdering a man, and not contacting her for days. She convinced me it was over."

"Suzie, in the ten years Anne and I have been together, she's never done anything like this. I'm truly shocked."

"If this is too personal, I apologize but, is everything okay between the two of you?"

He put his finger across his lips as if thinking intently. "To be honest, she has been distant, but that's been going on for a long time. We're getting older so our relationship has waned a bit; not so hot and passionate. Life is mundane. She has her interests and I have mine. When we get together, it's pleasant but we're more like roommates than lovers."

I understood exactly what he was talking about. "I think that's typical. Long time relationships tend to become less exciting and we just accept each other as we are. Before Bill died, we didn't have much in common anymore. We were comfortable with each other, but there was no excitement or intimacy. Okay, back to Anne. Do you think we should do something? I'll be with you every step of the way. She's my dearest friend."

"I was willing to wait a bit longer, Suzie, but if you think she might be in danger, then yes, we should go to the police and file a missing person report."

"None of this makes sense, Mark. Australia is a huge country and I don't even know where we would start to look for her," I paused. "Wait, maybe her book is still on her computer and she may have put his location in there. That would at least be a start."

"Gee Suzie, you might have missed your calling. Perhaps you should have been a detective."

I drove to Anne's house where Mark and I began reading the book. It was interesting and filled with drama and passion. After reading for a couple hours, we found some obscure information about the city closest to where Troy said he lived. We didn't know if he had given her his real name, but we had to try. We would be a team until Anne was home safely. I wanted to do everything I could to be supportive of Mark. It must have been awful to be left in such a situation. We closed the document as Mark touched my shoulder. "Let me take you to dinner, Suzie, for all your help."

"Mark, that's not necessary. Anne is my dearest friend and I'll do anything to find her. I'm sure it would put your mind at ease, too."

"If you go to dinner with me, I can cry on your shoulder a bit longer," Mark said. "How about a nice steak at Ruth Chris?"

"Now you're talking," I said. "You had me at dinner, actually." We laughed as we headed out the door for the restaurant. I felt happy, even snappy, for the first time in a long while.

Our conversation was mostly light except when Mark began talking about his relationship with Anne. "We really don't have much of a relationship, Suzie. We've grown apart and I have a feeling she'll be moving me out soon anyway. The house belongs to her so it's her call." He seemed somewhat indifferent about the situation.

"I'm really sorry, Mark, and shocked. Anne has never said anything negative about you." Looking into space, I continued. "Actually, she hasn't said anything about you, period."

"I thought we were going to turn a new page a couple weeks ago. She made a nice romantic dinner, candles and the whole bit. She bought a great bottle of wine and we enjoyed warm conversation. I was hopeful the feelings we had before would rekindle, but when I took her in my arms, preparing to kiss her, she refused me and went to bed. I knew then, it was over."

I felt deep compassion for Mark. I knew he was crushed even though he couldn't admit it. Ten years is a long time to be in a committed relationship and watch it crumble, feeling helpless to save it. He was such a good guy. My deceased husband Bill was Mark's best friend. On the ride home, I remembered all the fun we two couples had together and Bill always said Mark had such integrity he would trust him without regard.

Mark and I were both quiet on the way back to the house. I'm not sure what was on his mind, but I was glowing just being in a gentleman's company. I had to get my car. Pulling into the garage, he asked if I'd like to come in for a nightcap. He turned on a light and told Alexa to play some soft jazz. "Suzie, what would you like?"

Stepping toward him, not questioning my feelings, I softly said, "You, Mark," as I walked into his arms. Our bodies felt right together, like slipping on a warm mitten on a cold day. Entwined for hours, letting all our inhibitions vanish, nothing mattered but the comfort and caress of another human being. Morning would come too soon, as would reality and the guilt.

Chapter 21

Mark woke with a smile on his face and in his heart. He felt wanted and needed and he'd always had the utmost respect for Suzie. As he drove to the golf course, he couldn't help but think about her class and confidence. She has a master's degree in criminal justice and her career matched her intelligence. Becoming assistant DA, she's prosecuted the most heinous characters and brought them to justice. She knows the law from the inside out and could have become a candidate for the Supreme Court but her goals were not that lofty. She's been content to play in her own backyard to rid the neighborhood of wolves who attempted to strip the dignity from the weak.

Even at her age, she is often asked to glean through ongoing cases, helping close possible pinholes that might negate the chance of conviction. Integrity is the word most frequently used to describe Suzie. She has never left anyone wondering if she was a fake.

In her private life, she's faithful to a fault, with unquestionable loyalty to family and friends. When her husband Bill became ill, caring for him was the most important job she ever accepted without regret.

Now that Anne left the country, it was curious that, after only one week since Anne left, Suzie walked into his arms and bed. Only she knows what she was thinking, but she gave Mark confidence he hadn't felt in a long time. Suzie is human after all and she felt perfect in his arms.

****

After enjoying a breakfast better than any Anne ever had, they sat on the verandah, she enjoying her coffee and he, his tea. "When are you going to start drinking coffee like a real man, Troy?"

He feigned shock. "How dare you insult me like that! Tea is for the refined palette, unlike coffee. You just haven't been exposed to the finer things in life, have you?" he winked.

"I guess not, honey. You may have to give me an education while I'm here." After those words slipped out of her mouth, she gulped hoping he didn't take that comment in a sexual way. She had no intention of any physical relationship with him, even though, it was hard to admit there were some feelings stirring inside that she refused to acknowledge. "So, what are your plans for today?" she asked.

"I was going to talk to you about that. I have to make a quick run to town. Is there anything you need from the big city?" he asked with air quotes.

"I could go with you."

"Sweetheart, I can't take you this time. I have some personal business that can't wait but I won't be long. I am very sorry but next time I'll show you around. We'll do some sightseeing."

Anne felt a bit strange about that but everyone has things that can't be shared so she let it go and watched as he drove toward town.

She tidied up around the house, showered, and put a cool cotton blouse and shorts on. She peeked into Troy's bedroom and noticed a huge safe built into his massive closet. "I wonder what's in there. Maybe gold, diamonds. I wouldn't mind being treated to some of that," she said under her breath. She made his bed, fluffing his pillow. Though routine, she enjoyed making herself useful and the fragrance of his pillow was a reminder of how delicious he smelled. She wasn't about to give him false hope about their relationship. They were friends, and friends they would stay; at least that was her plan.

Anne was going to wander around outside but was hesitant being so unfamiliar with everything in this strange land. Maybe when Troy came back, he could show her his property. She would enjoy that. She got one of the books Troy had sent to the airplane for her, fixed a cool ice tea, and went to the verandah. The weather was perfect, a balmy 78 degrees with a gentle breeze whispering through the huge trees shading the house. She was so relaxed she began to doze in the overstuffed chair.

As she slipped into a slight slumber she began to dream of Troy. He put his huge hands on her face and gently pulled her toward him. His silky beard touched her face as his full, luscious lips covered hers. Suddenly, she was awakened by tires crunching the gravel. Troy was back and she was shaking. She can't get involved with him. She sucked in a deep shot of air, shook her hair out of her face, and was determined to get that vivid picture of the kiss, out of her head.

Troy was carrying a bag and smiled. "What have you been doing, my love? Did you miss me? Well, of course, you did; what a silly question. Your big handsome hero is home."

Anne smiled. She did miss him but wasn't about to say so. "No, I was hoping you'd be gone all day."

"That's not a proper welcome home greeting." He put the bag down on the verandah, and opened his arms, waiting for a hug.

"You're expecting lots of hugs, aren't you? What gives? Maybe we should put a limit on the number of kangaroo hugs you're allowed." She didn't mind in the least, but she couldn't expose the feelings that were beginning to stir in her belly.

He didn't respond to her questions; taking her hand, he helped her out of the chair and hugged her with such passion, she was nearly gasping. This can't be happening, she thought. 'He's trying to break down the barriers I am determined to keep in place. I can't allow this to happen,' she thought.

"So, what's in the bag? Did you do some shopping?"

"Yes, as a matter of fact, I did. I would like to take you on a tour around the property but you need the proper Aussie attire before we can go. Go ahead and open it."

It was like he read her mind. She opened the bag and squealed. A delightful wide-brimmed hat with mosquito netting was amazing but, the boots were the cutest ever. They were rubber, nearly knee-high with sunflowers all over them. "Troy, thank you. That's so thoughtful of you. Let me see if they fit." He smiled as she slipped her feet into them. They were a perfect fit. "How did you know what size boot I needed?"

"I have my ways," he said. "Don't ever underestimate me."

She reached for him and pulled him into a hug; probably a big mistake. Oh hell, she'd made mistakes before and so far, this is a fun one. She just hoped it continued and her good luck held out. She fixed him a frosty glass of tea and met him on the verandah while he relaxed a bit. The conversation was light; he didn't offer any details about his business in town, and she didn't feel she could push him.

Troy excused himself. "Anne, I have to make a quick call to Steve. You remember him, right?"

"How could I forget a guy looking like Crocodile Dundee, with a big black hat, a snakeskin belt, holding a big pink heart with my name on it? It was the pink heart that threw me. It didn't coordinate with his outfit, but then I thought of all the pink heart emojis you sent me while playing our word game. He was intimidating, to say the least. I was afraid to ask where he was taking me; he might tell me something I didn't want to hear."

Troy guffawed, "He's somewhat harmless, except when it comes to taking care of me."

"Yeah, it's the **somewhat** that worries me," Anne said, wrinkling her nose.

"He was born in Africa but is a true native Aussie at heart. He's been around the world a few times with me. He's faithful and fearless; I can trust him with my life, and I have. He's my nephew. I couldn't care more for him if he was my son. He's been with me for many years and nothing I ask him to do is too trivial or too big."

"Wow, you're lucky to have such a friend." Not sure if she was pushing too far, she asked, "Is he your sister Sharon's son, and does he have a family?"

"Well, Anne, it's a long story- a little too long for now, but yes, he has a wife and a darling redheaded princess sweeter than icing on a cake."

Putting the phone to his ear, Troy said, "Hey Steve. Anne and I are going to take a tour around the property. Will you come by and feed the animals while we're gone? I'm not sure I'm up to it. Anne is wearing me out," he chuckled.

"Of course, I will be over in a few minutes. Are you going up to the plateau? Just checking, in case you're gone a little too long," Steve commented.

Steve's allegiance was unmistakable; he had dedicated his life to protecting and caring for Troy. Nothing Troy asked of Steve was too great a sacrifice. If it was doable, Steve would find a way. It seemed they were closer than any uncle and nephew could be.

Anne wondered about the rest of Troy's family. "You have many siblings, right?"

"Yes, I sure do. With all the nieces, nephews, in-laws, and outlaws, we could start our own town. Two of my brothers died in a vehicle accident a few years ago and one sister passed away from health issues."

"I'm sorry to hear about those tragedies. Where are you in the link of ten children?"

"I'm the third from the youngest. It seems like I'm always spending money on those birthdays. We have seven birthdays in the month of July alone. I don't mind. We usually get together for a cookout or pool party and they're always happy to see Uncle Troy and his $5000 gift for the birthday honoree."

"I can't believe you give so much. You've managed to spoil them all, in my way of thinking," Anne said.

"I know, but I love the delight on their faces. It never gets old to me. Okay, enough about me and my family, let's go for a ride, sweet pea!"

Troy brought out his shiny new four-wheeler that looked as comfortable as a BMW. He had spared no expense on it. He handed her a can of insect spray. "You may need this. As we get into more foliage, the mosquitoes will be looking for fresh flesh." He laughed but she shuddered.

The vehicle was quiet so it was easy to hear his description of the property and all he had done. They moved slowly down the wide paths he had cut through the thick forest. He had taken the trees he cut down and ground them into mulch so the pathways were smooth and clean. He pointed out different trees and native flowers. Birds were plentiful and the sound of the woods was peaceful. It appeared he was heading for the base of the mountain when he stopped suddenly.

"Be quiet, Anne, and don't make any sudden moves."

She felt her heart begin to race. "What is it? What's the matter?"

"There's a group of Emus right through those trees there. See them? They're snacking on some mulberries. I make delicious mulberry wine. You'll have to try some. The birds can be very cantankerous so we don't want to startle them. They are aggressive."

"Really? I wouldn't have known that."

"That's why you're with your big strong protector. Maybe you should snuggle close to me," he whispered.

"I'll give you an A for effort; nice try," she said as she winked at him.

"Okay, we'll move on if you're not going to cuddle me."

"Put it in gear, buddy."

Chapter 22

Meandering through the forest, he shut off the engine. "This is a eucalyptus forest, Anne. It's a big part of the ecology here. We'll wait a minute and listen to hear the bellbirds tinkling their calls to one another. They are common but they prefer this environment. When they all start calling, it can be almost deafening."

Just then, the chorus began. Anne had never heard anything quite like that. Indescribable, loud, crisp, not quite a warble, like tiny tinkling bells. She got a glimpse of one sitting close by and soon another joined in. Before long there were about twenty singing their concert for them. It didn't take long for Anne to appreciate the unique call of these lovely little birds.

"This is so amazing, Troy. Thank you for making it possible for me to come. It's a trip of a lifetime and your generosity is more than astounding."

"You know what I find amazing, Anne?"

"What's that, Troy?"

"That you love nature and what I have created here as much as I do. Not many women, in my experience, really enjoy this sort of thing."

"I'm definitely in my element; more comfortable than any place I can be," she said.

He made a slight turn and drove up to a crystal-clear creek. "This is the creek that the dickhead neighbor dammed up to flood my place. I guarantee that will never happen again. He won't soon forget what that stunt cost him." She believed him; she wouldn't put anything past him although, she sometimes wondered if his stories were embellished like hers.

He pulled up next to the creek. She had never seen clearer water. Every little pebble was visible and polished like glass from the constant movement of the water. They looked like gemstones. She knew that this continent wasn't widely populated so humans hadn't polluted it like in the US. The musky fragrance from decaying leaves was a familiar smell to Anne. She had walked along many creek beds in search of the morel mushrooms, a delicacy in her area.

"Do you have edible mushrooms here that you pick to eat?"

"Oh yes. That's the best part of Fall for me. I love foraging for them. The two most popular ones are the Saffron Milk Caps and Slippery Jack. They make my mouth water just thinking about them. They're quite plentiful but not until the weather cools. One needs to be well-educated though because we also have some of the deadliest mushrooms anywhere."

He opened a compartment and pulled out a small bag with a drawstring. "Come here," he said. "How about some fresh watercress with dinner?"

"That sounds delicious. Is that what's growing there in the edge of the water?"

"Yep. I come here to get it a couple of times a week. It even grows in the winter, which isn't so cold, so it's something I can always enjoy. It seems like you and I enjoy many of the same foods. I like that about you. Are you ready to try snake for dinner?"

"No! No! but hell no! I will never do that so don't get any ideas. I'm adventurous but not that much." He laughed but she wasn't sure he took her seriously. She needed to be careful what he served her.

Driving through the jungle with sparks of sunlight peeking through, she felt alive and free. It had been years since she felt so liberated and excited about living another day. Troy made a sharp left turn and slowly drove to the base of a massive tree. The smell was familiar, the leaves waxy. It was more eucalyptus trees. He turned the engine off and whispered. "We'll sit here for a few minutes, okay?"

"I know koalas eat eucalyptus. Are you thinking we might see one in the wild?" she was as excited as a little school girl.

"There are several koala families living in this area. They move around from time to time giving the leaves a chance to replenish. Chances are good we could see a couple," he said. "There, look," he pointed. "There's a mama holding her baby."

Anne was mesmerized by the beauty and strangeness of this place. "I think I've fallen in love," she said.

"I knew you would fall in love with me; now how do you like my property?" he chuckled.

"Always the wise guy, aren't you?"

"Yep, matey, that's me." He put the four-wheeler in gear and headed toward the mountain range. Anne was amazed at how large his property was. She felt like she was in a different world, a world she could easily love, maybe even the man.

Troy maneuvered the machine like a racecar driver around sharp curves, through some wet gullies, and began a slight ascent. He stopped the machine and let it idle. He pointed toward the rise of the mountain. "Anne, there's a mob of kangaroos, probably about sixty. What do you think of that?"

"That's amazing! I never knew these animals we see on TV roamed free, especially in your backyard. A group of them is called a mob? Or did you just make that up?" she asked.

"There are other names like troupe or court, but the most common is mob. Okay, Anne, I need you to buckle your seat belt and hang on tightly to the side rail."

She felt slightly panicked but safe and, somehow knew he wouldn't put her in undue danger.

"We're going to climb this mountain here just to the first plateau. The view is outstanding. In fact, I wish I had a cabin up here to breathe it all in." He put the four-wheeler in low gear and ever so slowly, made the ascent. The higher they went, the cooler and fresher the air. She felt a slight mist engulfing her. The angle was very steep and she was more worried about going down. Approaching the plateau at a 30-degree angle, the machine growled but the tires bit into the dirt and kept traction. Leveling out onto the plateau, Troy killed the engine and sighed deeply. "Isn't it gorgeous?"

Anne was awe-struck. The beauty of nature was overwhelming. The only thought she had, at the moment, was how deeply she would miss this lifestyle when it was time to go home. She didn't want to admit it, but she was beginning to think she would miss Troy as well.

He reached into the built-in cooler holding a bottle of chilled wine and two glasses. "You came prepared, huh?" she asked.

"I try to be ready for anything so I thought this would be a perfect place to toast our friendship and this time we're able to spend together."

Watching the birds soaring high toward the setting sun, the shades of indigo were becoming evident in the west. Streaks of rose gold blazed through the clouds in one of the most beautiful displays of colors Anne had ever seen in her life.

After taking in the breathtaking view, Troy carefully and slowly allowed the four-wheeler to take them back to more level ground. Following the curves of the foothills, he stopped near a large area of freshly disturbed dirt, with a small cross in the middle of the grave. Anne silently gasped remembering the stories Troy told her about his disregard for human life. She wanted to make light of it and not sound as panicked as she really was. He stopped; she cleared her throat. "Well, how many bodies do you have buried out here, Bad Boy Troy?"

He tapped his finger on his cheek. "Hmm, it seems I've forgotten, but they are forgotten, too. No worries, sweetheart."

"I hope you're kidding because I don't think I could handle the truth, if, in fact, that's true."

He threw his head back and howled a hearty wolf-like laugh. "Don't be so serious, Anne. This is Ivor's grave.

Remember me telling you that my donkey got bit by a tiger snake and didn't survive? I buried him closer to the house but John, the pig, kept trying to dig him up. I finally had to move his body with the end loader and bury him here. God, I loved that donkey."

"Whew, I'm relieved. I was worried for a moment," she said.

"I'll let you know if you have something to worry about," he clicked his tongue and winked. "So far, so good, little gal."

They returned to the house just as the sun was dropping below the trees and the temperature was waning. "Anne, sweetheart, I think I'll freshen up a bit. Would you like to try my homemade mulberry wine? It's sweet and smooth on the tongue."

"That sounds like a wonderful plan, Troy. Is there anything I can do?"

"Yes," he answered. "I'd like you to relax, leave all those troubles you've yet to tell me about on the other side of the world, for now, enjoy the wine, while I enjoy the company of the most delightful woman I've ever met. My only regret is that we didn't meet years ago so I could spend a lifetime with you."

She smiled and patted his forearm as they headed into the house. He reached for her wrist and pulled her into his massive chest. She could barely breathe. His warmth and ability to express his feelings were incredible, considering how tough he claimed to be. His embrace was comforting and she felt as if she'd just been rescued. She was aware that his eyes always followed her with admiration. He never missed an opportunity to smile at her, tapping his heart or blowing her a kiss.

Chapter 23

Anne showered and put on fresh clothes. Troy was sitting on the verandah with two wine glasses set on the table along with chips and salsa. She had in her hand, a big carrot for Dolores and a slice of watermelon for John, the pig. She couldn't forget sweet little Maggie, Troy's tiny terrier. She brought one of her favorite treats which she promptly took and laid down near Troy's feet. He smiled to see her kindness to his animals. Giving Dolores and John their treats, she scratched them and said good evening. Dolores laid her head on her shoulder and brayed so loudly in her ear, that she was nearly deafened. Walking back onto the verandah, Anne sat beside Troy. "Can I do the honors of pouring your wine, sir?"

Ignoring her offer, he licked his lips. "You smell absolutely delicious. I may not need dinner if you come closer."

"Now why would I do that? I told you I'm a lady and you said you'd be respectful of me. You haven't changed your mind, have you?"

"Anne, I would never disrespect you or expect you to do anything that makes you uncomfortable, but you can't blame a guy for trying," he said with a twinkle in his eye. "After all, I'm quite a catch; a big strong hunka hunka burnin' love."

"Yes, and modest, too, I see," she laughed. "I guess you and Elvis have lots in common."

"Someone has to remind me how amazing I am and since you're not stroking my ego," whispering he said, "or anything else, I must do it."

"How's that workin' for ya, Bad Boy Troy?"

"Well, not so good, but you will soon come to realize I'm the best thing that ever happened to you. Not only am I devastatingly handsome and smart, but I could also be the best lover you've ever had. We're not getting any younger so we need to grab every juicy slice of the tender fruit we are offered. We never know when it could be over. I don't want to die with regrets from all the wonderful things I could have enjoyed."

"There's that modesty showing again. You know I can't go down that road with you. I thought I made it abundantly clear before I got on that airplane. Our relationship is friendship, right?"

"Maybe in your mind," he winked, "but a man has to have dreams and mine are of you, sweetheart."

"I need a drink. Open that bottle of mulberry wine you've been bragging about," she ordered.

"I know this may sound immature, but I was thinking about something. Maybe we could create a code that only you and I know that would be a term of endearment. If I want to say, I love you, I would use it and you could do the same. I'm not sure why I thought about such a childish thing, but it might be fun. It could be our own private secret."

"Okay, for a rough and tumble gorilla like you, you never cease to shock me; I'll play the game. What ya got?"

"Well, how about 01-22?"

"Huh? Why?"

"Because that's when we first started talking and playing the game. I'll never forget it."

"Okay, so show me how it works."

"It would almost be like signing if we do it with our hands. If we texted each other, it would be typing the numbers. What do you think? Is it stupid?"

"It's our game; if we like it, we go for it, and I like it." Anne made a zero with her thumb and pointer finger, a one and two twos. They both laughed.

"Anne, this is probably not the best time to talk seriously, but I want you to know a couple things. There are, of course, things I can't share with you, or anyone until I die, but I'm not the person you think I am. You only bring out the best part of me and that's difficult to do."

Anne interrupted, "Troy, I don't care who you've been or what you've done. It's who you are now that matters to me."

Shaking his head from side to side, his eyes dropping to the floor, "Listen to me. I don't deserve you. You're way too good for me; in fact, I don't deserve the breath of life. I've been a horrible, hateful excuse for a human being. One single event changed me forever and caused this disease that devours me from the inside. When I finally regained a conscience, I ran. I'm not a coward but I had to get away; I had to change. I'm running out of time to reconcile my past with the present and I know things can change in an instant. I'm, more or less, a cannibal now."

Anne sucked in a breath of horror.

"No, not like that, Anne. I consume myself; destroy every part of me that tries to earn forgiveness. I find I can turn on even the ones I love in an instant like a wild animal. I can't control the urge at times.

She noticed a tear in the corner of his eye. It was hard to keep her composure when he was obviously so deeply troubled.

"Let's drink and get happy, Mr. Troy! Enough of this awful pity party."

"I don't know why I'm laying open my heart; I've not let anyone in for such a long time. The walls around me are made of steel but, here I am, cutting them away with you. I guess I want you to know what you're getting yourself into. Oh, another biggie, my sweet. I am an alcoholic; have been for many years. For prolonged periods of time, I'm fine, although it's always nagging at me. When I drink, other than some wine, I drink for one purpose; to get drunk, to forget. That's my way of punishing myself. Alcohol is a rod that I use to flog myself."

"Wow!" Anne said, wide-eyed. "Should I be afraid of you?"

"You certainly should, but not in the way you think. You should be afraid that you're falling in love with the likes of me."

The wine was smooth, rich with undertones of mulberries and pear. It was something like she had never tasted. After the second glass, she was feeling a little woozy. Troy could see it in her eyes so it was time to see if her tongue was loose enough to answer some of his questions.

"Sweetheart, tell me about that partner you live with in the states. Is he good to you? Do you love him?"

"Hmm, getting personal, aren't you?"

"You know so much about me, I'd like to get to know you better, that's all," he said, almost convincing her his questions were innocent.

"Okay, I guess that's fair," she conceded. "His name is Mark and we've been together ten years. I met him after a crushing divorce. I was in a very bad way, depression as deep as a sinkhole. He too, had gone through a hurtful divorce, so I guess you could say, we rescued each other. It took a long time for trust to build between us, but our relationship has been good."

"It sounds to me like you're living in the past, Anne. What's your life like with him now?"

"I'm not sure, Troy. Sometimes people outgrow each other. We don't have much in common and my life has become like a fogged-up mirror. Things just aren't as clear as they could be. I love him for who he is and what he's been to me, but I'm not in love with him. In my mind, there's a distinct difference."

"I couldn't agree more. As evil as I seem and have been, there are many people I love. But I'm only in love with one woman." He spoke quietly as he took a sip of his wine.

Anne couldn't go there. Maybe he was talking about someone else. He had told her he still loves his ex-wife, though there's no hope for a relationship with her. That comment sent mixed signals like shockwaves through her body. She feared she was the woman he loved, but some part of her found a fire burning in her gut, hoping she was. This was not going according to her plan. He was savvier than she.

"I think I'll cook some chook for dinner," he winked as he ignited the grill.

Almost afraid to ask, "What is chook, Troy? I hope it's not something gross."

He laughed. "It depends on what you call gross."

"Well, you know…like snake or lizard or…or…bugs."

"I thought you told me you were a country girl. Why are you being so finicky?"

"Just tell me what chook is and we'll go from there," she said with her hand on her hip.

"Sweetie, it's chicken," he chuckled.

"Why the hell didn't you just say chicken in the first place?"

"I like it when you get cheeky so I like to tease you to see what you'll do."

"I'll bet you were a terror growing up with your sisters," she teased.

"Yep, that's what I do. Let's get cooking. What do you say?"

Chapter 24

Dinner was amazing. He was a great cook. The evening was quiet. He put on some nice listening music. The Casablanca ceiling fans made a slight swishing noise overhead and a gentle breeze blew through the open windows. The warm lamp light was comfortable, yet adequate; Anne curled up with a good book in one of the solid wood chairs Troy had built. The cushions were luxurious and comfy and Troy sat reading with his feet on his ottoman. What a lovely way to spend an evening, except for him throwing a small pillow at her, making her jump out of her skin.

"Hey, knock it off, you bully!"

"They're called 'toss pillows' for a reason," he teased.

Anne basked in another night of luxurious, restful sleep. She couldn't remember when she had been so relaxed. It seemed her cares had melted away, although her life back home was good. She had to stay focused on her real purpose of going home with a good chunk of his wealth, although he was making it more difficult each day to continue with her plan. His kindness, gentleness, and humor were wearing her down; she was almost feeling sorry that 'taking him to the cleaners' was a good idea.

Another beautiful day at the foot of the mountains, she walked to the kitchen to see Troy had brewed fresh coffee and there was a pan of homemade warm cinnamon rolls. She called for him but he didn't answer. Looking out the door, she saw him swimming laps in the aquamarine water. She was afraid to look too closely in case he was swimming naked like he said he always did. Assuring he had trunks on, she poured herself a rich cup of coffee and pulled an iced, gooey cinnamon roll out of the pan.

Walking onto the verandah, Dolores, the donkey began braying. She had fallen in love with Anne and the treats she brought her every day. Anne pulled a chair close to the edge. If this is what heaven was like, she was ready for the trip. Seeing Anne, Troy swam to the side, smiled, and shook his head. "Good morning, my love," he said.

"Hey! Thanks for the coffee. Can I get you some?"

"You know I don't drink coffee, only the finest tea. Coffee is for hillbillies."

"Ha! Ya think? Who's the kettle and who's the pot here?"

"What? That must be another one of those strange American sayings that make no sense. So, what's it mean? Translate, please."

"Gee, for a smart man, you're a bit dense this morning, aren't you? It means you're calling me a hillbilly, but you're a bigger hillbilly."

He pushed himself up to the side of the pool before Anne could make sense of what was happening. He grabbed her and pulled her into the pool with him. She came up sputtering but laughing. He put his beautiful hands on her face and gently pushed her wet hair from her eyes. His lips brushed hers; though she vowed this would never happen, she didn't resist.

****

Suzie

I've thought about the night I spent with Mark making love. Reliving it a hundred times in the last week, I tried to feel guilty but it didn't come. I should regret sleeping with Anne's man, but I had a feeling she was doing the same with Troy. I secretly hoped that was true so perhaps, I could have a relationship with Mark and not be shrouded with guilt. Before that night with Mark, I was only going through the motions of living. I may never be with him again but it gave me a zest for living that I hadn't felt in a long while. Hesitant to pursue finding Anne, I felt I needed to do the right thing by her. She had never done anything to me that would cause me to double-cross her. Since I hadn't heard from Mark, I decided to call Anne's daughter Kate.

"Kate?"

"Hi, Suzie. How are you?"

"I'm well but I'm so concerned about your mom. I haven't heard anything from her in over two weeks. I'm sick with worry."

Kate chuckled. "She's not very good at communication unless she needs something. A few days ago, I got a quick text from her. Wait, this is what she said; Hi, sweet girl. I'm in Australia doing research for a book. It's wonderful here and I'm having the time of my life. No worries. Love you! Mom. I never expected her to be so flippant and erratic, but hey, if she's having fun, she should go for it. I didn't expect this behavior from her."

Sighing under my breath, a slight smile invading my face, I said, "Kate, I'm thrilled to hear she's okay. Will you let me know if you hear when she's coming home? I can't wait to hear about her adventures." More importantly, I wanted to cover my bases and not get caught with Mark.

I know it was selfish of me to think of Mark at this time. I wanted to see him again. I texted him. "Hey, Mark! Wondered if you'd like to come over for dinner tonight?" He didn't answer right away so I felt I had overstepped my bounds and perhaps he hadn't enjoyed our night together like I did.

A half-hour later, my phone pinged. "Wow! We're in sync, Suzie. I was going to call you as soon as my foursome finished our golf round. I'd love to see you and dinner would be a bonus. Seven, okay?"

"Seven is perfect. See you then." I showered and did all the girl things we do and dressed in a soft jersey knit dress. I wore the prettiest bra and panty set I had, just in case. I was actually hoping we could have a replay of the lovely night we spent together last week. The tenderness in Mark's voice left me little doubt that our torrid affair would continue. It was a whole five days and I felt like I was starving.

I watched as his lights pulled into my driveway; a little nervous but a lot excited, I had the stage set perfectly for what I hoped would be another night of pleasure with Mark. I held the door open as he stepped inside, meeting his steel-gray eyes with mine. Without saying a word, he dropped his jacket to the floor, put both of his warm hands on my face, and kissed me more passionately than I thought was possible.

"Suzie, I've wanted you for so long, I'm almost embarrassed to admit it. However, not embarrassed enough to miss an opportunity to make love to you again. I've thought of nothing else," Mark whispered.

Before I could answer, his mouth covered mine as he walked me backward toward my bedroom. Dinner would have to wait; I had suddenly lost my appetite for food. I would feast on Mark.

Another romantic evening with a truly nice man had me reeling. He was a fantastic lover, thoughtful, and caring. He made me comfortable like he truly enjoyed my body and my company. I wasn't self-conscious and I found myself being more aggressive than I ever remembered. I wanted to squeeze every bit of pleasure I could out of this time, and I didn't want to think about what might happen when Anne came back. Her friendship was important to me, but so was the comfort and spark of life I got from embracing the man she left. I desperately hoped there was a solution or compromise.

****

Another spectacular sunrise in New South Wales, enjoying a delicious breakfast on the verandah, Anne expected there might be a note of tension between them after sharing a brief kiss. That didn't happen. In fact, Anne could only hope it was a precursor of more delightful encounters. She wouldn't be aggressive, nor would she turn him down.

Taking a sip of tea, dabbing his beautiful lips with his napkin, he asked, "When do you think we should plan on spending a day or two on the lake? Are you game? I've only had it on the water once and that was the day it was delivered for sea trials. You will be the very first person, except for

Steve, to experience my dream with me. How does that sound?"

"Why don't you tell me what you have in mind?" she said.

"I can't tell you all my secrets, but we can take some food, nice linens for the bed, fishing gear, games, and maybe a little wacky weed for relaxing. That's what we'll do, just relax and enjoy each other."

"You had me until you got to wacky weed. I've only tried it a couple of times and that was years ago but you never know. I've been surprising myself lately. The rest of it sounds delightful. I do love the water. We won't actually be going out into the open ocean, will we?"

"Let me assure you, Anne, I will never pressure you into doing something you're uncomfortable with. You can trust my word. I think we'll just stay in the lake, which is huge by the way, since I haven't handled the boat. Lake Macquarie is a saltwater lake so we should have a chance at catching some amazing seafood. I know a great spot to pick oysters, too, like the ones I left for you at the cabin."

Anne thought about the possibilities of what might happen on their outing, but her thoughts didn't include what kind of fish they might catch. Her anticipation was teetering on visualizing what would happen when they lie next to each other in the same bed. She was quite sure she knew the answer, but didn't know if she was ready.

"Well then, it sounds like a great plan. What do we need to do to get ready?"

"I need to have Steve take care of the animals while we're gone and handle any other emergency that might come up. We'll pack our provisions and be off on our adventure tomorrow morning. How's that sound, Anne?"

"Perfect," she answered, hoping he would allow her the choice of making love with him. She was hesitant, though very attracted to him, she had moments when she had second thoughts because of Mark. Only time would tell how this would all play out. Anne had a knot as big as a bowling ball in her gut, thinking about what would probably transpire on the maiden voyage. It had actually been a couple years since she'd been intimate with a man and she wasn't sure how she would feel. She thought about her age and the possibility of sex with this unusual man. Sex wasn't reserved only for the young. If the planet didn't have mirrors, she would think she was as young and sexy as she had been fifty years before. The feeling and twinge she felt stirring were the same and exciting as hell.

Chapter 25

Launching the 370 Aegean Stamas yacht was no problem for the dockmaster. Troy took the helm and she purred like a kitten. Three two-hundred-fifty horsepower Suzuki engines would handle anything that was required. The yacht was one of the highest-ranking seaworthy yachts and ideal for fishing and cruising. There were no predicted storms for the area so Anne felt no anxiety. It had been years since she had fished with her father on his Stamas boat and enjoyed reminiscing.

Anne sat next to Troy on the bridge in the luxurious leather chairs. There was no rush to get anyplace. Taking in a huge breath of the moist salt air, in her mind, she was carried back to the three years she spent on the Gulf of Mexico fishing for a living when she was a young widow with two girls to support. The memories were mostly good, but this voyage was perfect. She somehow trusted this man and his actions impressed her. He opened up the throttle for a mile or two, feeling the power and freedom of being alive. If this was the last day of her life, it would be a good one. This experience was worth anything she might have sacrificed to get here.

Shutting down to a slow cruising speed, it was obvious he was familiar with the lake and marine protocol. Pointing out his favorite bars and restaurants along the way, he explained the beauty of the lake like describing a lover. This is where his heart truly was. She noticed the look of contentment on his face; he belonged here. They visited as they cruised in the warm sunshine of early summer. Obviously in his element, he threw his arms in the air briefly, looking to the cloudless sky, and said, "Thank you, God, for the best day of my life."

Tears stung Anne's eyes. "I hope you have many years to live out your passion here. It's obviously your destiny."

A sad look blanketed his face as he looked straight ahead through the windshield. "I won't have many years, Anne," he said with a paleness overtaking his skin.

Anne felt despair in his comment; something she hadn't seen in him before. She didn't feel she could ask. "We already determined none of us will be here forever, big boy, so let's keep a positive attitude, plugging along until we run out of gas."

He inhaled a deep breath of salt air as if taking a bitter pill. "I plan to do just that, my sweet Anne."

Troy did everything with such enthusiasm and fervor; Anne found it hard to keep up, but she wasn't about to be outdone. Somehow, it seemed as if he was trying to squeeze every second out of each moment to the fullest. She wondered if maybe he was ill and hadn't shared that with her, or maybe, he just had a zest for life to live it with chili pepper spice.

"We'll go to Pulbah Island first and see if we can get a few oysters. It's nearing the end of the season and I'd like to have you taste the essence fresh from the water. After that, we'll try our hand at fishing so we can have a succulent dinner."

"Sounds like a great plan to me. I think we determined catching would be better than fishing," she flirted, and I'll be catching. "Throttle down, honey!"

Looking into her eyes, he said, "You already caught me, Miss Cooke. Hang on, baby!"

That beautiful new boat made Anne feel like she was flying. She hadn't felt this exhilarated in a long while. This was the 'shot in the arm' she needed to remember what living was all about. She twisted her curly ginger locks in a ponytail and let the brilliant sun warm her, sucking in the freshest air she'd ever breathed.

"Okay, sweetie. We'll go for the oysters first, then you'll get a bit of an education fishing for flathead. They're abundant here and delicious, a little tricky to catch, but you will probably show me up."

"I'll do my very best to make that happen," she grinned.

Anchoring a few feet offshore, Troy stepped off the swim platform in his white rubber boots, and carefully made his way to a sandbar with his oyster tongs and bucket in hand. The water was amazingly clear. Spotting a nice clump of mollusks, he pulled them loose. Checking for undersized oysters, he put the large ones in the bucket and returned the others to the water. This brought back memories of Anne's years in the Everglades where she made many meals of oysters she had hand-picked, just as Troy was doing now. Making his way back to the boat, he handed the bucket and his tools to Anne. She rinsed them in fresh water and placed them in the ice chest and couldn't wait till dinner.

"Now, we'll go after the rest of our dinner. Are you game?"

"Game? Game?" she shrieked, "I'm always in the mood for a game, as well you know. Is there a prize if I win?"

He looked directly and seriously into her eyes. "The prize can be anything you want. All you have to do is ask and it's all yours- no limits, sweet Anne."

Anne's mind spun like a child's striped top. His comment jolted her to remember her original goal to cash in, literally, but the other side led her to think about lying in his arms. This was a complicated situation she had gotten herself into. He maneuvered the boat to a channel that was flowing with the tide.

"Okay, Anne, we will be drift fishing, no anchor. We've got plenty of depth here so we don't have to worry about the draft. We will cast the lure upstream and it will move with the current as it goes to the bottom. The tricky part is to move the rod in a bouncing fashion, up and down. When you get that move down, we will have dinner."

"Sounds pretty easy. Kinda like dancing, shakin' my bootie, huh? Let's have a go of it," she winked.

"I'm sure it's exactly like that. Give me a demo. I need to make sure you're doing it right."

She punched his arm and cast her lure into the crystal water, as she watched him out of the corner of her eye. She was teasing him but it was so much fun. She didn't want him to know she was trying to figure out the proper up and down bounce. There's always a learning curve but she was hoping to impress him with her skills although it had been years since she fished.

All of a sudden, her rod bent down in a fury and Anne squealed. "I've got something, Troy. What should I do? Help me!"

"Naw, this is a game remember? We're competitors. I'm a nice guy but I love to win; you know that all too well. But I would suggest if you want to eat, you bring him in!" he said with a mischievous grin.

"You're no help at all," she yelled, "but I think I've got it from here!" Slowly reeling in the big fish, she was giddy.

After securing it in the boat, she jumped up and down. "I win! I win!" feeling like a kid again.

"Indeed, you did!" he smiled. "Now you'll have to figure out what you want your prize to be."

She didn't want to go there right now. Their expedition was delightful, and she wasn't about to spoil it by thinking about the possibilities this contest might open to her. She caught one more flathead and Troy pulled one in, so dinner would be fantastic.

****

<u>**Suzie**</u>

As hard as I tried to dissuade myself, I was having a full-fledged affair with my best friend's man. Guilt would sometimes override my pleasure, but I quickly kicked those thoughts to the curb. I was enjoying my time with Mark entirely too much to dwell on it. We were spending nearly every night together, having dinner, drinking wine, and indulging in each other. We had lovely days of bike riding, playing golf, going on picnics, and enjoying the perfect Fall weather. I didn't want it to end, dreading Anne's return and what might ensue.

I called Kate, Anne's daughter. "Hi, Kate. How are things? The kids?"

"We're all good here except for the usual everyday drama. What's up, Suzie?"

"I've been wondering what you hear from your mom. I miss her so much and wonder when she's coming home," I said with a small lie stuck in my throat like a fishbone.

"She sent me a text a couple days ago and said she was going on a boat for a few days. She didn't know if she'd have service but everything is great and she doesn't have her return planned yet."

"Really?" I asked. "She must be having a good time. Do you think everything is okay?"

"I think so, although she hasn't contacted me much. I'm surprised about that. I don't think we need to worry. She's good at taking care of herself, don't you think?" Kate asked.

"Yes, she's quite capable. Listen, honey, if you hear anything about her return, please let me know. I'd like to plan a little welcome home party for her."

"You're so sweet, Suzie. I sure will and I know she's always game for a party."

"Yep, games and parties; that's her thing," I said a bit relieved that her return wasn't imminent.

A boulder crumbled off my shoulders knowing Anne wasn't coming back any time soon. As much as I love her, spending time with Mark has given me a reason to wake up each morning. Most of the time, I'm looking at his handsome face and snuggling into his chest. I dread how devastated I'll feel when she comes home if he goes back to her. I will also have lost my best friend. I don't think she would tolerate my occupying his time and bed. Even if the outcome wasn't exactly what I hoped, this experience was worth it. We sometimes think about what we've given up, but forget what we've gained.

Two wrongs don't make a right. I've heard that expression my whole life; it certainly is befitting now. Maybe Anne is totally innocent there in Australia researching her book, but if she has crawled into Troy's bed, would that make my actions permissible? As much as I try to convince myself it's okay and Anne doesn't want Mark, I still suffer some guilt. But then again, the pleasure I find spending time with him makes me want him more and caring less about Anne. It's not that I don't care about Anne, I do. I don't want to hurt her in any way or lose her friendship, but, if she is doing what I suspect in Australia, I'll take advantage of the gift she left behind.

I didn't intend for this to happen between Mark and me. Not sure how he feels about the situation, but when Anne comes home, I hope he will give serious thought to our relationship. He's mentioned several times how he feels alive again and enjoys our time together. I'm sure it will be difficult to make a choice between Anne and me but, she's the one who left. If we're keeping score that should be one point for me. Maybe I'm more a game player than I thought.

Chapter 26

Troy grilled the flathead fillets and oysters while Anne made a fresh salad. The rich buttery texture of the fish finished with lemon, melted in her mouth. Paired with the scent of the ocean, carried by the warm breeze, arms of contentment enveloped her. She couldn't remember being happier. Anchored in a cove, there was a gentle sway to the boat as the waves gently rocked them like a hammock.

After dinner, Troy opened a bottle of Grand Marnier; it was the perfect blend of light citrus to top off the meal; each sip of the brandy warmed them. Small waves lapped the sides of the yacht as the sky was beginning to glow with colors of papaya and melon. Hints of aqua streaked across the magnificent kaleidoscope as imagined by a master artist. Breathtaking as the sunset was, Anne was hypnotized by Troy's soft voice.

"I can't remember being so happy in all my life, Anne. My soul is filled with peace, and the essence of love and appreciation for life and you. Thank you for this gift you have given me." He winked as he made the 01-22 sign.

Emotion swelling in her throat, she repeated the sign as she whispered, "More than you know, the pleasure is all mine."

He gently covered her hand with his and touched it in a way she'd never felt before. There was something so sensual and loving that she couldn't control the tear that ran down her cheek. She gazed toward the horizon where the brilliant orange ball was kissing the water, but his eyes never left her. She was aware of the tenderness and longing on his face, yet he didn't ask for more. A torch of passion was roaring inside her. He gently touched her chin and turned her face toward his, gazing into her hazel-green eyes. She touched his face and combed his silky beard with her fingers, falling in love with the scars on his face as the candlelight flickered across them. She moistened her lips and touched them to his; his response was unmistakable. She blew out the candle and took him down into the sleeping quarters where the crisp white sheets awaited their eager bodies.

****

As morning dawned, a sliver of sunlight flickered down from the stairway. Anne woke with Troy's arm still wrapped around her waist. His breathing was soft and gentle, just like the man. She was anguished by the dilemma she had created. She came here for the purpose of playing the ultimate game on Troy, swindling him out of a significant bankroll, but now as she touched his arm and relived the intimacy they shared a few hours earlier, her defense was all but gone. She thought she was winning this game, yet she couldn't imagine what her next move might be. She didn't know how this happened. As she lay next to him, trying to convince herself that she wasn't in love with him, that he wasn't the man she wanted to spend the rest of her life with, it was hopeless. Her game, her plan, had seriously turned on her like a tiger turns on its trainer.

Anne's thoughts turned to Troy's end game. As much as she didn't want to think he had an agenda, she knew he was a true game player, so there must be some other plot building just out of her sight. She would have to somehow keep her guard up to ferret out his ultimate intentions for this game. They were both playing for keeps, whatever that meant.

He stirred slightly and caressed her stomach, then kissed her neck. Her breath caught. She needed this man in her life. She hoped he felt the same. She turned to face him as his eyes opened and he smiled. "Am I dreaming?"

Anne smiled, "If you're dreaming, so am I and I like this dream." She put her moist lips on his and slipped her tongue into his mouth as he groaned. She hadn't been so aggressive in years; she couldn't get enough of this man. An hour later, the ache for each other sated, Troy brushed her hair from her face.

"I love your red hair and," he paused as if wondering if he should continue, "I love you, Anne."

Those words jumbled in her mouth but she chose not to say them. It was too soon.

Slipping on a light coverup, she went to the main deck, started her coffee, and heated water for his tea. The weather was glorious, cool enough to be refreshing, but balmy enough to jump in the lake; Troy soon appeared on the main deck wearing nothing but a smile. "Ready for a morning swim, my love?" he asked. "I don't want you to worry, but keep an eye out for sharks or saltwater crocs. They sometimes show up here so it's always good to be cautious."

"Oh, that's just great! Don't worry, he says. Just swim with the sharks and crocodiles. What is wrong with you? You expect me to get in the water now?"

He laughed. "I'm a superhero. I will protect you. Never fear, Big Bad Troy is here!"

"And I suppose that should make me feel better, huh?"

"Aw, come on, Anne. Watch this."

As he stood on the swim platform preparing to jump, Anne giggled. "Protect the family jewels, Troy!" Looking across the water, not a human or crocodile in sight, she let her garment fall to the deck and jumped in with him.

Swimming and playing together in the water, she felt like a kid again. He swam up behind her and embraced her ever so gently; turning her toward him, kissing her passionately. Anne couldn't imagine life, at her age, could be so exciting. He couldn't get enough of her either. After their refreshing swim, relaxing on the deck with their morning brew, Troy said, "I have an idea." "Oh I bet you do, sexy man," she teased.

"Well, yes, that's a great idea but I was thinking maybe I'd give you a tour around the lake. There's a little chickee bar and grill on the windward side that serves a delicious breakfast. Then we can cruise for a couple hours. I'd like to show you some of my favorite spots. Is that okay with you, Anne?"

"Sure, that sounds great. I need a few minutes to make myself presentable."

"You're perfect just the way you are, all messed up and sexy, but I understand a girl's gotta do what girls do. I'll just slow idle so you can take your time."

"Thanks for being so thoughtful and astute," she said, kissing him lightly before going down to the stateroom.

Mooring at the dock of a waterside restaurant called Chickee Charlie's, Troy offered his hand to her and helped her topside. The air smelled delicious, like fresh baking bread with cinnamon. Anne ordered a mimosa and French toast sauteed in butter made from that fresh bread that called to patrons like a siren. Anne could make a great breakfast but there was something about this that went above great. She finally attributed it to the fresh salt air, pure sunshine, and amazing company. She couldn't think, or say anything that would have made that moment any better.

The weather, and time spent with Troy, were ideal. As she looked across the sparkling aqua water, she wondered how she could have fallen in love with this strange man so quickly. It was out of character for her. When she had a mission, she always stuck to the game plan, but this turned on her like an F5 tornado.

Late in the afternoon, Troy pulled into a shady cove, close to a clean sandy beach. They had cocktails on the deck and visited about life and how precious each moment is. "When I was young, I thought I had all the time in the world, but now I know differently. This is the autumn of my life; soon winter will be upon me," Anne said. "I thought getting old would take longer."

"Geez Anne, nice way to bring down a perfect day," Troy said. "Do you have more pearls of wisdom you'd like to share with me? Or maybe another weather forecast?" he laughed.

"I'm sorry. This trip has allowed me to reevaluate everything in my life and stop taking it for granted. I've been pilfering away the years instead of dancing in the sunshine, my cotton dress blowing in the breeze. You probably don't get my girly adage, but it's the best way I can describe it."

Troy, nodding his head said, "I understand completely. I'd look ridiculous in a cotton dress but great on a Harley or in my boat; I should have bought them years earlier. I can't take my moldy money with me, so it's time to enjoy it with someone I love."

Troy lit the grill, baked some potatoes, and cooked two luscious filet mignons. Anne lit the candles and poured a full-bodied merlot as the sun disappeared into the ocean beyond the reef of the lake.

"I've got some things to do. Please excuse me," he said.

"Can I help with something?"

"No, I've got this. Relax, I'll have everything ready shortly."

Before long, he had two short beach chairs, a couple of white buckets filled with mystery, then pushed a button and launched an inflatable raft and secured it to the swim platform. The moon was nearly full, the sky as clear as crystal showing off millions of diamonds like Anne had never seen. They stepped into the raft and paddled to the beach. Securing everything, with Anne's help, Troy lit some tiki torches as they gathered some driftwood, started a fire, and sat comfortably in the chairs.

"I've been wanting to do this for a while and now I have my woman to share it with." He pulled the buckets closer and pulled out all the makings for S'mores. He had even found two sticks for roasting the marshmallows.

"Wow! You thought of everything, didn't you? I suppose you even ordered the weather. It's perfect. I love everything about this," she said. Being overwhelmed at his thoughtfulness, she leaned to kiss his sticky marshmallow lips and said, "I love you, Bad Boy Troy."

Suddenly, interrupting this magical moment, Troy's satellite phone pinged. "Hello? Ya David, sure. When? Confirmed? How long do I have? I thought I had more time. Thanks, buddy. I owe you my life a second time. Be in touch." He disconnected the phone and his whole demeanor changed. He sighed deeply and felt the life he hoped to live with Anne disappear like dandelions in a breeze. He couldn't tell her the danger they were in; he had to protect her. Anne knew it was something serious. The air changed, the world stopped spinning, a heavy blanket of ominous fear came over her but she couldn't imagine what the problem was. If Troy wanted her to know, he would tell her. She remembered David from his recent visit to Troy's house when Troy gave him $75,000. If she recalled the story correctly, David was the comrade who had carried him for miles after Troy had been shot. This must have something to do with Troy's past although Anne didn't know much about it, she was sure she knew all she needed to know.

Chapter 27

<u>**Suzie**</u>

I was watching the news and drinking my coffee this morning when my phone pinged. I don't use WhatsApp often. I don't really know anyone overseas so what's the point? I checked it; what a surprise.

"Suze, Hi. It's Anne. How are you?"

"Is it really you? We were beginning to think you were lunch for an Australian crocodile, or worse."

She laughed. "I know, I'm sorry. There's just been so much going on, that I haven't taken the time. How's everyone there?"

"Well, let's see… we had a 7.5 earthquake, a volcanic eruption, a major flood, your house exploded and I got pregnant by an alien and had a kid!"

Laughing uproariously, Anne said, "I guess I wasn't very good at keeping in touch. You're so funny. You make me happy just hearing your voice, not to be outdone by your dramatic sense of humor. You got your point across so can you please fill me in on what's going on back home?"

I was pissed, to say the least. It wasn't fair how Anne had left us all hanging in limbo with no information about where she was, if she was even dead or alive. "Everyone seems to be fine. Kate told me you had messaged her. She and her family are fine; finally getting back to normalcy since Covid. Mark and I, you remember him, right? read some of your book trying to figure out if we could find you."

"I didn't intend to make anyone worry. I guess I didn't want any of you talking me out of the trip, so I just hopped on the plane. How is Mark, by the way? I hope he's not too lonely. He's such a good man."

"Mark? Oh, Mark is fine…just fine. Why? Are you rethinking your relationship with him?" I asked a bit cautiously.

"Actually, yes. I think we may have outgrown each other. To tell you the truth, as I know it now, we probably should have moved on a while ago. It's nothing Mark said, or did. He's an amazing guy and I want nothing but the best for him. I truly hope he finds someone who appreciates him for the sweetheart he is. Please don't tell him this, but I think I'm in love with Troy."

"What? I can't believe it! I don't know what that means. What about your family, your friends, your property? Are you planning to leave everything behind and be a Bush Bride, or whatever they're called over there? That's crazy, Anne."

"Suze, none of this is a done deal. We haven't discussed any kind of future so I don't know where this might go-maybe nowhere but I want to stay long enough to give it a go or I might regret it.”

“Well, what will you do about Mark?” I asked, not wanting to sound too desperate. “I’ve been keeping him company and I know you two have had a long relationship.”

“I really appreciate you helping him through this transition, or whatever we may call it. You’re a true friend, Suze. I just hope he’s not too sad.”

“Oh, I think he’ll manage, Anne. I have a feeling he’ll be just fine. To be fair, you need to tell him when you’ve made up your mind.”

“I was hoping you could gently break the news to him,” Anne said.

“No, no! This is all you, girlfriend; you started this dance, now you have to face the music.”

Our call ended and I felt like I wanted to do a happy dance. Did she just give me permission to take her man? That’s my interpretation of it. And away we go!

****

It felt like she threw ice water on Troy. He shut down like a balloon stuck with a pin. They packed up and made their way back to the yacht, almost in complete silence. Anne didn’t know what happened but saying she loved him had not affected him the way she hoped; perhaps it was the phone call, an emergency. She felt foolish and insecure. Something was wrong that she didn't understand.

Troy throttled up the boat and anchored in a protective cove for the night. Sitting on the upper deck, they had a cocktail. Troy leaned toward her. "Anne, I'm quite tired. I think I'll go below to sleep."

"Of course, Troy but, if there's something we need to talk about, I'm here. You can say anything to me."

"Not tonight, honey, but we'll talk soon. I have to sort through some things in my mind and then I will tell you more than you probably want to know."

"Okay, Troy. I won't push you. Is it okay if I come to bed with you? I don't want to stay up alone."

"Sweet Anne, you don't ever have to ask my permission to lie down beside me. It's the joy of my life."

She felt comforted that he had things on his mind, and it was nothing she said or did. They snuggled contentedly together, though her sleep was fitful wondering what could be so bad that triggered his reaction.

Morning came too soon; Anne knew they'd be going back to Troy's home. The good thing about it was perhaps Troy would open up and tell her why the sudden change in his behavior. Radioing the dockmaster, two deckhands met the yacht, securing it and unloading their personal items. They would clean, refuel, and get the boat ready for the next outing. She hoped they could go on more boat trips. It was wonderful…until the phone call that changed everything.

Troy made a quick call to Steve announcing their return. He was so dedicated to Troy, that Anne wondered how someone could be so faithful. There was no doubt, however, that Troy was extremely generous to Steve for his services. Their relationship seemed respectful and comfortable.

Steve, as usual, had everything under control waiting for Troy. He unloaded the vehicle while Troy and Anne went inside to take showers and prepare for lunch. Anne hoped the air would clear now that Troy was home, but the tension still hung like fog over a bog. After lunch, Anne retired to her bedroom, cuddled up with a book instead of Troy, giving him some space. That seemed like the proper protocol. A couple hours later, Anne heard a crash in the kitchen and ran to see what happened.

Troy was teetering, eyes glassy and his hair a frightful mess. He had dropped a bottle of slivovitz on the slate floor and the sticky, purple liquid and shards of glass were everywhere. Before Anne could stop him, Troy staggered across the floor suddenly screaming in pain as broken glass embedded in his feet. He was clearly drunk. This was a problem. Not only did she have to clean up the mess, but she also had to be his doctor.

"Stop, Troy!" Anne screamed. "Don't move! I mean it!" He looked at her with squinted eyes but obeyed her order. She rolled a chair over to him, crunching glass under her shoes, and made him sit so she could roll him out of the mess. Two hours later after something resembling minor surgery, she had most of the glass out of his feet, medicated and covered with gauze. She put him to bed and shut the door. So, this is the alcoholic rod he uses to flog himself with. Not a pretty picture.

Checking on him several times during the night, it seemed like he had slept. In the morning, she dressed and prepared to make a good greasy breakfast. She knew he'd be hungover. When he came out of his room, looking sheepish, he gave her a small wave but didn't speak. She poured him a cup of strong coffee and a large glass of water. Serving breakfast, she wasn't sure what to say and thought it best be left to him. Finally, he looked over his cup and said, "I'm so sorry, Anne. I guess I'm not the strongest hook on which to hang a hat." She wanted to smile but wouldn't stroke his ego.

He wasn't very perky what with the headache from the slivovitz and sore feet. She felt sorry for him but it was self-inflicted and she wasn't going to tolerate it. He hobbled to the verandah with ice tea and a book, spending most of the day until late afternoon. Very little conversation was exchanged, she knew something was bothering him and had been for days. Each time she looked at him, it was clear he was in deep concentration. He turned to look at her and said, "It's time for me to talk, Anne. It can't wait any longer."

"Go for it, Troy. I'm a big girl; I can handle whatever you have to dish out."

"There's no way I can express how much this hurts me; you will be hurt, too, if I'm reading your signals properly. I can't completely explain why this has to happen; I'm not sure myself. I've made a reservation for you to fly back to Houston tomorrow."

Anne couldn't believe what she was hearing. With every bit of courage she could muster, she kept her emotions from showing on her face. This was devastating, excruciating, and humiliating all in the same breath.

"Do you want me to try to explain?" he asked. "I owe you an explanation, but I'm not sure I can be truthful."

"Don't bother. You've said enough. When I'm not wanted, I'm smart enough to let it go. No big deal, Troy. It was fun while it lasted. What time is my flight and will Steve be taking me?"

"Anne, please. Your coldness is killing me. You act like this was just a fling. It means so much more to me but I don't know how to tell you. I can't put you through the nightmare I will soon be facing; the pain would be so much worse than this. I need you to leave to protect you."

"Oh, please! That's bullshit and you know it. Better yet, I know it. Just call it what it was – a fun fuck! Pretty expensive for you, huh?"

"Listen, Anne, and listen good. I'm only going to say this once. When you said you loved me, I knew I had made a terrible mistake. Remember when I went to town and didn't take you with me a few weeks ago?"

She nodded.

"My doctor told me I have stage 4 cancer and I have a very short time to live. I should never have let our relationship get to this level but I was selfish; I needed your love. Please try to understand why you must go. I couldn't bear to have you see me in the end stages of my life and it's coming quickly."

"If it's true, I would want to be with you; if it's not true, it's a good yarn, Troy." She went to her room, not able to hold back her sorrow much longer. She had been duped, fooled, tricked, deceived, and….loved. She couldn't imagine, at her age, she could be so gullible. She had been catfished but not out of money. He stole her heart instead. She didn't believe for a minute that he was ill, as he said. She became angry with herself that she let this happen. He was sending her home, leaving her heart and his bankroll in Australia. Her plan had turned to shit and he had totally outwitted her. As she packed her Louie Vuitton bag, the tears began to flow. Even angrier that she would allow herself to be crushed by this man, she would walk away with dignity and not allow him to see that he had reduced her to a sniveling idiot.

At 8:00 AM the following morning, she pulled her suitcase toward the kitchen. Troy was sitting on a stool at the island. He turned with love and deep emotion whipping him from the inside. His eyes seemed red and swollen but he should be happy he managed to get rid of her. She would never give a man the satisfaction of knowing he ripped her heart out and threw it in the trash like a piece of rotten meat.

"Anne, please try to understand. This is for your own good, though I know you're crushed. There are some things we can't foresee or plan on; they just happen, and this is one of those things. I'll be in touch with you; I promise." His heart was wrenched but he knew there was no other way to handle this. He'd gone over it a thousand times in his mind. The danger was real now and he couldn't put Anne or Steve in such terrible jeopardy. He had to make it believable.

With all the flippancy she could manage, she looked straight into his tear-stained eyes. "Don't bother, Troy. I can handle whatever you dish out and then some. Have a nice life…or what's left of it." She glanced one final time at Troy as he gave her their secret 01-22, I love you, code. She walked out the door just as Steve pulled up in the Land Rover.

A two-hour trip to the airport in Sydney seemed like forever. She wanted to be on her way, back to her real life. Steve attempted small talk but Anne wasn't in the mood. It wasn't long before he turned the radio on to quell the deafening silence.

Traffic was picking up; they were getting close to the airport. Anne felt like a bird in a cage and wanted out. She wondered what life would be like back in Houston. She and Mark were finished as a couple but she had no regrets. That was probably one of the good things about her trip. She wanted him to be happy and, as of late, neither of them had been happy together.

Steve's phone rang. "Yes, hi. Hmm, okay. Anything you say. You're sure about this, right? I'm sorry. Sure thing." He took the next exit off the highway and turned around heading back the way they came.

Panicked, Anne screeched louder than she intended. "What's going on? Where are we going? I can't miss my flight."

"Miss Anne, please trust me. This is a good thing; you'll see."

"I don't want to see anything but the airport. Take me there now."

With a nearly desperate look, he touched her hand. "Please, Anne. I know you've been hurt but this is for the best."

Flames of anger licked at her. She wanted to explode; exasperation eating her gut. What in the hell did Troy want now? Did he want to further humiliate her? Whatever it was, his tactics weren't going to work. She didn't have a choice at the moment, but she would find her own way to the airport. He could not keep her there against her will.

Arriving back at Troy's home, he was waiting on the verandah. Steve got her luggage and placed it near the door. "Thank you, Anne, for coming back. I know I have put you through hell and I'm so sorry."

"I didn't have a choice now, did I?" She was angry; not only at him but at herself for allowing this to happen.

Troy looked at both Anne and Steve, "Will you both come inside with me? I haven't been totally honest."

Chapter 28

Sitting around the beautiful wood table Troy had made himself from the timber on his property, he folded his hands together. It appeared he was very emotional dropping his head. "I don't know how or where to start. Steve, you've been my faithful friend and companion for most of your life and I can't thank you enough. There's nothing I can say or do to repay your loyalty. I'm not afraid to say I love you."

Steve, in his quiet way, reached across the table and touched Troy's arm. "I love you, too, man. I always have. Thank you for all you've done for me."

Anne tried so hard not to cry when Troy reached for her hand. She didn't pull away. "Anne," he said tenderly, "I never expected this kind of love again in my life. Who could have ever guessed that a silly online game would bring me love? I know your initial intent was different than how it's turned out. I know about your plans, but you fell in love with me, too. I would give you anything you ask for; you know that, right?"

She nearly choked on her tears. Sobbing she said, "How can you leave us? You can't just drop a bomb like you have."

"I know, honey, but as I said, some things just aren't planned and there's nothing we can do about them. I have brought much of this on myself so please don't feel bad for me."

Troy reached for Steve's hand. "There's something very important I need to tell you. I only hope you won't hate me for waiting so long. I wanted to say…"

Steve interrupted him, squeezing his hand. "I know, Dad. I've known for several years that you are my dad."

Troy couldn't hold the tears back, flooding his face. They embraced each other and bonded as only a father and son could. Anne was flabbergasted. This was better than any book she could write. The worse thing about this story is that Anne always liked a happy ending, which, obviously, was not the way this would end.

"Steve, how did you find out? I've kept my distance all these years because I didn't want to put you or your beautiful family in danger. My life is volatile and could explode at any minute."

Steve pulled away from his dad, "I've always felt a deeper connection to you. I had a feeling you were more than my uncle. I sent samples to one of the DNA places and it came back as I suspected. I questioned Mom and she told me she's not my mom but my aunt, but you know, she's been an amazing mum and Grand mum to little Ginger."

Troy gasped, unable to comprehend it all. "I should explain, although I'm sure you probably know, being the detective that you are. I had a one-night-stand and you were conceived. I didn't know about you until you were nearly three when your mother died. When I found you, your aunt Sharon adopted you and vowed to keep my secret. I guess she wasn't very good at that."

"Don't blame Mom. I was blatant and direct and I kept questioning her until she finally broke down and told me the story."

"It's past time to become a family, Steve….and Anne, if you'll join us," Troy said. "I can't wait to spend time with your little redheaded princess Ginger and hug her like I've wanted to since she was born. I want her to know who I really am. Is that okay, Steve?"

"Of course, Dad, I want Ginger to know her Grandpapa."

After all the raw emotion was sopped up and sighs of complete peace filled the room, Troy stood, rubbing his hands together.

"Okay, here's what we'll do. I don't want to be presumptuous, but, Anne, will you stay here with us for a while?"

"I wouldn't want to miss a minute of this, Troy," reaching to kiss him gently.

"I don't know how much time I have, but I want to make the most out of every second while I'm still feeling good. We are going to be a family, a real family. We are going to play, eat, party, and go to the lake. We'll cram as much into every day as we can. How does that sound? Are you game?"

"Game? Game? You know I love games, Troy. This is how this all started," Anne winked. She turned to walk outside to give the two men some space. As she did, she turned back to meet Troy's eyes and flashed their secret 01-22 code. He blew her a kiss.

"Steve, I've decided to hire someone to give us a hand here. We shouldn't have to work around here when we have so much catching up to do. What do you think?" he asked.

"I've often wondered why you work so hard when you can clearly afford to pay for help. I know you enjoy it, but you should do the things you like. You love working in the gardens, but all the other things can be done by someone else," Steve suggested. "Do you have someone in mind?"

"Yes, as a matter of fact, I do. The Driscoll boy, Tommy I think is his name. He just got laid off from his job. He helps support his mom so I thought I'd talk to him. Do you know anything about him or his family?"

"He seems like a nice kid- seen him around town some. Wouldn't hurt to talk to him. If he's a good worker, why not?" Steve said.

Tommy Driscoll was nineteen years old and lived at home with his single mom. They had moved to the area about six months before. He couldn't afford college, even if he wanted to. He wasn't college material; he enjoyed working with his hands. He was tall and lanky without much meat or muscle on his bones. Troy interviewed him and was impressed with the boy's respect and hired him on the spot. Troy set a schedule; Tommy would work four days a week. His pay was $350 per day. He had a list of chores that needed to be done each day he was there, and he'd be given odd jobs as needed. Troy's little dog Maggie, who had never been aggressive, had issues with Tommy. Whenever he came close to Troy, Maggie would snarl and snap at him; it was an unusual reaction.

Troy instructed Tommy on feeding the animals, mowing the acreage, repairing the split-rail fencing, spraying for weeds and insects, and general maintenance. He was supposed to begin at 7:00 AM but he was always there early, excited to work. He was conscientious and eager to take instruction from Troy about anything that needed to be done. Troy truly liked him and was impressed with his work ethic and potential. When Troy liked someone, he was very generous. After a couple weeks, Troy bought him a brand-new pickup truck to use as long as he was in his employ. Money was never an issue with Troy. His excuse for the purchase was that Tommy's beater of a car, made Troy look bad.

Anne knew her time with Troy was short; she wasn't sure if his health or his past would catch up with him first. Something was hanging in the air like a guillotine waiting to fall. Anne was determined to make the most of every moment they could share. They took walks through the woods, along the trails, rode the ATV up the mountain and to the plateau, and peeked in on the koalas often. They were a wonder to behold in the wild. When Anne was sure no one was around and Tommy Driscoll had gone home for the day, she would strip down and skinny dip with Troy. They played volleyball in the pool, but mostly, they kissed, laughed, and breathed. Every moment she spent with Troy made her realize she had never really lived until now. Why now? She was old and he was dying.

One afternoon for lunch, Anne had prepared a delicious shrimp salad with some green onions, tomatoes, red peppers, and fresh dill from the garden. It was a lifestyle Anne had quickly fallen in love with. She baked up some flavorful flatbread and made fresh hibiscus tea. She set the table outside on the verandah; the weather as perfect as could be. Troy groaned in delight a dozen times enjoying the feast Anne had set before him. He knew he had found a good thing when we found Anne, in spite of the fact that she had planned to pad her bank account at his expense. All that had changed now. They had both changed. Life was sweet but their moments together were ticking like a timer on a bomb.

"Anne, honey, why don't you go get your ukulele and play a bit for me? You've only played a couple of times since you got here and I really enjoy your music."

She was happy he suggested it; she loved to play and knowing he enjoyed it, was a bonus. She played a couple songs inspired by the glimmer coming off the gurgling creek. Watching the birds fly in for a drink of cool, fresh water was amazing. She had been quietly practicing a song at night after he went to sleep. This seemed like the perfect time to play it. It was a love song for the ages, 'I Will Always Love You'.

As she played, he began to hum in perfect pitch. She hadn't heard him sing. When she got to the chorus, his voice, melodic and soothing, sang to her, 'and I will always love you'. She felt tears well in her eyes. She couldn't imagine love, and losing it, could hurt so badly. All things considered, in spite of his generosity and kindness, and his romantic attention, there was still something that rubbed Anne a little wrong. She tried to dismiss any doubt she had, but it gnawed at her, even at their most intimate moments.

That night as they lie in each other's arms, remembering the sweetness of the moment he sang to her, filled her with joy. Why did life have to be so unfair? She didn't know what to expect next. She would do anything to change the situation, to give them more time together. She wanted nothing more than to give herself completely to him and satisfy and comfort the pain that was locked inside of him like a fortress. She gently lifted her leg over his firm tanned body and lay on top of him kissing the breath out of him.

Chapter 29

<u>Suzie</u>

I haven't heard from Anne in several weeks so I assume she is still enjoying herself. Her daughter, Kate, said she'd called and had no immediate plans to come back to the states.

That plan is fine for me because I'm thoroughly enjoying the time spent with Mark. This is the first relationship I've had since Bill died and I had forgotten how fulfilling it is to have someone to share dinner with, dip my hand in the same popcorn bowl while watching a movie, or snuggling up together in a big tub of bubbles.

Sipping a glass of wine in our robes after an impromptu lovemaking session, Mark said, "Suzie, I don't want to throw ice on our "got a cigarette?" moment, but I got a call from Anne a couple days ago."

I felt snakes in my belly, fearing the worst. I'm sorry to say, the worst news would be if Anne is planning to come home to reconcile with Mark. She's been my friend forever, but I think I've fallen for Mark. "That's interesting," I said, my voice cracking. "What did she have to say?"

Mark reached over and gently ran his finger down my cheek. "You look a little pale, honey. Are you okay?" He was teasing her and having a hell of a lot of fun doing it.

"I'm fine. So, what's she up to? Does she have plans?" I asked, not wanting to sound overly anxious, while I could feel every beat of my heart.

"Relax, Suzie. It's all good. Take a deep breath for me, please. Sip your wine and listen."

I tried to do what he instructed but wasn't sure I wanted to hear what was coming next. "Go ahead, Mark. Where do things stand?"

He smiled with a sexy little quirk on his face. "Where would you like them to stand?" he asked teasingly as he touched my bare leg.

"Oh no, mister. This is your show. You started this; now it's up to you," I said.

"Okay, so you're throwing the ball back in my court, huh?"

I responded, "I didn't know we were playing ball but, if that's what you want to call it, sink it!"

Mark laughed. "I just did. Did you forget so soon? Maybe I should refresh your memory before continuing this conversation." He laughed. "First, I want to tell you how very much you mean to me, Suze."

I felt like someone put a plastic bag over my head as I tried to get air.

He continued. "I forgot how much fun being in love could be. I know this sounds corny but you've brought sunshine back into my life and, if you're willing, I'm ready to see this through, until….whenever."

I was so relieved; I didn't want to lose him. "I agree with what you just said, but what about Anne?"

"When she called, she tried to be very gentle and I appreciated that. We both knew our time together had come to an end. I told her about us."

I sucked in a gasp. "Oh, no! What did she say?"

"Suze, she's very happy for both of us. She loves us, we know that, and is perfectly fine that we've found each other."

"Really? I can't believe it. Well, what is she going to do? Stay in Australia?"

"It seems Troy is terminally ill. Unless he sends her away, she wants to stay with him until the end. It seems she's really in love with him," Mark said.

"How do you feel about it?"

"Suze, I couldn't be happier on all counts. It's funny how life twists us in knots and all of a sudden, everything straightens out. I don't know what I'm trying to say, but you get it, right?"

"I sure do, and I like it," I answered.

He got a serious look on his face; I didn't know what was coming next. "Suzie, how do you feel about moving in together?"

I couldn't contain the smile that washed completely through me. "It's perfect, Mark; just perfect!"

****

Troy couldn't remember being happier in many years. This feeling compared only to the overwhelming knowledge that he had a son and family he could enjoy. Now that the truth was out and Troy could truly be a father and grandpapa, the only thing standing in his way was his past; it was stalking him like an apparition in the night. He had to deal with it quickly. Details were imperative and time-consuming, but he wanted a bit more time to enjoy Anne and his family before he disappeared. Some might think his punishment was unfair, but he knew it was justice and retribution for the man he had been. He had hopes that his past would never catch him, though unrealistic. He had always been good at finding solutions but this was an extremely difficult one. He had to make sure no harm came to Steve's family and Anne was safely back in the USA; his affairs needed to be in perfect order.

A few weeks wasn't long to plan the end of one's life but that's what it was coming down to. He gave Tommy Driscoll extra duties around the homestead which he fulfilled without incident. However, each evening as Tommy was preparing to leave, he would attempt to shake Troy's hand but the problem with Maggie persisted. She would nearly attack him, a total mystery; one that left Troy wary. He felt animals had a certain intuition; maybe something wasn't quite right. He would never let his guard down. He couldn't afford to.

A beautiful cool morning welcomed Anne as she stretched in her bed. She and Troy had intimate times of great love and passion, but they found they both slept better in separate beds. She lifted the shade to see the glory of the birds flying in for their breakfast near the creek and the seed that was available for them. A heavy morning fog drifted up from the ground as the rising sun coaxed it to disappear. Suddenly she caught a glimpse of movement toward the open, park-like area just off to the east of the house. Slipping her robe on, she walked to the door to get a better look. Troy was talking to some men who had arrived in several trucks. They unloaded things onto the grass that were unfamiliar to Anne until she saw a very large basket sitting off to the side of one of the trucks. It appeared someone was going on a hot-air balloon ride.

Quickly dressing and twisting her hair in a messy bun, Anne had a feeling this was going to involve her. She stepped outside as the men continued to set up. Troy motioned for Anne; hesitantly, she complied. She cowered like little Maggie did when Anne called her to administer her medicine.

"Good morning, my love. Look what I have planned for us today. Won't it be amazing? I'm so looking forward to it- been thinking about it for a while now."

Her legs shaking, she said, "I'm not a big fan of heights, Troy. Seems like you've been thinking of lots of things for a while now. I wish we had discussed this before you did all this. I'm not sure I can do it."

"What?! Of course, you can. Our pilot is one of the best in the land; it will be an experience we'll cherish the rest of our lives."

"I hope it won't be the last thing we'll cherish," she said. "Do we have parachutes just in case?"

Troy laughed, "Naw, we'll be fine. I'll protect you."

"That's nice of you to say, but you can't protect me from falling a thousand feet."

"Maybe you should have a little hit off my pipe to relax you; you could really enjoy it then."

"You're a bad influence on me, but I might just take you up on it."

"We'll be ready in about fifteen minutes while the temperature and winds are perfect. See you in a few."

Soon after liftoff, Anne forgot about the apprehension she felt. The cool air, the mastery painted by the sun streaking through the clouds barely above the horizon, was breathtakingly beautiful. She felt like nature was breathing.

Looking below at the patchwork of patterns created by God and skilled farmers, she had never seen anything more stunning. The vineyards below were soaking in the sun to grow and ripen some of the best fruit on the planet. The magnitude of it all was astounding. Colors of emerald, peridot, yellows, the color of liquid sunshine, and hints of mulberry and golden citrine were a wonder to behold. The silence was calming and welcoming.

Drifting over Troy's acreage, her eye caught the sparkling creek and the hills they had climbed in the ATV many times to view the beauty. Soon, Lake Macquarie came into view, the sun coaxing its colors to bloom into shades of azure. Tiny boats dotted the still water. Troy put his strong arm around her; Anne's heart was flooded with emotion, remembering her first night on that lake with Troy holding her in his arms. They both relived it at that very moment. "You've given me everything I need to take me through eternity, Anne."

"I know exactly how you feel, Troy." She could never have predicted she would fall so in love at her age. What a voyage her life had taken; no pun intended. She needed nothing from him except more time to love him. In the back of her mind, sorry to say, she hoped when he passed and his will was read, that he would be generous to her. That might make it seem worthwhile.

The next couple of weeks seemed like Troy was coming and going nearly every day. Trying to understand the stress he must be under, Anne supported him whenever she could. She understood he had legal matters to discuss with his solicitor and family. She didn't need to know details; she was just happy to be part of his family. She tried to put herself in his place, wondering how she would handle the knowledge that her life would soon be over. She prayed his suffering would be minimal and his journey quick when it came down to it. She squinted her eyes tightly closed, thinking about watching him take his final breath, feel his heart beat its last time. He had given her so much in the short time they had known each other; it didn't seem right that he was being taken from her so soon. Physically, he seemed to be doing quite well; his breathing was a bit labored from time to time but didn't seem excessive.

Not understanding how the disease progressed, she hoped this was the worst until he went to sleep one night and didn't wake up. She knew she was being naïve, but she didn't want to know anymore. She would just wait and be a comfort to him when he needed it. He was spending a lot of time with Steve which was perfectly understandable and sad at the same time. She didn't understand how those two men could think, all these years, that keeping the secret of being family was the right choice. She thought of the wonderful

family times they probably missed because of what? Fear?
Or just being men?

Chapter 30

Troy bought some delicious-looking steaks from the local meat market. "I know I haven't been around much trying to look over all the details, but maybe we can cook these for dinner. Would that be okay with you? We'll just relax and enjoy the evening together. I have to ask Tommy to do some extra things and then Steve and I have things to discuss. I'm sorry to leave you alone for the afternoon."

"Please don't worry about me. I'm happy to be here and I'll do whatever I can to make things easier for you." Anne smiled lovingly at him. "It sounds like the perfect way I'd want to live the rest of my life. Tell you what. If you let me know what time you'll be here to eat, I will totally take care of dinner. Deal?"

"I haven't had a better offer since Tuesday, when you crawled into my bed," he winked as he bent down to kiss her, wrapping his massive hand around the back of her neck.

"You might just get yourself in trouble, Mr. Kent, if this is the way you're going to act."

"You know, that's my favorite kind of trouble. I'll be daydreaming about that." As he left for the afternoon, he turned and signed their secret code, 01-22 to Anne. Her heart couldn't be fuller with love.

Troy had always trusted Steve, knowing he came from "good stock". He was relieved knowing now they had an understanding; Steve would take care of any detail that needed attention. So many specifics needed precise execution and there were few people he could rely on to do what needed to be done with expert accuracy. His wealth was to be distributed in certain ways, to assure nothing was left to chance. This was more complex than Steve knew but he'd seen his father come through many hard things through the years; he was confident in his ability. He knew he was very rich but when he was trusted with the actual figures, he was shocked. That kind of money didn't register in his brain.

Anne wanted to make a special meal for Troy. She didn't know how many nights they would have together; it grieved her, but tonight they would celebrate. She perused his pantry to inspire her, then went to the succulent garden. Red ripe tomatoes nearly fell off the vine, bulbs of garlic were ready for the taking, an abundance of fresh herbs, a savory onion, and a couple fresh carrots to spoil Dolores the donkey, as Anne did every morning.

She knew Troy loved pasta so, after locating his pasta machine, she googled a recipe and went to work. She dipped the tomatoes in hot water to peel them, roasted bulbs of garlic, and began simmering the sauce that needed hours to come to perfection. She made a marinade for the steaks, trimmed them, and put them in the fridge. Adding a fresh salad would top it off so she returned to the garden with her shears. Cutting some bib lettuce, spinach, and pulling a few radishes, all that was left was to make a delicious orange vinaigrette and chill the wine.

When Troy got home from his busy day, the sun was shedding its golden crystals across the blades of emerald green grass, flickering underneath the sway of the trees overhead, a beautiful time of day. Tommy was finishing up his chores, so Troy dismissed him for the day but not before Maggie could go on the attack, as she did every day. Troy was unsure why she acted like that. Troy's internal radar picked up on her reaction.

Anne had the table set with items Troy didn't even remember he had. She had walked through a part of the woods to gather wildflowers that she braided into leis to decorate the table. The house smelled like a five-star restaurant; she was freshly showered and, according to Troy, smelled more delicious than the food.

Troy freshened up while Anne lit the candles and plated the food. She had outdone herself. She loved to cook but this steak, side of pasta, and fresh salad were out of this world, if she did think so herself. By the look on Troy's face scanning the spread before him, he was impressed with the many sides of Anne. He had a few surprises up his sleeve for her, too if all went according to plan.

They retired to the verandah, Anne serving up a chocolate mousse with just the perfect amount of Amaretto teasing the tongue. The meal was perfect, the company perfect, the weather perfect. The only thing that wasn't perfect was the elephant in the room, Troy's imminent death.

They went inside; the candles burning down, it had been an evening to write about. Anne hadn't been spending much time on the book; she was too busy living the book. Tonight was different, she could feel something in the air. As she walked toward the table to clear the dishes, Troy caught her wrist. "I think those dishes can wait till tomorrow, don't you?"

Anne was anxious about this surprise. She had learned to love passion, maybe even more than when she was young. Troy was so different and just his touch lit an uncontrollable fire. He spun her like a doll on a dance floor as she fell into his arms. The silkiness of his beard against her face, the moistness of his soft lips, and the desire that she was aware of below his waist, excited her. He made her feel young and sexy, a feeling she hadn't experienced in years; maybe never. There was something about the way he touched her, ate her with his eyes, and adjusted his breathing to match hers. It was so incredibly sensual in the way he touched her.

He never lost eye contact with her as he moved his fingers down her arms and up her back. They kissed passionately all the way to his king-size bed, undressing each other, in anticipation. This was how love should be at any age, and lovemaking was an added bonus.

They laid in each other's arms for a long while, not speaking, but listening to the rhythm of their heartbeats nearly in sync. Anne felt Troy's body relax and drift into a light sleep so she slipped out of his bed. As she got to the doorway, he quietly called her name. When she turned, he gave her the 01-22 sign and she returned the "I Love You" sign right back to him. She was crushed inside knowing she would lose him forever; the love they shared would have to last the rest of her life.

Troy was settling in for some welcomed sleep after an evening as pleasant as he could ever recall. He had been gifted with this amazing woman. Grief haunted him knowing their time was limited and he dreaded the pain this was causing all of them. He had come to trust her, something he vowed he would never do. He was wise to deception so he reserved a slight bit of caution to be safe. He sighed, then pulled the sheet over his naked body just as Maggie, his twelve-pound terrier jumped onto his bed. She never slept on his bed; this was curious. He reached down to comfort her but she was shaking, never taking her eyes off the doorway.

Troy was so sleepy and began to doze, just as Maggie growled. She continued the throaty warning relentlessly. Troy silently slipped out of bed and put his pillows where his body had been, tiptoeing across the large room, to hide behind the door. Something was amiss.

He listened, barely breathing and then he heard the gentle swish of clothing moving toward him; a small light pointing toward his room. His heart thundered in his chest; he knew they were coming for him but he hoped he had more time. If not for faithful Maggie, he may have been caught unaware. He didn't know what he was facing but he was as ready as he could be. He hoped his African name of Quick Fist was still viable; he was out of practice. His eyes adjusted to the darkness; he heard the slight wheezing of the intruder on the other side of the door just inches away. Suddenly, a large machete preceded the assailant's arm heading for Troy's bed. Troy stepped from behind the door and tackled the tall man to the floor, throwing the deadly knife to the side. Grabbing the light, he thrust it into the man's face; shockingly, it was Tommy Driscoll. "Tommy! Tommy!" Troy puffed. "Why? Why would you do this? I've been so good to you."

Fear was written on Tommy's face; a stare as cold as ice, looking into Troy's eyes he said, "You're my million-dollar golden ticket." Without even thinking, in one swift, expert movement, Troy snapped his neck and watched the last breath of life slip from Tommy Driscoll.

Winded, Troy sat on the floor next to the lifeless body. Visions of his past flooded him with emotion. He had been the assassin to do the president's bidding, but now the hunter was the hunted. A tear escaped his eye; he had truly loved that boy, Tommy. He actually reminded him of a young Troy, when he was just coming into manhood. The most ironic part of all was they had both been enticed by an evil regime and had eaten the fruit, though poisonous in the end. Unfortunately, Tommy didn't have the skill or experience Troy did. The evidence lay on his bedroom floor.

Troy waited till near dawn to start his tractor with Tommy's body in the bucket. It would seem odd to hear a tractor in the middle of the night, but not so, in the early morning. He slowly made his way to the base of the mountain where Ivor rested. He hoped they wouldn't look for the boy here, but that was the chance Troy had to take. He didn't have the convenience of time to work out a better plan. Using the backhoe made quick work of digging the grave; a painful weight filled his chest as he lowered Tommy's body into the earth and covered him with soil. "God be with you, Tommy. I'm so sorry."

Troy was back in bed when Anne woke with no trace of the horror that occurred during the night. Troy didn't sleep but his body needed rest nearly as much as his mind. He had to continue with his plan and move on it faster than he thought. Most of his financials were in place; he was grateful he had people he could trust to help with his plan. "Money talks, bullshit walks," one of his favorite sayings. He was smart enough to know anyone's loyalty can be bought with a big enough carrot dangling in front of their nose, and he had no shortage of carrots.

Chapter 31

He hated to spend time away from Anne but his final plans needed tweaking to assure all went off without a hitch. He had the best in the business to work out the details; they needed to strategize together to fine-tune it all. Timing was critical. He left her a few hours a day while she worked in the gardens, and tended to the animals, though her mind never left Troy, and wondered if there was something she wasn't understanding. She wasn't sure she wanted to know and planned to take each day as it came. It wouldn't do any good to worry; there was nothing she could do to change the situation, whatever it was. She was sure there was more to the story than she had been told. She had the sense to stay vigilant in case something affected her.

One afternoon, as she was watering the rose bushes, a car, tires squealing, spinning gravel everywhere, screeched into the driveway. The car barely came to a complete stop, when a woman jumped out and ran toward Anne. A petite woman, but muscular, her hair a frazzled mess, probably in her late forties, grabbed Anne's arm. "Where is he?" she screamed. "Tell me now or I'll break your arm! NOW!"

Anne panicked and could hardly speak. "I don't know who you're talking about!" she panted. "Are you looking for

Troy? Steve?" She tried to pry her arm loose from the woman's grasp but she was strong as a plow horse.

The woman tightened her grip. "Don't play coy with me. You know damn well who I'm looking for."

Anne, shaking her head, tried to speak, but the woman interrupted her. "Tommy! Tommy Driscoll, my," she hesitated as if searching for a word, "my son!" she shrieked. "Where is he?"

Trying to catch her breath, still trying to free her arm, Anne said, "He quit a few weeks ago. I didn't know the boy. Mr. Kent said he probably found a better job and just didn't show up anymore."

"You liar bitch," she yelled, as she doubled her fist and hit Anne square in the face. Anne whimpered but was determined not to let her weakness show. "You'd better be telling me the truth or I'll be back to settle this score!" She released Anne's arm, spun on her heel, and sped off in her rusty red Toyota.

Anne, shaking from head to toe, slowly treaded into the house, grabbed some ice and a clean kitchen towel, making a cold compress for her swelling eye. She wanted to cry but she was tougher than that. She couldn't understand why this woman was so violent; of course, a mother's love is unquestionable. She was going to call Troy, but not knowing the seriousness of his business, this could wait until he got home. She poured herself a glass of tea, took her ice pack, and went to the verandah. She tried to imagine how Troy would react; she was terrified about what he would do. From his many stories, his tolerance for bullies was non-existent.

An hour after the attack, Troy and Steve pulled into the driveway. Anne didn't want to make a big deal out of the situation because she knew Troy was as volatile as a vial of nitroglycerine. She remained seated as the two men entered the verandah. Troy, walking toward her, concern on his face, asked, "What's wrong, Anne? Why are you holding that rag on your face?" He bent to gently kiss her.

"I have a headache- no big deal," as she put her feet on the deck and scooched out of the chair. She stood, and when she did, Troy touched her arm and saw her flinch. She tried to pull away, but he carefully lifted the sleeve on her cotton blouse and saw a massive bruise on her arm. He touched her hand holding the ice and looked at her eye.

He turned and stomped his foot, "Damnit! Those fucking thugs! How dare they?" Looking straight at Steve he said, "Son, I might need a little help."

"Anything you say, Dad. I'm always here for you."

After considerable coaxing, Anne finally told Troy what happened. It painted an immediate picture, all too familiar to Troy. That woman was not Tommy Driscoll's mother. She was an assassin teaching him the ropes. She didn't do a very good job; he didn't survive his first attempted target. Troy's past was chasing him like a rabid animal and he had to carefully think through this scenario. Things were too dangerous to make mistakes now. A few days passed, giving the woman a chance to be off-guard, a critical error. When she least expected it, that's when she would meet her demise. People tend to get complacent, a huge mistake.

Steve staked out near her home with binoculars and night vision glasses to journal her routine. After logging her everyday habits, he reported to Troy and they made a plan. She wasn't from the area, so it was unlikely anyone would miss her for quite some time, especially since she was sent here for a mission.

It was simple, really; no muss, no fuss. Something Anne had been curious about tripped Troy's memory. Mushrooms. Perfect. He carefully selected the deadliest fungi on the planet which grew just about everywhere in Australia, including on his property. Cooking a delicious cut of beef in a delectable sauce, he added freshly sauteed mushrooms to the sauce and hired an old woman who had done "favors" for him over the years. She delivered this beautiful meal to Anne's attacker as a 'welcome to the neighborhood' gift. Problem solved, for now.

Chapter 32

There were so many places he had wanted to show Anne. The beauty of his area was amazing but he didn't feel the risk was worth it. He knew he had a huge target on his back and that endangered everyone he loved. They took regular tours around the property always spotting a new bird Anne had never seen or getting a closer look at some koalas. Some of the luscious red grapes in his vineyard were ready for picking as were strawberries. They spent one morning picking the perfect fruit and preparing it for fermentation. Anne had never made wine but Troy had a talent for it. Another day, they rode the ATV to a small nearby lake where some of the best clams could be found. They dug in the sandy bottom and found enough to cook a delicious batch for dinner. Anne had nearly forgotten about Troy's illness. Things seemed normal; better than normal, perfect. She did feel that Troy was on edge a bit more and thought it was probably because Tommy had quit working for Troy and he was trying to find someone else to help.

Steve came over Monday morning just as Troy and Anne were getting ready for breakfast. Anne cooked extra eggs and bacon for Steve. She had squeezed fresh juice and made a pot of tea for the non-coffee drinkers. As they were enjoying light conversation, Steve spoke, "Dad, I was wondering if later in the week, we could all go to the lake for a day. I'll take my boat and you and Anne can be on yours. We can have a cookout, do some swimming, take the jet skis and just make a day of it."

Troy smiled, "That would be great. What day were you thinking?"

"I thought Thursday might be good before the weekend crowds start pouring in. I don't like to go when it's so busy. What do you think?"

"Thursday sounds amazing. We'll work out all the details and plan an amazing day. The weather is supposed to be perfect all week," Troy said. Anne was excited; she loved being on the water with her new "family" and spending a day with them would be delightful.

Ordering weather was sometimes tricky, but someone got it right this time. Barely a cloud in the sky, the temperature in the mid-eighties, and a light breeze; couldn't be more perfect. The water was cool enough to be refreshing but with no real chill. They anchored their boats near each other in a deep part of the channel and tied them together so they could step from one boat to the other. Anne was so happy to spend a day getting to know Brooke, Steve's wife, and Ginger better. She hadn't spent much time with them but they were both incredible. Ginger was a red-headed tiny firecracker, but not in a bad way. She was smart, energetic and brought sparkles of light every place she went. Troy was in love with her; it made Anne's heart swell with joy for all of them. A sob swelled inside her wishing Ginger could have more time with her Grandpapa and experience what an amazing man he is.

It had been years since Anne had been on a jet ski but, it's like riding a bike, they said. HA! When she started it up the first time, it nearly got away from her. When she looked back at the boats, they were all laughing. "I wonder if they set me up," she thought. Troy got on the second PWC but not before Anne insisted he put his vented neon-yellow shirt on to protect his sensitive skin from the intense sun. Anne didn't know how much more fun she could endure without bursting like popcorn. They grilled food, drank beer, played games, and pulled tubes behind the jet skis. It was glorious; truly a day to remember.

The sun was sinking in the west covered with distant clouds creating a glorious palette of color. They were all sitting on Troy's deck when they heard a splash and scream off the back of the swim platform. They all jumped up at the same time. Little Ginger had fallen into the water and the outgoing tide was pulling her toward the sea. Troy dove in, grabbed her and began swimming toward the boat when Steve yelled, "Croc! Behind you! Croc!" Troy kept swimming to bring Ginger to safety with no apparent concern for his wellbeing. Anne and Brooke were screaming, pure bedlam ensued. Steve was ready to jump in when Troy yelled, "NO!" just as he flung Ginger into the arms of her panicked father. In one fluid moment, Ginger was safe, but a massive flop of a tail beside the boat pulled Troy out of sight and into the dark water.

"Please God! Somebody HELP! No, please. This can't be!" They were all screaming at the same time. They could make no sense of the horror they had just witnessed. Tears, screams, and hysteria took over, praying Troy would resurface, but the lake became deathly still. The sun disappeared with a sizzle below the horizon and Troy into his watery grave.

Stunned, tears flowing like summer rain, no one spoke. There were no words to say; nothing to do, just staring into the water at the arms of death.

A few minutes later, when Steve could catch his breath, he got on the marine radio.

"MAYDAY! MAYDAY! MAYDAY! This is the Ginger Lei on Lake Macquarie."

"Come back Ginger Lei," the Coast Guard operator replied.

Steve tried to clear his throat, his voice cracking with emotion, "My little girl fell overboard and my father dove in to save her. He got her and threw her to me just as the croc pulled him under," he choked, not being able to continue. This was a day they would never forget.

Paxton Daily Reporter Obituaries

A day of family fun on Lake Macquarie turned tragic for the Kents. Troy Kent, his friend Anne, son Steve, daughter-in-law, and granddaughter were enjoying a celebration Thursday when tragedy struck. Just before sunset, three-year-old Ginger fell into the water. Her grandfather, Troy Kent, 62, long-time resident of Paxton, dove in to save her. Just as he flung the child to her father, a large crocodile grabbed the man and pulled him under. Croc attacks on Lake Macquarie are rare but do occur as witnessed by this grieving family. The Coast Guard reported the only evidence of the attack were pieces of Mr. Kent's neon-yellow shirt. He was an undisputed hero. A private celebration of life is being planned.

For the next few days, Anne was in a fog. She would sometimes forget the horror they had witnessed and expected him to come through the door. After the tragedy, Anne sat on the edge of Troy's bed, hugging his pillow tightly to her chest. Reminding herself to breathe, she inhaled the essence of the man she had come to love. The house was lifeless and cold without him. She felt as if there was a hole as big as a soccer ball completely through her that would never heal. There were no more tears to shed; they just wouldn't come. The heart, which was filled with love for her gentle man, was missing. There was no room for love, for hate, for indifference, only grief and the realization that her life would never be the same. Taken, ripped from her arms; this was too cruel to comprehend.

Anne had trouble finding her voice to speak to his faithful animals, though she knew they felt his absence, too. Little Maggie laid on his slippers beside his bed and whined most of the time. When Anne sat, Maggie lay on her feet. Dolores, Troy's donkey, brayed nearly constantly since the accident. The only comfort she had was when Anne let Dolores rest her head on her shoulder. Even John, the pig, seemed to have lost his appetite and needed an extra scratch or two. Life is painful. She wallowed in her agony for days, wishing her life had ended when his did; in reality, it seemed it did. Aimlessly, she ran her fingers over every surface in the house, remembering that his hands had lovingly crafted most of the beautiful items in his home.

She walked down the trails Troy had carefully cut through the forest. He had touched nearly every tree, bush, and flower and laid the mulch on which she walked. Sometimes she stood and thought she could hear his tender voice whispering her name through the breeze. There were times when the trees sang to her in Troy's soft, melodic tone; longing and imagination is a powerful sense. She couldn't even think about what her next move would be; she was completely numb to her own life, and not really caring.

Steve, being a man of few words, stopped by twice a day to do the chores and check on Anne. "Is there anything we can do for you, Anne? Anything you need?"

"No, Steve, I'm okay, but thank you for checking on me. I guess I just need a little time," she told him.

"I know what you mean, Anne. When you're ready, we should sit down as a family and talk. It might help all of us. Let me know."

Anne had planned to make this paradise her permanent home, but now she had to rethink the plans she and Troy made together. As much as she adored Steve, Brooke, and Ginger, she had a family back in the US that needed her; she needed to be needed. Everything that happened these last few months was never on her radar. She had plans; she had an agenda. All of it changed when her heart got in the way. She knew the time was coming to make some difficult decisions.

Two weeks after the accident, Anne stepped outside to greet Steve as he was feeding the animals. "Morning, Steve. How are you doing? And your girls?"

"Hi, Anne. We're managing. It's a really tough transition, especially since we had just recognized our relationship."

"It must be heartbreaking for you. I can't imagine," she said.

"I know you're hurting, too, Anne, so thank you for your kind words."

"I was wondering, Steve, how you would feel about having a little family memorial service for him. I think it would help me achieve some closure, but if…"

Steve interrupted her. "That would be perfect, Anne. We all need it. How about the area at the base of the mountain where Ivor is buried? He loved that area."

"Yes, I would love that. How about next Tuesday?" she asked.

"It's a date. See you later," he said. "I'll go check it out before then." A few minutes later, Anne heard the roar of one of the ATVs heading up the trail toward the mountain. It was impossible to miss the newly disturbed dirt next to Ivor's grave. Steve had a job to do. It wasn't the first time for such a chore. People like Steve are commonly known as 'Cleaners'. He would take care of it.

Chapter 33

That afternoon as Anne and Maggie were outside watering the gardens, a Sheriff's car pulled into the driveway and two officers walked up to Anne. "Afternoon, Ma'am," one of them said. The other seemed preoccupied looking around the property.

"Hello," Anne answered. "Is something wrong?"

"No, Ma'am, we'd like to ask you a couple questions."

Nothing registered with Anne. "Sure, no problem," she said.

"Did Tommy Driscoll work here awhile back?" the officer asked.

"Yes, he did. Seemed like a nice young man."

"He's not still working here, is he?"

"No, Mr. Kent said Tommy quit and had another job lined up. Mr. Kent seemed sad because he really liked the boy."

"Hmm, I see. When was that? When did he quit?"

"I'm not sure. A lot has happened since then but I think it was perhaps a month or more that he left. Is something wrong?"

"His mother called our office a week or so ago and asked us to check around. She said she hasn't seen him for over a month, so we're trying to locate him. We've been busy so this is the first chance we've had to come out. We'd like to look around the property if you don't have any objection," the officer said.

Anne immediately relived the attack the day Tommy's mother came looking for him. She hadn't heard any more about it, so, as far as she knew, the situation was over.

"I'm not the owner so I can't authorize that. I'm sure if you talk to Mr. Kent's son, Steve, he wouldn't have a problem."

"That's understandable. We know Steve. We'll talk to him. Thank you, Ma'am."

Early the next morning, as Anne was pouring a cup of coffee, Steve backed his truck up to the loading door of the barn. He was stacking buckets of potted flowers into the ATV and drove off in the direction of the mountain where the memorial would be in a few days. Several hours later, he returned hot, sweaty, and dirty. Anne shouted, "Steve, can I get you a cold glass of tea?"

"That would be amazing, Miss Anne. I'll be there in a minute."

He went to the hose bib and let the ice-cold water run over his head and face, soothing his sunburned cheeks. Shaking the water off, he walked up to the verandah and sat on a bench. "Thanks, Anne. This will really hit the spot," he said as he guzzled half the glass.

"You're welcome. I knew you must be thirsty. You've been outside for a while." Not asking, she was curious what he was doing and hoped he would tell her.

Raking his fingers through his wet hair, he looked off into the distance. "I guess you're wondering what I was doing, huh?"

"This is your home, Steve. You don't need to tell me anything,"

"Since we're having a memorial service for him, I decided I would plant a small flower garden there in his honor. It's obvious how he loved flowers. I covered an area with some of his favorites and I'm making a cross with his information on it."

Anne was deeply touched by Steve's sensitivity. "That's wonderful, Steve. He would be so pleased."

Three days later, the two deputies pulled onto the property accompanied by Steve. They looked through the barn and announced themselves as they walked through the house. Paying particular attention to Troy's bedroom and bath, Anne was confused as to why they were even there. Did they think Tommy was here or met an ill fate? Outside, the men got on the ATV and headed up toward the mountain.

One of the officers spoke, "Steve, thanks for humoring us with this investigation but it seems like something has happened and we're trying to get to the bottom of it. As a matter of fact, do you know Tommy Driscoll's mother?"

Steve nonchalantly answered, "No, never met her. Why do you ask? She reported him missing, right?"

"That's right," the officer in the front seat said, wiping beads of sweat off his forehead. "Funny thing is, Steve, we went to the house they were living in yesterday and found her body, decomposed."

"Oh man," Steve looked shocked. "That's terrible. What happened?"

"The medical examiner will need a week or more to determine the cause of death," the deputy said.

They were gone over an hour and Anne's curiosity was piqued. She knew Troy had alluded to a questionable past, but he didn't seem capable of serious crimes. On second thought, recently he had spent two stints in jail for assault. One was on a police officer when they destroyed his Harley and the other was the neighbor who flooded Troy's property. He definitely had a hair-trigger, though Anne had not personally seen that side of him. She wasn't even sure she believed those stories. He had mentioned his solicitor several times and he always did a good job of getting him out of jail. That just wasn't the man Anne had come to know and love.

Steve had done a good job protecting his father's final legacy by planting the flowers over the grave of Tommy Driscoll, disguising it as a tribute to his father. The deputies were satisfied with the explanation.

On Tuesday morning, Steve and his family greeted Anne at the door. The girls were dressed in fresh summer colors, but of course, Steve donned his usual black outfit. It was his signature, Anne believed. Anne also wore a pretty flowered dress, with no drab colors. They truly wanted to celebrate the man they loved. That man Troy had been a lover of nature, though Anne knew there were many dark memories that haunted him. He was at peace now and that comforted Anne.

When they got ready to go to the memorial site, little Maggie was on Anne's heels, as if she knew. She jumped on the ATV with the family, the breeze filling her nostrils and flapping her ears. As they neared the site, Maggie became excited and hopped off before they even got to the spot. She began sniffing and digging around the newly planted flowers. She barked and growled. Anne had not heard her act like that except with Tommy Driscoll. A strange feeling crept up the back of her neck. Steve knew this was going to be a problem.

"Maggie, come, girl," Anne commanded. Maggie had no intention of listening but continued to try to dig into the soil.

"I can't imagine why she'd do that. She never bothers the flowers back at the house."

Steve gave her a half-hearted smile. "Maybe she feels Dad's spirit. I don't know why animals behave the way they do." He found a small piece of rope and tied her collar to one of the seats so they could have their service uninterrupted by a snoopy little dog who instinctively reacted to evil.

Steve brought a cloth bag from the ATV. Opening it, the sentiment hit Anne hard. It was a beautiful cross, handmade of copper. Steve had engraved it with vines and his name. It read:

TROY KENT

1960 - 2022

Man of Integrity

They each spoke from the heart. Anne hadn't known Troy long so she didn't have much to say but Steve's words melted her. She had never heard him say more than a few words at any given time so this was an anomaly.

"Dad, though you're not here in person, you're here in our hearts. I have loved you since I was a little boy and I knew you loved me, too. It didn't matter that the words were never said, that you didn't tell me you were my father, love runs deeper than that. Yes, I have helped you through some difficult times that were kept between the two of us, and, at times, I questioned why certain things happened the way they did, but I could never question your compassion for people in need. You held out your hand to lift them from their filth, you bathed them in kindness, fed them from your table of wealth, and prayed for them like family."

There was nothing left to say. It was closure, for all of them. Even little Ginger gently touched a flower reaching its petals toward heaven and said, "Bye, bye, Grandpapa. I love you." Anne's heart was bleeding inside knowing how much Troy loved that little red-headed doll. He didn't have enough time with her. It wasn't fair. She relived the scenario a thousand times in her mind. They all knew Troy was sick and would probably suffer untold agony but, a crocodile? Seriously? There was no chance to say goodbye, no last touch, kiss, or hug. Perhaps this was God's way of sparing him the pain he would experience if he died from his illness. There was no real conclusion that could be drawn from the whole situation. There were times when Anne's mind fixated on these months of conversations with Troy, all the things that had been said and done, the hopes they shared, the love that bloomed from the beginning, like a rare flower in the night. In one breath, she wished she had never played the word game with him because none of this would have happened; in the next heartfelt breath, she wouldn't have missed one moment of the time knowing him. Though he was gone, for the first time in her life, she felt she had truly loved and been loved.

Chapter 34

Brooke, Steve's darling wife, and Ginger were such a help sorting through Troy's things. It was a heartbreaking task, but best to do it quickly to dismiss some of the reminders of him. Ginger was a cut up one day as she began going through all of Papa Troy's hats. She tried on each one and paraded around his bedroom with a different stride for every hat. She invented different voices and created scenarios for the hats. Putting on a wide-brimmed Aussie hat that hung down her back, she pointed her finger and, in the deepest voice she could muster, she said, "Mr. Crocodile, give me my Grandpapa back!" Wow, that hurt. It was evident she understood what had happened.

They had several meetings with Troy's solicitor, discussing all the legal mumbo-jumbo that Anne didn't care about, although it was a formality that needed to be completed. His homestead, and all of his other properties, were left to Steve but he had left considerable amounts of money to his visually impaired brother and his other siblings. They were well-cared for. The will was read; there were no surprises, although Anne was disappointed Troy hadn't left her some money. The only shock was that this happened so quickly. The one thing left was to open the safe and no one knew what to expect. They all gathered in Troy's home around the steel fortress. The solicitor had a small strongbox to be opened by Steve and the solicitor. They each had a key and they were both needed to open the small box that held the combination to the safe. Troy had obviously executed a well-planned strategy.

Inserting the keys, turning and carefully lifting the lid, an envelope facing up said, "Please Read".

To my dear family and Anne Cooke:

This is, more or less, a confession, of my troubled and hideous life. If you are sensitive to violence or would rather not know the full truth, please don't go any further. There are some collectibles and monetary treasures in the safe but also, the journal, in which I have poured out my heart. I hope you and the God of Heaven and Earth, can allow me forgiveness, though I am undeserving.

Troy Kent

It was only fitting that Steve have first and sole access to the contents. He carefully turned the large wheel and heard the tumblers falling into place. The large steel door creaked as he pulled it open and peeked in, not knowing what to expect. They turned a light on to shine inside to better see its contents. Steve reached in and placed his hand around one of twelve velvet pouches that held assorted natural, uncut gemstones; diamonds, rubies, sapphires, emeralds, opals, alexandrite, tourmaline, and aquamarine. Even though uncut and raw, the solicitor had the value estimated to be $9,000,000. There were instructions as to how they should be distributed. To say the family was stunned was an understatement. Troy never bragged about his wealth or how he accumulated it, although, he did tell Anne he was very rich.

Next was a very heavy box about the size of a loaf of bread, filled with gold coins called Krugerrands. He explained they were African, and the government wanted them back but wasn't willing to pay their true value. He explained about his jeweler friends who would buy them at a fair price. There were 1260 coins that had an estimated value of $3,800,000. The majority of the coins were left to Steve, the others were left to his remaining siblings.

There were three wooden boxes the size of a tissue box. They were beautiful in themselves with a hand-polished finish, gleaming hinges, and carvings on the top. Anne wondered if Troy made them. She wanted to touch them thinking his hands had been there. Inside each box was a breathtaking find, Faberge Eggs. A note inside stated there were only seven eggs in the world that weren't accounted for and he had three of them. They would bring a fortune when they were ready to sell. Troy estimated the value to be about $30,000,000 or more depending on the collector or museum who wanted them most. There was no explanation for how he came to have these near priceless items, but he stated that his estate had every legal right to sell them if they wished. If there was a majority consensus to sell the eggs, the money would be distributed among his son Steve, brother Keith and his brothers and sisters in equal shares.

There were artifacts from many parts of the world that were sure to be very valuable though, at this point, they were all so flabbergasted, that they couldn't comprehend anymore. Steve carefully picked up the leather-bound journal, and held it to his chest; a small tear escaping his eye. "I'd like to read it first if you don't mind," he said. "I have many unanswered questions so I hope this will answer some of them." They all agreed that Steve should have all the time alone with his father's journal that he needed to process, and come to grips with everything.

The family gathered on the verandah discussing the generosity of the man they loved and lost. They all seemed to have a special story about Troy and some of his crazy antics. They agreed that his family was his priority and he never left any of them wanting if their needs could be met with money. Anne busied herself preparing a big platter of finger food, giving them privacy as a family. She felt it was respectful to give them time to process their loss and also their inheritance.

She prepared slices of summer sausage, prosciutto wrapped around cheese, ham with a hearty mustard sauce, crackers of every kind, and slices of decadent cheeses. She cut fresh vegetables from the garden and put together two dipping sauces. Pairing it all with luscious fruit and Troy's homemade mulberry wine, it looked fit for the, now rich, people she was serving. She carried it to the large table, then made her way back inside. Before she reached the door, one of his sisters called out to her.

"Anne, please join us. You're part of our family, too."

Grateful, Anne said, "That's so nice of you all, but I want to give you time to enjoy your memories without me."

Sarah, a younger sister said, "Anne, without you, our memories would be limited to the Troy we knew before. He became so much more to us since you entered his life. Please sit with us."

Anne was touched by the love and compassion of these people who had touched her life.

Too much emotion wouldn't allow Steve to open the journal. He would wait until the pain subsided a bit and he had quiet solitude to try to understand the man inside the armor he wore. He knew there was so much more to his father, but never felt he could ask. He didn't want to push him, out of respect and fear. He knew, from experience, that his father was capable of unspeakable acts when a situation presented itself.

A few days later, Steve sighed deeply knowing he needed to read the words his father had written. Dread filled his soul. There were things he wanted to know, but much more that should die with the man he loved. He carefully wrapped the journal in a soft cotton cloth, laid it on the seat of his truck, and drove to Troy's home.

****

<u>Suzie</u>

I was just getting out of the shower when my phone rang. I knew it must be Anne because the app we were using had a different sound. I grabbed a towel, shuddering, more from what news she might have, than cold.

"Anne, honey! Hi! How are you?"

"Hi, Suze." Her voice caught. I knew there was a problem.

"Tell me what's going on, Anne."

Sobbing her words so that I could hardly understand, she said, "Troy is dead."

As her sobbing slowed a bit so she could hear me, I said, "You must be devastated and I don't want to make things harder for you, but can you tell me what happened, or is it too soon?"

276

"If it was twenty years from now it would have been too soon. This is cruel, a cruel twist of fate." She was choking her words out of her body as if they were stuck in a vacuum that she had to force.

"Did he die of his cancer, Anne? Is that why he died so suddenly?"

"No, damnit, that's why it's so twisted, crushing, heartbreaking. He had just decided to try a clinical trial for his illness that was showing great promise; we were hopeful. Four weeks ago, Troy's family went out to the lake with us to spend a lovely day together. Just before sunset, Troy's little granddaughter fell into the water; he dove in to save her, which he did. Before he could get into the boat, a huge crocodile pulled him under and that was it." Anne was wailing. I have never heard such agony come from a human. I wish I could have said something, done something, to comfort her, but I couldn't find words to speak.

After she gained some control, she began to speak. "Suze, I'm coming home. It's pointless for me to stay here. I love it but without Troy, I'd rather be with my family and all of my dear friends like you…and Mark. Please don't let my decision have any effect on your relationship with Mark. I'm very happy for both of you and I'm looking forward to spending time with you once I get through this mourning if that ever happens."

I felt my face contort, not knowing how to react. Of course, I was happy she was coming home, but I knew I'd be uncomfortable around her since I was now her man's bedfellow. Maybe time will fix that although I was still a bit insecure about my relationship with Mark. He may want to go back with Anne. I could only pray we could stay together, but I needed to prepare myself, just in case.

"Anne, please let me know when you've got your schedule worked out. I'll make sure everything is ready for you at your house. You know, just get things freshened up and aired out."

"I will, Suzie. You're the best. I knew I could count on you."

I still felt a hint of guilt for being in love with Mark, but Anne had left him for another man, so I needed to let time soothe this for all of us. We're at an age now where we need to grab happiness when it comes our way. Happiness is like a big handful of cotton candy that dissolves in your mouth instantly. It can be gone before we realize what happened.

Chapter 35

Steve dragged a lounge chair down to the creek under the shade of a huge weeping willow tree. Journal in hand, he wasn't sure he was ready for this, yet hoping unanswered questions would become clear. He didn't know what to expect and hoped his father's words weren't too graphic. He opened the journal. His hands shaking slightly, inside was a sealed envelope addressed to Anne Cooke. He would give it to her, but this was his moment, alone with his father, under the worst circumstance.

To my family, and any of you who feel the need to know the real Troy Kent, this is who I have become and how. I've never spoken these things aloud. Fuck, I spend each waking moment trying to forget my life, but now I'm going to confess. I've tried to earn forgiveness but I'm probably in hell by now. My life was hell but I guess you can all benefit from the hell I caused and lived.

Hate permeated every cell of my body. I hated Africa, I hated my father, I hated my life. I hated everything and everyone, but disobeying my father was not an option. My mum had sent me to him from Australia; she couldn't control me. Fuck, knowing what I know now, I would have cleaned up my act and I may not be the despicable wretch I am. Truth be known, I probably loved my father, but since he had no use for me, it was my way to protect myself from the rejection I felt each time he looked at me with disgust. Grief was painted on my face like the native Aboriginals, even at the age of fourteen. Why the hell do I feel I have to tell this? Shit, maybe it's my way of purging.

Anyway, hang on. This ain't pretty.

I was snatched from the street as I was running an errand for my father. A bag was thrown over my head by the assailant. I was terrified and angry, kicking and screaming, but the son-of-a-bitch was a large chiseled man, out of my league. I was helpless to free myself. Shit, I was just a kid, fourteen, I think.

An icy cold concrete floor became my bed; my only covering was my underwear. Rats, half as big as cats would run across my near-naked body and squeal, taking small nibbles of my flesh. Cock roaches crawled in my ears and eyes when I dozed, looking for moisture. I shivered and cried like a little girl trying to make them leave me alone. Each day, though I became weaker, I was more determined I wouldn't die like this.

Hell, I lost track of days and nights; they were endless. I began to look forward to the stale slice of bread and water I was allowed. No one would find my body after I died in that hole. In the cold, gray darkness of my prison, the big asshole would enter and chase me, taunt me, try to rape me, mock me, and beat me. He laughed and that pissed me off. I never knew when to expect him so I rarely slept. Oozing sores dripped pus from my body rubbing on the jagged concrete. I had no peace, just fear. Each time he came in for the attack, I was reminded of my father's mantra; kill or be killed. Sooner or later, this cat and mouse game would come to an end for one of us, and it wouldn't be me.

I used every bit of wit and strength to devise a plan that would allow me to overtake him. He never spoke to me, just tortured me. I had, little by little, stripped a heavy lead pipe from the water system above my head and planned his demise; it was him or me. Sitting by the door, I waited; he didn't come. I drifted to sleep and jerked awake thinking I heard him; he didn't come. After two days, I was sure he would let me starve or freeze to death.

Suddenly, I heard his large bare feet quietly shuffling toward the door. I was so frightened I wasn't sure I would remain conscious but I stood against the wall where the door would rest near me. Today was the day it would come down to it, no turning back now. He began clicking the many locks open as I waited with terror burning my insides. As he came through the door, he flung it open hard against me, the bones cracked as I felt the blood spurt from my nose and a groan escaped my lungs. He whirled around to face me; I ducked and hit him in the knees with the heavy lead pipe. He went down. I was weak from lack of food but somehow a surge of strength poured through me. I was ruthless and never allowed him to get to his feet. The monstrous, muscle-bound man peered into my eyes with every deadly blow I administered. As I felt the life leaving his body, he whispered, "You win."

My life changed that day. I was destined for the family business. Father was an assassin of the most calculating kind. He was strategic, planned every move he must make to accomplish the task he was well-paid to do. The hell I had endured in the rat-infested dungeon, where I made my first kill was orchestrated by my father. If I was cut from the same cloth, he would teach me the business and recommend me for a similar position.

I worked, I practiced, I calculated, I concentrated on every possible scenario. Father was a good teacher. By my seventeenth birthday, I was a full-fledged, highly-paid executioner. It wasn't an easy life; there were times when eyes full of pleading tears touched my heart but it was "kill or be killed." The regime always had information on the victim and the evil he, or she, had committed. They were heinous crimes and, in my mind, I felt I was purging the earth of evil and satanic vices. I made mistakes; I have scars and bullet holes to prove it, but the more money I stashed away, the more jobs I completed. I was becoming very wealthy.

My last professional job was a day of abhorrent bloodshed. The details are too graphic for me to put on paper; the blood of twelve people still on my hands. That was the day my father's hands were tied behind his back and he was hit in the forehead with a large caliber shell. The last flicker of life left his eyes as I held him and whispered the words I had always wanted to say. "I love you, Dad."

Many more hideous stories fill this journal and, personally, I hope no one feels the need to read them. I only wrote them as a sort of confession, hoping for forgiveness and redemption. I don't deserve either but I pray the God of Heaven and Earth will have mercy on me.

Troy Kent

Steve let the journal slip to his lap as he looked into the woods, not seeing anything but the horror he could only imagine was the life his father had been forced into. The same beautiful trees and breeze that blew through them to sing their song, went unheard that day. The only thing Steve could hear and feel was the agony his father had suffered his entire life by no fault of his own. He hesitated to turn the page, not knowing if he could tolerate the hurt his father had suffered; the wind caught the page and gently turned it for him.

Steve, my dear son,

As I write this, the weight of the years I kept our relationship from you has crushed me. I can't begin to tell you how fucking sorry I am for lots of shit, but mostly I'm sorry I couldn't fully share myself with you and now it's too late. Doesn't matter too damn much, does it? I'm not sure why I felt the need to keep it from you. I told myself it was for your protection which is certainly true, but the real truth is, I was ashamed for you to know that this despicable man you worked for, was your father. You have cleaned up my disastrous messes for years, covered for me, been a witness when I may not have had an alibi, and protected me without question. Many of those things I should not have burdened you with but now, I am gone and it's too late to make amends. I hope you're not too pissed to remember some pleasant times we had throughout the years.

I would like to tell you how you came to be. I was working for a very vile man in Uganda. Seems like I always gravitated to those sorts. I had been there for several months, doing his bidding. Completely focused on my job, one night I decided to go out with my friend Omer. He knew all the hot spots around the city and I was ready for "hot" if you know what I mean. I've always been a sucker for redheads and when I found one that night who was willing to share her body with me, I was all in. She was a very nice lady by the name of Lila, and I'm quite sure I would have pursued a relationship with her but, a few days after our encounter, I was transferred several hundred miles away. Not long after that one glorious night, Omer told me she was pregnant. I had no way of knowing if Lila was carrying my baby, but I asked Omer to keep an eye on her for me.

She delivered a beautiful baby boy and was caring for him as best she could. As you got older, Omer told me you looked so much like me, he was sure I was your father. I sent money for Omer to give to Lila on a regular basis; I needed to make sure you were well cared for. I was planning to travel to see you when I got word that Lila was very ill. Before I arrived, your mother passed away and you were in a government orphanage. The instant I saw you, my heart melted; I knew you were mine. Your Aunt Sharon and I made arrangements to adopt you. You were three years old and Sharon became your Mum.

Though we didn't acknowledge my paternity, I truly hope you knew how much I've loved you. There were times, it pained me, to ask you to help with certain things, which I find hard to write on paper. You did so, without question or compromise, as any good son would. You have made me so proud over the years; I could never have asked for a better son. My only regret is that I did not share my true story and love with you but I didn't want you to know you may have those seeds of ruthlessness inside you. Fortunately, you didn't inherit those traits. I'm quite sure your goodness comes from your dear mother, Lila.

By now, the will would have been read, my assets accounted for, the property spoken for and you can live the rest of your life in comfort and peace. You won't have to clean up after me any further and I've left you enough to care for you and your family for the rest of your life.

Regarding Anne, she will probably go back to the US but, should she decide to stay here, I'd like her to have full access to the cabin and I've left a separate account at the bank for her needs. If she leaves, you have full access to it.

Oh, one other thing; sweet little Maggie loves Anne. If Anne would like to take her, please allow that to happen.

I'm sure you'll take good care of the farm, the animals, and your family. Enjoy your life the way I never could and know I loved you completely until I drew my last breath.

Your father, Troy

Steve leaned his head back and gazed up into the tree overhead. Damn, he would miss him. Life just wouldn't be the same, but no one could change it. He wished they could have more time together as father and son, but that wouldn't change either. Troy's letter brought back memories of sketchy, unspeakable things he was asked to do for his father. These were crimes he tried to forget and had to let roll off his back and wipe from his memory. He had to let go of the past. He was so blessed with his family; Troy had been generous. Steve had managed to save a good amount over the years. Steve wasn't sure he wanted to read the journal. There was probably more than he wanted to know. He still had some questions that he was hoping would be answered. He inhaled a couple deep breaths and continued to read.

As he swallowed the sorrow of his father's pain, Steve wiped tears flowing down his cheeks with the back of his hand. He didn't want or need to know anything more. He took a deep breath, gently closed the journal, placed it into the fire pit, and set it ablaze. No questions, no judgment, just closure. None of it was an issue now. Let him rest in peace.

It was time to give Anne the letter his father left for her. He hoped it would give her some kind of relief though he knew how much she loved him and the suffering she was enduring. He went to the house and tapped on the door. Anne answered, but without Steve saying a word, he handed her the envelope with her name written on it, put his arms around her for a few seconds as a sigh escaped his lips. He turned and drove away.

Chapter 36

My dear sweet Anne,

It was a twist of fate that we met each other. No one could have predicted that I would have found such love and delight from playing a silly little game online. You were the reason I woke in the morning and the reason I stayed awake at night, just for a chance to hear a few more words from you. You won me over almost immediately with your compassion, sense of humor, and wit. My life completely changed by playing the game with you, as crazy as that sounds. You lifted me from my depression, gave me reason to breathe, made my life feel significant, helped me believe I could achieve forgiveness for my sins and, most of all, made me fall in love with you. Your words were so sincere; they helped me accept the personal things I was going through. You convinced me that I was worthy. You never judged me; however, you don't know the person I was. Even then, I think you would forgive me, love me and leave the judging to God.

If you're reading this, it means I am gone from your life and this world. I wish I could have had a million years with you but perhaps, in Heaven. Please know that I want you to find someone else to share yourself with. He would be the luckiest man alive. Be careful; you tend to be too gullible and sweetly naïve.

I investigated you before I bought the ticket to bring you here. I probably knew more about you than you could imagine. I know about a couple men who became your victims. I thought about that for a while and here's what I deduced. In order to get their money, you had to give something as well. You paid, in essence, for what you got. An honest day's work for an honest day's pay, so they say. Maybe not quite as honest as one would like, but who am I to judge? You became a challenge for me and I was a challenge for you. I knew you were coming to tap into my wealth but I was determined to change your mind and convince you to fall in love with me. How did I do, sweet Anne? It was the ultimate game and you know how I love games. I never held any of that against you or thought less of you. As a matter of fact, I'm also an opportunist, always searching for an easy target, a competitor, so my respect for you became more intense. You were not exactly easy, you kept me wondering and all I could do was to continue to play the game until you were persuaded to see for yourself. If you want to read the journal, my confessions, you are welcome to do so, but I would prefer you remember me as the man you knew, not the man I was. I'll leave it to you to decide.

My biggest regret is that we didn't have more time together but fate can be as cruel as she is kind. She brought us together and tore us apart. I want you to know, that I've made sure there is a surprise for you when you go back to the US. You have a family there so I'm confident you'll leave Australia. I only hope it was an experience you will cherish until we meet again. Give little Maggie an extra hug from me.

I will always love you, Anne.

Troy

Anne sat frozen in place; the tears falling from her eyes should have iced over. A chill as cold as a Siberian winter filled her spirit. The realization that Troy was, indeed, gone was more than she could comprehend. Fate was cruel, as Troy stated. Anne wanted to fight back and kick her ass. She became stomping mad that she had been teased and taunted with the relationship she had sought her entire life but was stripped from her before she could blink. What was left for her now? She had decisions to make.

Waves of grief would hit Anne like a tsunami without warning. She spent days helping Steve and Brooke do a few things to make the big house more suitable for their family. A song would come on the radio or some simple word would be uttered and the flood gates to her heart were ripped open. She didn't know such agony was possible. How many ways are there to grieve, to say "I can't breathe without you?" She wondered if she would get over it; at best, she prayed she could get through it.

Troy's little dog, Maggie, wouldn't let Anne out of her sight. She followed every step she took and snuggled close to her at night. It was clear Maggie was grieving for Troy; Anne could certainly relate. She went to Troy's bedroom and took his pillow from his bed. Hugging it to her lonely body she breathed in the essence of the man she loved. The fragrance of fresh spring rain with soft woodsy undertones carried her on clouds of ecstasy to the last time she had kissed his beautiful lips and laid her head on this pillow with him. As she lay cuddling the pillow, Maggie gently laid her head on a small corner and whimpered. Somehow, she felt Maggie was her final connection to Troy; it would break her heart to leave her here. Perhaps Steve would allow her to take Maggie home with her; Troy loved that little puffball and Anne prayed she would have the opportunity to love her the way Troy did.

As Anne was packing to go back to the states, she had to stop every few minutes to calm herself.

Folding her clothing, she remembered the short set she wore on their first trip up the mountain; she cried. She tucked the sunflower boots Troy bought her into the outside pocket; she cried. The satiny aqua nightie she wore the first night Troy held her in his arms and gently made love to her on the yacht; she cried. She clung to it, held it tight to her face and breast, and she could almost smell him, even in her clothes. She had to stop this; she must move on with her life, though she didn't want to forget a moment he was in her life. She was ready to close her bag when she remembered something; she hesitated. Reaching into a drawer next to her bed, her hand trembled as she reached for a small piece of neon-yellow fabric the Coast Guard had found from the shirt Anne had insisted he wear that fatal day. This would be her four-leaf clover, her good luck charm forever. It appeared to be the only evidence left of Troy.

Hugs, kisses, and lots of tears were shared with Brooke, Ginger, and Troy's brothers and sisters. They all considered themselves lucky to have come to know and love each other; they promised to keep in touch. Steve loaded her Louie Vuitton bag into the Land Rover. That had been such a statement piece for her; now she wouldn't care if it was a Walmart bag. It's amazing how she had changed. Monetary things held no importance for her anymore. She didn't need to dress to impress; she wanted the pain of her loss to end but time was the only hope she had. The drive to the airport in Sydney was quiet, although a few minutes before their arrival, Steve reached for Anne's hand.

"Thank you, Anne…for everything," he said with a slight catch in his throat.

"No, thank you, Steve, for your graciousness and acceptance of me. I've never been treated better. This experience changed my life."

"You gave my father something he hasn't had for many years. You gave him love and hope and confidence. You let him see that he was only a victim of his environment, not the monster he believed he was. We will always love you for making him so happy."

Anne couldn't respond; tears choked her. She squeezed his hand tighter before she pulled away to wipe the tears from her face. It was time for her to go. "Goodbye, Steve. Love you."

He tipped his big black hat in respect and mouthed, "Love you, too."

****

As she settled in her luxurious sleeping room aboard the plane, an emptiness filled her. Unlike the trip to meet Troy, she had no anticipation, no excitement that something good was about to happen. She had no plans for her future except to remind herself to open her eyes in the mornings and get through each day for as long as her destiny allowed. Life felt so unfair but she couldn't complain. Even though their love was short-lived, she knew some people never find the joy and fulfillment that she and Troy shared, even if for only a few short months; it seemed like only days when she reflected. At least she had sweet little Maggie, who was a great comfort.

Getting Maggie cleared for the trip to the US took some major politics, not to mention the cost, but it was worth it, like taking a bit of Troy home with her. Perhaps someday her grief would subside and she could enjoy her memories that were cut short. She and Maggie had a long plane ride, plenty of time to think about what her life might be like now after all she'd been through. Time would tell.

Anne's oldest daughter Kate was picking her up from the airport. Her anticipation of seeing Kate and her grandchildren gave her spirit a sentimental lift, as the big silver bird brought her closer to reality. It almost felt like she had been a character in a book or movie; sometimes she would wake and wonder if her experience was real. This book that she started, based on some conversations with Troy, was hanging in limbo. There were times when she thought about the words she had written; were they actual conversations she had with Troy or from her own imaginative mind? It was difficult to decipher fact from fiction. She could only hope, that being back home, would clarify all she had been through and perhaps, even, soothe her grieving soul.

There were times, even though the experience was amazing, the man was amazing, she always felt there was some kind of angle. She couldn't put her finger on it but, though she knew he loved her passionately, there was this little devil on her shoulder trying to tell her a story. She was always cautious of Troy; until the day he died, she was looking to uncover something she missed; a plan, an agenda, an angle, some reason he was using her. Maybe someday she could finish the book and dedicate it to his memory, but there was something she couldn't quite identify so the end of the book would still be a mystery.

Back in Houston, her home felt adequate but empty. Walking from room to room, it felt like a house, no longer a home. "Home really is where the heart is," she repeated to herself. It was her heart that was empty, but nothing to fill it. Sweet little Maggie made the trip without incident and seemed to be adjusting well. Lots of snuggles and doggie kisses were in order every day. It was strange seeing Mark's closet empty with nothing left but hangers and a couple of shoe boxes. She had no ill feelings; she wanted Suzie and Mark to be happy. She would find something to fill her days; find a new hobby, and volunteer more frequently.

Keeping busy would be a key to filling the time before sleep gave her respite; it seemed she saw Troy's face in every cloud, heard his gentle voice in every breeze, every bird on the wing, every breath she took. She had never experienced anything like this before. When she was driving her car, she thought she would see him on a street corner or whizzing by in another car. She would glance at her front door and gasp, thinking she saw him. Many times, at night, she would wake up feeling like he was there with her. Is that what a person's mind is capable of when grief is the fuel it operates on? She was going to seek counseling. There must be help to relieve her torment.

****

Suzie

This is going to be a hard phone call to make but I've put it off long enough. I've got to call Anne and welcome her home.

"Anne, Hi, my dear friend!"

"Suze, it's nice to hear from you. What's up? Everything okay?"

"That's why I'm calling, to make sure you're okay. Is there anything I can do? I thought about calling sooner but I wanted to give you a chance to get settled in."

"That was thoughtful. It has been hard but I expected it to be," Anne said, trying to hold it together. Suddenly she blurted out tears and anger and frustration like Suzie hadn't heard come from her before. "Suzie," she wailed, "I'm so lost. I don't know how this happened. I never knew I was so vulnerable or could fall so in love. What's worse is to realize, at this stage in my life, what love is like, and then have it snatched, literally, right before my eyes," she sobbed. "Damnit! What the fuck will I do?"

On my end of the phone, I stood shaking my head, looking at Mark who had just walked in from golfing. I couldn't find words to say. I fumbled. "Honey, I'm so very sorry. Honestly, I don't know what to say. I love you so much and can't stand to know you're in this kind of pain, but what can I do to help?"

There was silence for a few long seconds. Anne sighed deeply to reel in her emotions so she could talk like a human. "There's nothing anyone can do; it's just the shits. Excuse me. Life sucks, then you die."

"You know I'm here for you, anytime day or night…and Mark," looking at him he shook his head, yes.

"I know, Suze, but this is something that will take some time. As painful as it is, I think I'll finish the book and perhaps that will give me some closure. Shit! Everyone talks about closure like it's a good thing, so maybe I'll give it a try. I guess it's the acceptance that the person you loved is gone forever. What the hell is so good about that? I've decided closure sucks, too."

We said our goodbyes and I love you, but I felt bad like I had failed our friendship; like I should hold myself partially responsible, though that didn't make sense. Then Mark spoke up.

"Suzie, hear me out, please. I feel I should go see Anne. I need to clear the air with her, see if I can help, and establish our relationship with her. Is that okay?"

I didn't want to answer; I wanted to panic. I was so afraid of losing him but that was a chance I knew I had to take. "Mark, you do whatever you feel you need to do. I don't dictate your life and, if Anne needs you, or us, we want to be there for her." I hoped I was sounding sincere.

"Suzie, you are amazing. This is why I fell in love with you." He leaned in and sweetly kissed me which I felt was a down payment, like insurance, that it would all work out.

Several days went by when he announced he would call Anne and ask to see her. I knew it was coming and had to deal with whatever the outcome was. An hour later, he drove to Anne's house.

Opening the door, tears filled her eyes as she threw her arms around his neck. "Mark, oh, Mark," she cried. He held her, patting her back with a familiarity of their ten-year relationship. She was different; he had never known her to be so emotional. Always the strong, and courageous one. He hoped he could comfort her somehow. She pulled away and motioned him toward the kitchen as she grabbed some tissue to dab her eyes and blow her nose. "Let's have some coffee."

"No, you don't need to wait on me, please. Let's sit and talk," he said.

"I need coffee Mark, and if I remember right, you like coffee, too." She burst into tears again.

"What's wrong, Anne?"

Trying to stop the tears from flooding her face as she filled the coffee pot, she said, "this conversation reminded me of times with Troy when he said, sophisticated people with a more refined palette drink tea, and coffee is for hillbillies. He was quite the fellow," she laughed lightly through her sniffles.

As the coffee brewed, they sat at the island as she held his hand. Mark felt his muscles tighten uncomfortably. "Mark, seeing you is like putting on an old comfy sweater that you've waited all summer to wear."

"Geez, Anne. Thank you, I think."

"That's a good thing. I feel so much better just sitting here with you. You are my closest friend, the one I know I can count on through anything," she said. She stood to pour the fresh, roasted coffee. Looking at him she said with a little glimmer in her eye, "Don't worry, honey. I'm happy for you and Suze. I felt for a long time that our relationship had become more of a solid friendship. Don't you?"

Releasing the breath he didn't know he was holding, he affectionately looked at her. "Anne, I would do anything for you, and Suzie loves you like a sister. I want our relationship to be solid, knowing we can depend on each other."

"That's perfect, Mark. Life is strange, isn't it? Things sometimes don't work out the way we planned; they work out even better. My mom used to say, 'be careful what you pray for…you just might get it'. Just be good to my dearest friend," she winked. Mark left that day knowing they were in the right place. They had been good for each other for many years; he was a fine man. Now her darling friend can enjoy the privilege of his company. Anne was happy for them, truly.

Chapter 37

The days droned on, some better than others. The late fall weather in Houston was a welcomed relief from the brutal, oppressive heat of summer. Anne could start planting a few of her favorite winter crops. Little Maggie got right in the middle of it, rooting the fresh soil with her nose and chasing a few late-traveling butterflies. Anne was so grateful she had Maggie. She was an incredible companion and a true pleasure having a pet for comfort and a reminder of Troy. After seeing a good counselor several times, Anne's sightings of Troy were diminishing. She was beginning to deal with the truth that he was really gone; it was agonizingly hard.

Anne had gone to the senior education center a couple times to play the ukulele with her friends but the only thing she could think about was the last time she played. Sitting under the shade of the big willow tree by the creek in Australia, she played 'I will always love you' while Troy sang it to her. It was a moment branded into her memory; one of the sweetest, most treasured of her life. It was unbearable to play now, remembering that moment with the man she loved. Eventually, she would play again, in his honor.

Several weeks had passed since Anne came home. The days ran together and it was hard to motivate herself to accomplish much of anything. She opened the book she had been writing about Troy on her laptop; perhaps she could work on it. She didn't get two pages into it before the tears were dripping on the desk. It was too soon. She closed it, fixed her makeup, and walked from room to room looking for something that might soothe her a bit. She heard her phone ring in the kitchen where she had left it. She wasn't in a rush to answer; it was probably some telemarketer. She answered on the last ring.

"Hello?"

"Ms. Cooke, this is Raoul at Third Fifth Bank. I'm the representative that oversees your account."

"Yes, Raoul. I remember you. Is something wrong?"

He hesitated. "Well…no, not really. Would it be possible for you to come and see me at the branch? There is an issue with your account and my supervisor and I need to speak with you in person."

"Oh no," panic in her voice. "Did someone hack my account and take my money?"

"No, ma'am. Your money is secure. I'm not at liberty to discuss this over the phone. Can you come in today?"
"Raoul, you're not trying to sell me another IRA or something, are you? I'm not interested in anything."

"It's nothing like that, Ms. Cooke."

An hour later Anne was greeted by Raoul and the branch manager as she walked through the door. After greeting each other, they escorted her to a private office, offering her refreshments. She was feeling aggravated and wished they would get on with their spiel.

The branch manager spoke. "Ms. Cooke, this is an unusual situation. Were you expecting a wire transfer?"

"No, why do you ask?"

The manager and Raoul exchanged glances. "Well, ma'am, we received a very large sum late yesterday that was transferred into your account."

"What? There must be some mistake. Who is it from?" Anne asked.

"It was sent from a lawyer in New South Wales, Australia as an inheritance from an estate there. Are you familiar with this, Ms. Cooke?"

"I spent some time there a couple months ago and someone I was very close to passed away, but I'm not expecting anything from the estate. How much is it? Can we send it back? I don't need anything from their family."

"Ma'am, you might want to reconsider and accept this most generous gift. It's one hundred million dollars."

****

Anne was stunned, shocked. A million questions ran through her mind. No, make those one hundred million questions. She had no idea how such a thing could be. Obviously, Troy had set this up before the crocodile ended his life, but why? She left the bank, not hardly remembering how to drive or where she lived. She parked in the garage, turned the car off, and sat for a few minutes, trying to comprehend this news. Shaking her head, trying to make sense of it all, she wondered why he had been so generous. He didn't know a crocodile would eat him. One fact was apparent, she was a very rich woman. She got what she went to Australia for, his bankroll. It turned out better than she could have ever planned or speculated. She heard Maggie barking and scratching at the door, bringing her back to reality.

When Anne went inside, Maggie bounced and jumped like a puppy. She barked and twirled in circles as if she was trying to tell Anne something. She never acted this way. From the laundry room, Anne walked into the kitchen with Maggie nearly tripping her, still barking and hopping. As Anne bent down to pick her up, she was stopped dead in her tracks. There was a hint of fragrance on Maggie that smelled exactly like Troy. That sweet aroma was etched in her memory. She gasped. This couldn't be. This was her imagination playing tricks on her…. again. She walked from room to room holding Maggie close. No, she must be hallucinating. Anne and Maggie walked into their bedroom and there, on her bed, was her small piece of yellow-neon fabric that had been in the top drawer of her nightstand.

Setting Maggie down, Anne collapsed on the bed, her heart racing. She couldn't think; couldn't imagine what was happening. Her phone suddenly pinged, notifying her of a text message. Reaching into her pocket, hands trembling, trying to make sense of what was transpiring, she opened the text. It read:

01-22 followed by kisses and pink hearts.

NO! NO! This can't be. Troy is alive! He's alive? She immediately texted him. "Troy, where are you? Come to me, please." She got an immediate notification that her text was undeliverable. What the hell? What did that mean?

She wrang her hands, paced the floor, and checked every inch of her house for some sign of him. The doors and windows were all secure, though it was clear he had been in her home. What was his game? Aha, that's it. The son-of-a-bitch! It's another one of his games. The problem was, that Anne didn't know if this was a good game or a bad one. She was in a panic, not knowing what to do. The only choice she had was to wait, try to stay awake, outwit him. If he was here once, he would be back and she had to be ready for whatever his game was. Did he come to spend his life with her or end her life? That was the ultimate question.

She discreetly opened the drawer on the nightstand and went into her closet, shutting the door behind her. She slipped her bra holster on that held her pistol and checked it. There was no ammo in the gun. Anne knew this was a very bad sign. Someone had removed the bullets; it could only have been Troy. She reloaded it and put her shirt over it. With crime at an all-time high, she had practiced her moves many times, in case of an emergency. She hoped this wasn't that kind of emergency. She put some pillows under her duvet to appear she was there but sat in a small chair in an obscure area of the room. She had a full view of her door and windows, but an intruder couldn't readily see her. Her heart thumped in her chest; this was a simple waiting game. Seems they were always playing games.

Anne was heartbroken that he had come to do her harm, but he had told her many times about the red fog that descends on him that he can't control. He had told her more than once he had little regard for human life, especially if that person he pursued was a bully or a user. This was a well-executed plan that Anne was now putting together in her mind. The little devil on her shoulder was a warning that something was wrong but she was too in love to allow herself to see the truth.

She sat in the darkness with Maggie at her feet. She felt herself starting to nod off but that couldn't happen. She must stay awake and alert in case he showed up. She felt like worms were crawling inside her body. Call it fear, or anticipation, she imagined this was a bad horror movie, and the tense scary music playing in the background, makes your heart race, knowing something was about to happen. For the first time in a long time, she prayed she was wrong. There were too many signs that ripped hope from her. She knew this was going to end badly, one way or another.

Clever boy. He had totally set her up. Their love affair was amazing for being part of a scripted game. He not only spoiled her, but also loved her, and lured her, he hooked her. But what was his end game? The cliché, hook, line, and sinker came to mind. It had all come down to this. He could win an Oscar for this performance. He had warned her numerous times, telling her how ruthless he is. She, an emotionally loving woman, let her heart rule her mind. Now she had to face her folly, coming, in the flesh, to make her pay.

Exhaustion was starting to overtake her when she felt Maggie's little body tense as she lay across Anne's feet. Immediately Anne became alert and could almost feel the presence of someone. She silently removed her gun from her holster and held it in her hand. Maggie began shaking, then a low growl came from her mouth. This was it. She hoped he was coming to love her and share her life, but this was not the proper way to continue a romantic relationship. She had become his victim and she didn't see it coming. She thought she was more astute than that. Troy gave her lots of rope to hang herself and now was the moment of truth.

Staring thru the partial darkness, his huge body filled the doorway. She stopped breathing. She knew that silhouette. Then he spoke.

His voice, dripping like sweet honey, he said, "Anne, darling, I've been watching you, waiting for this perfect moment. You were a minx, a deceptive little predator, but I will love you till I draw my last breath. From the first word you wrote me, to this very moment, my heart belonged to you. I knew I had met a worthy competitor and you would keep me on my game. Your game was as good as mine so you challenged me to stay a step or two ahead of you. I want you to know, I will always love you and hold you dear to my heart," he smiled, touching his chest.

Anne's blood pressure soared, the sound of blood squishing in her ears. At this moment, it appeared she had been outsmarted by a true professional. "Why, Troy? What did you want from me that would cause you to play this deadly, sick game? This is a strange way to show your love for me."

He released a throaty sinister laugh. "I didn't have an end game in the beginning, but as things went along, I realized you could be my ticket to a new identity. I had hoped I could be free of my past and disappear here in the US. I've worked very diligently to put all the pieces together perfectly and I have succeeded. Here we are, you and I, face to face, and I'm quite confident only one of us will be breathing when our confrontation is over."

Anne was short of breath. "So, after everything we shared, the wonderful times we had, the grief you allowed me to suffer thinking you were dead, you've now come to kill me?" Again, he was ripping her heart out. "I don't understand how you can be so ruthless. I love you, Troy." As she looked into his lavender orchid eyes, she saw evil for the first time.

"I don't need to explain it to you. You were a user, sweet Anne and I've never tolerated that. Your fate is in my hands now and I'm sorry to tell you, your future is short-lived. Remember, my name was Quick Fist in Africa." He stretched his fingers inside the leather gloves and made a circle with his hands as if putting them around her neck. "This reminds me of Tommy Driscoll and how he met his demise on my bedroom floor when he had come to kill me. I felt bad looking into his eyes as the life escaped them. But that was another time. I put a clause in your estate inheritance, that if something happens to you, the money goes to Lee Fitch. Say hello to Lee, Anne. He's my new identity and all the blood money I earned has come back home to daddy."

Anne carefully lifted her gun and pointed the laser dot directly at his heart. Two hands securely on the weapon, it had come down to this when Troy laughed. "What do you plan to do with that, throw it at me? I removed the ammo, so a very wealthy Lee Fitch is the new man in town." He stepped toward her.

Anne sighed deeply, sorrow eating her heart out, she knew this was the ultimate game of life or death.

"Stop!" she commanded. "You've underestimated me again, Troy. I replaced the lead and you have to be alive to spend your filthy money. Games? This was a great one but….I WIN!"